The Normandy Run

by Brett Hoskins

Published by Treacle Moon

Cover illustrations by Katy Cambridge

ISBN 978-1-9768-7323-2

"Have you news of my boy Jack?"
Not this tide.
"When d'you think that he'll come back?"
Not with this wind blowing, and this tide.

—*Rudyard Kipling, My Boy Jack*

Chapter One

Brighton, England - 0210 BST Sunday 29th May

Can you imagine what it must feel like to desperately hang on to the wire guardrail of a moving yacht with your feet dragging in the water while someone prises your fingers away one by one? Imagine the terror as you finally drop into the black, chilling, muscle numbing sea and watch as the yacht slowly sails away into the darkness, all of your shouts for help ignored, until only the dipping and the rising of the yacht's white stern light is visible? Then, as the light also vanishes, the sense of desolation when you accept that you are going to die slowly and cold, miles from everything you love, with no one to help you. That's what happened to Jack McCabe. Jack was Chad McCabe's son and, when it happened, Chad was playing a late gig at Reinhardt's wine bar. It was the last Saturday night in May or, to be more correct, early on Sunday morning, and The Reinhardt's Bar Allstars were winding up the set with their final number.

Reinhardt's is not somewhere that you would come across by accident. It stands in a side street of two-storeyed, terraced Victorian properties in the North Laine of Brighton. Apart from the wine bar, all of the properties have shops below and flats above. To the left of Reinhardt's, as you face it, is a small shop that sells vegetarian shoes, and on the right is an even smaller shop cluttered full with books on the occult, crystals and bundles of joss sticks, all covered with a fine coating of dust. The vegetarian shoe shop is run by two trendy and ambitious twenty year old girls who will probably never be able to repay the money they borrowed from their wealthy parents to start the business because, even in Brighton, most people don't have a problem with wearing leather. Neither shop is open when the wine bar is, because Reinhardt's is closed during the day with the exception of Sundays. If it was open more often, Julia who owns it would have a far more successful business than she does, and she wouldn't constantly wonder aloud about how she'll pay all the bills; but selling lunches is not why she opened the place. If you asked her, she would tell you that she runs it for the music not for the money, and it's true. She loves that retro jazz swing stuff from between the two World Wars, which suited Chad McCabe because that's what he played.

Julia started Reinhardt's when her husband left her after thirty two years of marriage, and when she found it the place was a dump, empty and abandoned, having finally failed as a pub. She lives upstairs and opens the bar at seven every evening of the week. The music starts at nine. Sixty people can sit in relative discomfort on bent cane chairs at fifteen circular tables, and six more can sit on high stools at the bar. Anyone else can stand for all Julia cares, as long as they don't get between the tables and the band. The wine bar is L shaped and the colour scheme is predominantly brown and cream, except for the tablecloths which are red gingham. The walls are lined with French Art Deco music posters, and black and white photographs of Django Reinhardt in different poses but always with a Selmer-Maccaferri guitar. At intervals around the room huge mirrors in gilt frames reflect the room itself, giving the impression that it's twice its real size. Above the diners hang Tiffany uplighters, and two wide, twin bladed tropical fans suspended from the ceiling slowly rotate and stir the leaves of the tall aspidistra plants in their brass pots placed, seemingly at random, around the edges of the room. In a corner by the shopfront style window is a small stage, which is really just a dais raised twelve inches above floor level, with room for a double bass, four more bent cane chairs, four small amplifiers, and not much else.

Reinhardt's has a style reminiscent of Nineteen Thirties' Paris and, that night at the end of May, it was full so it was uncomfortably hot. How Julia gets away with cramming so many customers into such a small place is a mystery. She won't open the front door to let some air through because the neighbours complain about the noise, and the fans in the ceiling just move the warm air around without cooling it. It's also a mystery why the customers keep coming back to pay over the odds for indifferent wines and average food while they endure the heat and the lack of space. It can only be for the music.

There were five of them playing on the dais that night, the full complement. On some gigs it might just be McCabe on rhythm guitar with another guitarist to do the solos, but to make the full sound it takes five: three guitars, a double bass, and a violin. That was always the Saturday night lineup at Reinhardt's. As they swung into the head for the final time they were cooking a passable version of "Django's Tiger" in the style of The Quintette du Hot Club de France, a type of music made famous by Django Reinhardt and Stéphane Grappelli and called Jazz Manouche. In English, that translates as Gypsy Jazz.

McCabe was never going to set the world alight playing guitar, but it was a sort of living and it satisfied two of the main interests in his life - making music and drinking. Not like Andy who was playing solo guitar that night. Andy was obsessed with hitting the big time, practised all day every day, and played the solos almost like Reinhardt himself. Stewart on acoustic double bass was a school teacher and he did the gigs for fun and a bit of cash. George played the violin like Grappelli and was an example of how hard it is to make money in the music business; all that talent but still playing gigs in wine bars. Bronek was Polish and he was playing rhythm guitar alongside McCabe. Nobody knew much about Bronek because he didn't speak much English and just turned up to play, leaving as soon as the gig was finished. Andy decided what numbers they played, he collected the money from Julia, and paid the others when he got around to it. Not an ideal arrangement but it was his gig.

They were booked to play until one o'clock, but the doors were locked and they'd carried on because they were enjoying themselves and so was the audience. McCabe could see them tapping their feet and bopping their shoulders in time with the music as the quintet rounded off with an outro which they nailed as if they'd been playing together forever. The set finished to the type of rapturous applause which only comes after you've given it your best shot and the audience has been steadily drinking alcohol for five hours. They were hailed as visiting music gods. McCabe switched off his AER amplifier, stood up and leaned his Gitane oval hole guitar against the wall behind him, then he stepped down from the dais and weaved his way between the tables. He smiled at the customers as he passed and nodded thanks as the applause slowly died away leaving only an excited hum of conversation. When he reached the bar, he saw that Jimmy the barman had made sure that a large glass of well chilled Chablis was already waiting for him; the staff in Reinhardt's knew what he liked, and this first one was on the house. He turned and leaned back against the bar, took a sip of the wine, saw Bronek go through the front door guitar case in hand without even a wave, and watched as the others from the band linked up with their wives and girlfriends. They always came to watch the band play when they were at Reinhardt's, and sometimes McCabe envied the guys with their homey partners and sensible lives. He was about to walk over to join them when the girl standing to his left spoke.

"Hi, Chad."

Girl or woman? She was petite and fashionably dressed. She shouldered an expensive red leather bag, had an attractive impish brown-eyed smile, straight, shoulder length, well cut brunette hair, and she was gazing straight up at him. He'd seen her before at Reinhardt's but he couldn't tell whether she was fifteen or twenty five. He hoped it was the latter.

"How are you?" which, said with a friendly smile, was his standard reply. When people have seen someone play a few times in small venues they sometimes think that they know them, and expect to be recognised.

"I'm good thanks," she replied as she continued to smile up at him. She was toying with an empty wine glass, and he thought that she might be worth spending some time with.

"Would you like a drink?" he asked.

"Thank you."

What a sweet smile. McCabe attracted Jimmy's attention, and the barman refilled her glass from the already opened bottle of Chablis. Then he topped up McCabe's glass and winked at him. McCabe paid for the drinks, handing over a note and waiting for his change, and then turned back to her but she wasn't beside him any more. He could see that customers were crowding the door as they were leaving and he thought for a moment that she had slipped out ahead of them but, as he looked around the room, he saw that she was sitting at an empty table by the window and was waiting for him. Carrying the two glasses he joined her and sat facing her across the table. They sipped their wine in silence for a few moments until she spoke again.

"You probably don't remember me Chad, but I've often watched you play here."

What he might say in this situation, when an attractive girl from the audience may be about to proposition him, could make or break the deal so he was careful with his reply and smiled.

"Of course I remember you, but I've got a really bad memory for names…"

"You don't know my name, we've never spoken before. It's Caz … Caz Knight."

"Unusual."

"Short for Casablanca. My parents were crazy about old black and white films."

She smiled at him again, a sort of coy, sideways smile that promised a lot of good things if he jumped through the right hoops.

"Well it's great to talk to you at last Caz," and they flirted and chatted for another few minutes about music, about Brighton, until suddenly she looked him in the eyes, serious now.

"This isn't a good place for me to be seen, Chad. Can we go somewhere? Back to your place?"

When Chad played music in public, occasionally he would meet women who had been so moved by the experience of listening to him that, while they may not actually want to have his babies, they at least wanted to go through the preliminaries. When that happened and if they were attractive, being eight years divorced and still unattached, he didn't like to let them down.

"Sure we can," he answered, and that's how people like McCabe, who are basically decent, get suckered.

***

They didn't speak in the taxi that took them along Brighton seafront to Lewes Crescent, and McCabe sat there in the darkness feeling that small tingle of anticipation which always started when he was on his way to his flat late at night with an attractive girl. He paid off the driver who retrieved McCabe's guitar case and the lightweight AER amplifier from the boot of the taxi and handed them to him. Caz took the amplifier from McCabe and followed him up the short flight of steps, waiting patiently while he struggled to fish out the door key from his hip pocket. A chill wind swept through the deserted Crescent and continued into Sussex Square chasing the taxi as it disappeared around the corner, and McCabe opened the splendidly oversized panelled front door. He stepped aside so that Caz could pass him and enter the lobby, which he shared with the ground floor/basement flat. The wall lights flicked on automatically and displayed the spacious carpeted entrance hall with the door to the neighbours' flat to the left; good neighbours, a couple of well off gay guys who kept themselves to themselves. To the right, the wide staircase curved up and left to the first floor, a reminder of how grand this house once was. He gestured to the stairs with the guitar case and they started up.

If you didn't know McCabe you would think that he was wealthy, living in an apartment on the top three floors of a Grade 1 listed Regency building at one of the best addresses in Brighton. If you then discovered that less than a mile away in Brighton Marina he kept an immaculately restored classic sailing yacht, you would be convinced that he was seriously rich. It was true that he owned the flat and the boat but in cash terms he was just about broke. At the beginning of each January he was always amazed that he'd got through another year and still managed to hold it all together. His life revolved around sailing, attractive women, playing his guitar, and drinking, not necessarily in that order, and for years he'd managed to do all of that and financed it with property deals. At one time Brighton was full of small time property dealers and he was one of the more successful ones. As the last recession started he managed to pull off his biggest deal ever and then the market collapsed leaving him with huge debts and no cash. By selling off his houses and nearly everything else he owned at fire sale prices he managed to survive, and at the same time he hung on to this property and also his boat. So now, his only income was the rent from the flat downstairs, which paid all the bills, and whatever he could earn playing gigs. He'd never been happier in his life.

They reached the first floor landing and McCabe unlocked and opened the door to the flat. He thanked Caz as he took the amp from her, and he went up to the next floor and dumped both amp and guitar in one of the spare bedrooms; there were five bedrooms in total. When he came back Caz had gone into the lounge and he could see that she was puzzled. She saw him watching her.

"No furniture?"

Not strictly true really because she could see that he had a sofa, a low coffee table, and a flat screen wall mounted TV.

"Minimalist," he replied.

There was no point explaining that he'd sold nearly everything except the double bed in his room and two single beds in one of the other rooms. The dining area had a breakfast bar and a couple of stools, and there was a refrigerator, cooker, microwave, a radio and cupboards in the kitchen, a washing machine and dryer in the utility, wardrobes with drawer units in the bedrooms, and bedside tables. The only reason that the cupboards and wardrobes weren't sold was because they were built in, and he'd also kept the curtains. The carpets were still good; as thick and comfortable underfoot as they were when he'd bought them in the good times.

"Glass of wine?" He couldn't offer her anything else because if he had booze in the flat he just drank it all, but he was still disciplined enough to keep a dozen bottles of white, and a half dozen reds in case he had visitors, which was unusual these days.

"Yes please."

"Red or white?"

"Dry white please."

Caz kicked off her shoes and settled into the far corner of the leather sofa with her feet tucked up under her. As she did so her skirt rose up to reveal bare tanned legs, which he saw as a good sign that she was getting comfortable.

McCabe found two wine glasses and, in the fridge, an unopened bottle of Sauvignon Blanc. He removed the cork without fuss, half filled the glasses and carried them through to the lounge and gave one to Caz. Then he sat beside her on the sofa, keeping a respectful distance between them.

"What was it you wanted to talk about?"

She gave him a puzzled look and then, as if she suddenly understood what he meant, gave him a smile.

"Sorry. I can't remember what it was now. Can I stay here tonight, please?"

"Of course you can."

Caz swung her feet to the floor and turned slightly to face him. She moved closer to him but not close enough to touch. He faced her with his left arm along the back of the sofa and his right hand holding the wine. He took a sip and she smiled at him again, a mischievous smile as if she knew something that he didn't. She downed her glass of wine rapidly and then held the empty glass out to him. This girl liked a drink.

McCabe took the glass to the kitchen, half filled it again, and then topped up his own glass. He returned to the lounge and gave her the wine. Caz was still sitting in the same position but her skirt was hitched up slightly higher than when he'd left the room, revealing her thighs, and she still had the mischievous smile. He sat on the sofa but closer to her than before.

She suddenly looked serious, "I'm frightened, Chad."

"There's no need to be frightened of me."

"Not you. I'm not frightened of you," she said with emphasis on the word you.

"What then?"

"I can't explain why, but I'm being hassled by some guys who want money from me."

"Do you owe it to them?"

"Yes."

"Can't you pay them?" he asked.

"I can now, but I think they're watching my flat. They're violent, Chad. They won't listen to me. I've told them I'll pay them but they don't believe me any more. I'm frightened to go home. I've got some cash there but they'll get me before I can get to it, then make me pay them after. I don't know what they'll do to me."

She moved closer to him, held out her hand and he took it. It was small, delicate, and warm.

"Would you go for me Chad?"

"What now?"

"No, not now," she laughed. "In the morning."

"Of course I will, Caz." Something about this girl made him want to protect her.

"I'm so grateful," she said. "I can't tell you what that means to me. I've been so worried," and she looked as though she was about to cry.

At that moment he wanted to scoop her up and make sure that she would never have to worry about anything again, and he put his glass on the coffee table and shifted along the sofa towards her. Caz sat up straight, put her glass on the coffee table, and picked her shoulder bag up from the floor. She rooted around in the bag and pulled out a set of door keys from which she removed a single Yale key and handed it to him. She found an expensive looking gold roller ball pen in the bag and a small notebook. She scribbled in the notebook then tore out the page and gave it to him.

"That's the address."

He glanced at the note and saw an address near Brighton Station.

"There's an antique writing desk in the living room, which is at the front overlooking Queens Road. In the right hand drawer you'll find a cash box with the money in it. I'll wait here until you get back. I'm so grateful, Chad," and she leaned over and kissed him on the cheek. He moved to put his arms around her but she was already on her feet.

"Where will I sleep?"

"With me?" he asked as he stood up.

She put both arms around him and he was aware of her slim young body fitting perfectly against his.

"You're a lovely man, Chad, but I'm too strung out tonight. Let's take it slowly shall we? Another time maybe?"

They separated. What a let down.

"How old are you, Caz?"

"Twenty four. Why?"

"Just wondering. You look a lot younger."

He showed her upstairs to a guest bathroom, and gave her a towel, apologising that he didn't have a spare toothbrush. Back in the kitchen he washed up the glasses and left them to dry on the drainer and, when Caz came out of the bathroom and called down the stairs to him, he showed her to the room with the two single beds. At the door to the bedroom she kissed him on the cheek again, and for a moment he thought that she'd changed her mind.

"Thank you for going to the flat for me, Chad. I have a flatmate, so you'll need to be quiet if she's still asleep. I'll see you here when you get back."

Then she smiled and went in, coyly peeping around the door at him as she closed it.

So mesmerised by her that he hadn't thought to ask why her flatmate couldn't bring her the money, McCabe went to his bedroom. He used the en suite bathroom then undressed and got into bed. Switching off the bedside light he lay there in the darkness thinking impure thoughts about Caz in the next room, and feeling slightly foolish. As the desire slowly faded, common sense took its place. Why had he thought that an attractive girl of twenty four would want to sleep with a man of forty seven when she'd only met him a couple of hours ago? Suitably chastened, he gradually drifted off to sleep completely oblivious to the fact that she had set him up.

Chapter Two

English Channel - 0804 BST Sunday 29th May

The boat hook tore through the synthetic fabric of the red flotation jacket and Jack McCabe's corpse fell back into the black, glass smooth sea with a suck and a splash, rolling slowly until it lay face down in the water yet again. The old fisherman hooked the collar of the jacket once more to prevent the corpse from floating away and rested, oblivious to the flock of gulls circling and screaming overhead as they anticipated a catch being landed. Angrily he cursed at the young fisherman standing next to him, "Come on boy, get a grip, and this time we'll 'ave 'im."

Grunting with the exertion, he hauled the body half out of the water. His young crewmate, fighting back the impulse to throw up, managed to tie a rope under the corpse's arms and secured the other end to the boat. Again, the old fisherman rested for a few moments and then, together, they hauled the body of the dead yachtsman out of the water. It rolled over the starboard gunwale and, with a thud and a wet slap as it hit the deck, they dumped it face up like a huge stranded fish. The younger man backed away until he was stopped by the gunwale on the port side of the boat. Breathing heavily, he pressed himself back against the rusting steel and stared at the corpse with a look of horror on his face. It stared vacantly back at him.

The fishing boat's skipper, who had been watching this from the wheelhouse, picked up the telephone shaped handset of his VHF radio, pressed the red button on the radio marked 16, put the handset to his left ear, pressed the send button with his thumb and spoke.

"Dover Coastguard, Dover Coastguard this is fishing vessel Marie Anne on 16. I have traffic for you. Over."

He released the send button and waited.

The call, although asking for Dover Coastguard in Kent, was received at a radio mast 22 miles away on the cliffs at Newhaven in East Sussex, and was then relayed to the National Maritime Operations Centre at Fareham in Hampshire 60 miles from the fishing boat's position.

A Coastguard radio operator on watch at Fareham selected VHF Channel 16 and replied, "Marie Anne, this is Dover Coastguard. Go to Channel 67 please. Over."

The skipper of the Marie Anne selected Channel 67 on his VHF set and waited for a few seconds before replying, "Dover Coastguard, this is Marie Anne."

Immediately, the Coastguard came back, "Marie Anne, go ahead."

"Dover Coastguard, this is fishing vessel Marie Anne. My position is bearing 077 degrees five miles from the Greenwich Meridian Light Vessel. We've discovered a body floating in the water. Over."

There was a pause.

"Marie Anne, we've had a report of a basking shark in that area, are you sure it's not that?"

"Only if the shark was wearing a red jacket. Over."

There was a silence for a few moments then, "Marie Anne, are there any signs of life? Over."

"No. Dead."

The Coastguard timed the transmission at 0707 GMT, and there was a slight pause until he replied, "Marie Anne. Stand by please."

The skipper gazed through the glass of the wheelhouse at the harsh sunlight glinting from the water, and the unusually flat calm of the English

Channel in late May. During the night the wind had been a steady force four from the West, but had died away just before dawn and now the day was already still and sultry as both the barometer and the temperature rose steadily. It was going to be a hot one. Immediately in front of him, on the deck of the small fishing boat, he could see his two man crew staring at the corpse in its yachtsman's clothes, and he considered that nobody should have been abandoned to float alone in the sea on a day like this. The VHF broke the silence.

"Marie Anne. Where do you intend to take the casualty please?"

"Nowhere! I've got another twenty four hours of fishing to do."

"Marie Anne, I would like you to bring the casualty to the nearest port please. Over."

"Sorry, can't do that. I've got a living to earn. Tell you what, why don't I put it back in the water and mark it with a buoy, and you can arrange for it to be picked up when you're not so busy?"

"Stand by please."

Thirty seconds of silence passed.

"Marie Anne, Dover Coastguard."

The skipper keyed his VHF handset, "Yes sir?"

"Marie Anne, I'm sending a lifeboat to you. Can you describe the casualty please?"

"Fresh, not long dead. Young male adult, wearing red oilies, looks like a yotty. He's got a mini-flare pack attached to his wrist. Bluish pink skin. I'd say he recently drowned."

There was silence for a few moments and then the Coastguard came back, "We've had no Maydays reporting anyone overboard from a yacht. Is there anything unusual about him?"

"Yes," replied the fisherman. "His flies are undone."

Chapter Three

Queens Road, Brighton - 0927 BST Sunday 29th May

Chad McCabe had left Caz sleeping at his flat and had walked from Lewes Crescent to Queens Road, a distance of just under two miles. He was enjoying the relative stillness of the almost deserted street which, during the week, teemed with traffic and pedestrians. An occasional car or bus passed but that was all. Brighton is a nocturnal place at weekends and the population emerges slowly in the mornings. He glanced at the clock above the scrolled Victorian ironwork on the facade of nearby Brighton Station the top of which gleamed white as it caught the sun. It was still early, and he hoped that he could get in and out of the flat without disturbing Caz's flatmate.

The street where McCabe was standing was still in shadow. This part of Queens Road comprised a parade of small shops and offices each with two storeys above. The only person that he could see was a cafe owner, a few doors along, who was sweeping and setting up some well worn chrome tables and chairs ready to entice the day trippers from London who, in an hour or so, would start pouring out of the station. On the right hand side of the shop in front of him was a faded blue wood panelled door badly in need of repainting. Above the door was a borrowed light window, a few inches high, its clear glass thick with dust. Checking the piece of paper that Caz had given him, he double checked that the number was correct and then put the paper back into the pocket of his fleece jacket. He put the key which she had given him into the lock and turned it carefully, entered, closed the door quietly behind him, and put the key in his pocket with the note. Directly in front of him was a narrow gloomy stair covered with carpet, which had a surprisingly expensive feel underfoot. He started up, feeling his way as the murky light from the window above the door gradually faded.

When he reached the first landing McCabe stopped. The stair continued up to the next floor and to his left was a corridor so lacking in natural light that he could see nothing. Taking his phone from his pocket he switched on the torch function, at the same time suddenly remembering to turn the sound off in case it rang. Shining the light along the corridor he could see now that it was thickly carpeted and that there were three closed doors, one on each side and one directly ahead. Which one was the living room with a writing desk in it and which one was Caz's flatmate in? McCabe reasoned that if the flatmate was asleep then that was likely to be in a bedroom on the floor above him. Careful not to make any noise, he moved slowly along the corridor to the furthest door. Reaching out he slowly turned the old fashioned door knob, pushed the door open gently and peered into the room. It was big, extending from the front to the back of the building perhaps thirty feet or so. To his left was a large bay window with the writing desk he was looking for and a swivel chair in front of it. The windows were covered with translucent white curtains thin enough to allow some light in but too thick to see through, and on one side of the bay was a folding partition pulled back but there to be pulled across, if needed, to seal the room from outside light. Leaving the door open, McCabe stepped into the room and glanced around. It contained the same thick carpet as the stair and hallway and, in the centre, was a king sized bed, stripped of any bedding, with a mattress covered by a white sheet. Spread out around three sides of the bed were an array of studio lights and three professional looking video cameras. At the back of the room was another bay window, again with translucent curtains and a folding partition. The walls were painted brilliant white and there was enough light filtering through the curtains to see that at the far end of the room stood four director chairs. McCabe crossed to the desk and pulled the right hand drawer open revealing a ledger book on top of which was the grey metal cash box containing Caz's money. Its thin steel handle glinted dully in the light of the phone torch. He leaned forward, as with his left hand he reached into the drawer, taking hold of the cash box handle. At the same time the studio lights all fired up together and the walls blasted dazzling white reflected light at him. McCabe stopped, rigid with his hand in the drawer.

There was a brief silence and then, "Well who the hell are you?"

The calm female voice from somewhere behind him had put an emphasis on the word you.

"I've got a gun. Turn around slowly, stay still, and let's have a look at you then."

He straightened up and turned carefully to face her. With the studio lights behind her, she was a silhouette about ten feet away. He was careful not to move as she stepped backwards to a control box, which was on a small table behind the door, and pressed a master switch dowsing the studio lights and at the same time switching on the normal domestic ceiling lights. She faced him with her feet slightly apart, completely naked except for the wavy auburn hair which flowed down over her shoulders. She was petite, in her mid twenties, about five feet two inches tall and beautifully shaped.

She had striking green cat like eyes, nipples that were a very light shade of pink, and slightly freckled skin. A genuine redhead although, as she had no body hair, you would not have been able to immediately check whether that was so, but McCabe didn't see any of that as his eyes recovered from the blinding glare. All he saw was the Smith and Wesson 38 Special Airweight revolver held steadily in two small, slim, manicured hands, which was pointing straight at his chest.

Ignoring the stomach clenching flight reaction that had swept over him, McCabe tried to think rationally. She hadn't fired the gun at him so he assumed that the flatmate wasn't going to murder him in cold blood. Not yet anyway, but she simmered with suppressed anger.

"I asked you who you are?"

The gun didn't waiver.

"It's not what it looks like. I'm collecting some cash for Caz."

"Oh, really?"

" Really. She gave me her door key. I've got a note which she wrote the address on. Would you recognise her writing? I can show you."

"Put your hands up and move over to the bed."

McCabe did as she instructed and edged to the side of the bed while she slowly followed him with the revolver, keeping it steadily aimed at him.

"Where is this note?"

"In my right jacket pocket."

"OK then. Keep your left hand up and very slowly take the note out of your pocket with your thumb and forefinger, then put it on the bed."

McCabe carefully did as she said and, now that he was recovering from the initial shock of being discovered, he started to take in the fact that she was naked.

"Put both hands up and move back to the desk."

McCabe shuffled back to the desk and watched her as she sidestepped to the bed, picked up the note with her left hand, glanced at it, and dropped it back onto the bed, all the time keeping the gun trained on him. She held the revolver with both hands again.

"What's your name?"

"McCabe. Chad McCabe."

"OK Chad. So you let yourself into my flat to do a bit of burglary and you say you've been sent here by Caz Knight. Is that right?"

"Exactly."

"That's me, I'm Caz Knight. So how does that work then?"

Chapter Four

Brighton Marina - 0932 BST Sunday 29th May

The yacht Tiger Fish passed between the Brighton Marina breakwaters and entered the harbour. She was a Swedish built Hallberg-Rassy 46 centre cockpit sloop, dark blue hulled, teak decked, sixteen years old and in immaculate condition. Her foresail had been stowed below decks and her mainsail was rolled into her mast. Fenders were hanging over the port side and mooring ropes were ready fore and aft as she motored over the calm waters of the marina at five knots to her home berth on the hammerhead at the end of Pontoon 9. On deck were two men and a woman.

The man standing by the mast was in his late thirties. He was tall with an untidy mass of curly blonde hair and he looked like a body builder. He wore a blue denim shirt, navy blue cargo pants and brown deck shoes, and he stared fixedly ahead as they turned and approached the mooring.

The man at the wheel was in his fifties, short and expensively dressed in a light blue checked cotton shirt, navy blue fleece jacket, navy blue tailored cotton trousers and blue deck shoes. His white hair gave him a distinguished look and, as he turned the wheel, the sun glinted from the gold watch on his left wrist. He peered intently ahead through spectacles that had thick pebble lenses looking like the bases of two jam jars.

The woman standing by the cockpit on the port side deck was in her early thirties, tall, blonde, and with a classically beautiful face. She wore designer sun glasses and identical clothes to the man at the helm.

None of them spoke and, as they slowed and reached Tiger Fish's berth, the body builder and the woman dropped onto the pontoon, tied the warps to the mooring cleats in figures of eight, added springs to curtail any forward or backward movement, and then climbed back on board. The engine was cut by the man at the wheel and all three went below.

Five minutes later, two men appeared in Tiger Fish's cockpit. They had tanned complexions and they wore yachting clothes. Both had baseball caps, peaks forward, pulled down over their eyes, and they each carried a rucksack slung over their right shoulder. They stepped down onto the pontoon and, without hurrying, walked the length of it to the gate at the far end. They turned left through the gate, walked along the massive concrete West Jetty, exited through the main gate and walked up the ramp to the road. A nondescript Volvo estate car, parked in the berthholder unloading spaces on the left, started its engine. The men climbed into the back seat of the car and it drove away at legal speed and disappeared out of the marina. If any of the five people they had passed on that walk had been asked to describe the two men later - and they weren't - all they could have said was that they looked like yachtsman and were sun tanned. None of them would have been able to describe the car, not even its colour.

Another six minutes elapsed, then the woman and the man with the pebble glasses appeared on Tiger Fish's deck. They climbed down onto the pontoon, and walking then half running they hurried to the first gate. Instead of following the men to the road they crossed the West Jetty, climbed a flight of metal stairs and, fifteen minutes after Tiger Fish had tied up, burst into the Marina office. The man, who now appeared to be in a state of agitation, rushed to the reception desk.

"Quickly, I need a telephone. It's an emergency."

The startled receptionist pushed a telephone towards him. He grabbed the receiver and punched the buttons 999 and immediately a female voice answered him.

"Emergency. Which service do you require?"

"Coastguard. Quickly."

He heard the operator talk to the Coastguard and then he was connected and answered by the Coastguard operator.

"What is the nature of the emergency please?"

"My name is Graham Allerton. I own the yacht Tiger Fish and I wish to report a man overboard, nine miles off of Brighton."

Chapter Five

Queens Road, Brighton - 0933 BST Sunday 29th May

"You'd better start talking. I asked you how that works. I'm Caz Knight and you say I've sent you to burgle my flat."

McCabe's gaze remained fixed on the revolver aimed at his heart as he tried to work out how he'd got into this mess.

"I met a girl last night who said she's called Casablanca Knight. She asked me to come to this flat and collect some cash for her from the desk drawer. She gave me the front door key and told me to come in quietly so that I don't wake her flatmate."

"I don't have a flatmate. I live on my own which is why I'm pointing this gun at you. Sit on the chair, keep facing me, and put your hands behind your head."

Slowly, Chad backed towards the desk chair, sat on it, and put his hands behind his head realising that he still had the phone in his left hand.

Keeping him covered, Caz edged her way to the door and reached up to take a thin white robe from a hook on the back of it. She slipped it on, changing the gun from one hand to the other while still keeping it trained on McCabe, then resuming her two handed grip she moved back to the bed and sat on it facing him.

"Tell me about yourself, McCabe."

"What do you want to know?"

"Everything you can think of to stop me shooting you."

"I'm forty seven years old, I live in Brighton at Lewes Crescent. I'm a musician, I'm divorced, I was doing up and selling houses until the last crash came but

I just managed to get out without going under. I don't have a car. I sail, I've got a Hillyard 12 Tonner at Brighton Marina..."

"OK," she interrupted. "You're a regular guy, you're just over six feet tall, slim, black hair no sign of any grey, good looking. I've got it. You're not a burglar. You've met my sister Tricia and she's conned you into coming to my flat to get some cash to bail her out of the latest fix she's got herself into. I recognised her writing on the note."

Caz tossed the revolver onto the bed.

"It's not real, it's a film prop, but don't get any ideas. I'm pretty good at self defence."

McCabe gratefully relaxed and sat back in the chair while shaking his hands to get the blood circulating in them.

"A film prop?" he asked, putting the phone into his left jacket pocket.

"Yeah, I make movies here, of the adult type but with a storyline."

McCabe took in the room again. Of course, video cameras, studio lights, bed, imitation firearm, flimsy robe. He imagined for a moment the fantasies that must have been acted out here with this beautiful redhead playing the lead while, outside, commuters and shoppers passed by oblivious to what was going on behind the nondescript Queens Road facade.

"Why would she send me to get the cash instead of coming here herself?"

"Did she tell you that there were people watching the place so it wasn't safe for her?"

"Yes."

"Well, she might be right about that. She upsets a lot of dodgy people. She stays here sometimes, which is why she has a key, but I haven't seen her for about a month. I'll have that key now if you don't mind."

McCabe fished out the key from his jacket and tossed it onto the bed.

"Time for you to leave," said Caz, "and when you see my sister tell her to call me."

"I'm really sorry about this, I really…" he started.

She stood, "Don't worry. Just go. It's not your fault and it's not the first time she's set some random man up to do something stupid."

McCabe got to his feet and headed for the door, relieved to be leaving. As he reached the doorway she called out to him.

"Chad?"

He turned and she was standing facing him, feet apart again but this time with her hands on her hips. The robe had fallen open and she was smiling.

"If you ever want to do some acting come back and see me. I'll always be able to fit you in."

McCabe turned and felt his way along the darkened corridor and down the stairs. He let himself out into the daylight of the street closing the door behind him, thankful to have escaped. It had sounded like a genuine offer, but he wondered if she meant with or without the cameras.

Chapter Six

Paris, France - 1058 CEST Sunday 29th May

The terrorist known as Angelos sat on the edge of the single bed and waited. Twenty two years old, dressed in jeans, trainers and a black rugby shirt, the short jet black hair, dark brown eyes and olive skin creating a Mediterranean appearance which could have been Italian, Greek, or Arabic; a student perhaps.

The apartment in which Angelos waited had originally been a large salon on the first floor of what was once a town house close to the Gare Saint-Lazare, one of several main railway stations in Paris. One quarter of the salon had been partitioned off to create a bathroom, leaving the rest in the form of an L shaped bed sitting room with a door into the bathroom and another into the corridor. The room contained the bed, a bedside locker, a small wardrobe which also contained drawers, a coffee table, a TV, and an old armchair. In one corner were a sink, a refrigerator and a cooker.

On the bedside locker, in a tall, clear glass vase sealed with cling film, was a mouse which Angelos had trapped the night before by laying the vase on its side and baiting it with a piece of chocolate. The terrorist was surprised that the animal was still alive, and was waiting to see how long it would take for it to suffocate. From time to time a vigorous shake of the vase added to the mouse's torment and it would run round and round using up the precious oxygen in its trap. If it didn't die soon, Angelos would try snipping its feet off with kitchen scissors to see what would happen. The terrorist listened to the street noises filtering through the tall glazed double doors which opened onto the balcony and were ajar a few inches in a vain attempt to ventilate the room. For three days Angelos had not ventured out onto the balcony, not wanting to be seen even though, due to the unseasonably warm weather, the heat in the room was becoming oppressive, unable to escape past the net curtains. Renard the agent handler was already thirty minutes late but there was no hurry. He had been waiting in the apartment when Angelos had first arrived, and was just the latest of many handlers that the terrorist had met on the circuitous route which led to this place. Renard was typical of the handlers and enablers in every country which Angelos had passed through in order to get here, and the terrorist despised them all for being nervous, worried figures, constantly afraid of being caught by the authorities. There was a knock on the door.

Angelos stood, crossed the room, peered through the small spy hole in the door, opened it and stood to one side without speaking to allow the short, fat, sweating man to pass, then closed the door behind him. Renard was red faced and wore a crumpled beige linen suit and a dark blue open necked shirt. He mopped his face and neck with a large red handkerchief as he looked around the room, pausing for a moment when he saw the mouse in the vase then, choosing to ignore it, he crossed the room and sat down heavily in the armchair. He placed a black leather briefcase on the floor beside him and spoke in heavily accented English.

"It is hot out there my friend."

The terrorist returned to sit in the same place on the bed and, ignoring Renard's attempt at conversation, replied, also in English, "What do you have for me?"

This one made Renard nervous. He had met many young fanatics, all of them dangerous, but all of them respectful and eager to please him. Angelos had an air of menace like an explosive charge that would destroy you if you mishandled it. The sooner he was rid of this particular courier the better he would like it. He picked up the briefcase, placed it on the coffee table and opened it.

"These are for you."

From the briefcase he took a French passport, a French driving licence, a cheap mobile phone and a charger, a bundle of Euros in used notes of various denominations, three sets of door keys, a typed sheet of A4 paper, and placed them all on the coffee table. He leaned over the table and handed the passport and driving licence to Angelos.

"You are now a French citizen."

Angelos idly flicked through the passport, glanced at the driving licence and tossed them both onto the bed.

Renard pointed to the phone, "This pay as you go phone is new and has never been used. It has 50 Euros of credit in it and only one number in its memory. It is the number of another mobile phone and that is the number you use to contact me, but only in an emergency, otherwise I will contact you. You will not use it for any other calls. You will switch the phone on for the first time at noon eight days from now, and every day at noon after that. You will switch it off again after two minutes if I do not call you. That is how I will contact you. As an extra precaution the phone has voice distorting software added to it in case anyone should listen to our call. I don't need to explain phone security to you. You know that you must disable the phone after use to avoid having your position tracked."

The terrorist eyed the phone suspiciously. An intense aversion to anything that could be traced ensured that normally, when working, Angelos never carried a personal phone or tablet, and never used credit cards or anything else that left a trail which the authorities could follow.

"You must read what is on this sheet of paper and memorise the three addresses which are typed there."

He passed the paper to Angelos who studied it carefully for a minute and then passed it back. Renard produced a cigarette lighter, touched a flame to the paper, and held it as it burned into the empty ashtray on the coffee table. When it was just ash he stood, picked up the ashtray, walked to the bathroom, tipped the ash into the basin, broke it into pieces and washed it away. He walked back into the bedroom and sat in the chair again, then passed the three sets of door keys to Angelos.

"These keys fit the locks of the safe houses whose addresses you have just memorised. You will leave here and travel to the first address in five days time."

Angelos took the keys and put them on the bed.

"And here," said the handler, "are five thousand Euros. This is for expenses in addition to your substantial fee which we have already paid into your nominated bank account."

Finally, Renard took out of the briefcase a box 15cm square by 5cm deep, and carefully placed it on the coffee table. It was smooth with rounded corners, was made of metal the colour of aluminium, and was heavier than its size suggested. Closing the briefcase he said, "Now I will tell you the details of your mission."

For the first time Angelos appeared to be interested.

"As you know, in the past, the toxin ricin has been used in terror attacks against civilian populations, and also by certain governments to assassinate their opponents. The box on the table contains 250 grams of abrin powder, which is approximately 30 times more toxic than ricin. There is enough in that box to kill at least half a million people if it is delivered correctly. Inhaled, swallowed, or injected it breaks down the body's cell structure, and there is no antidote for it.

"Don't be alarmed, the box is sealed but on no account are you to attempt to open it. Even a microscopic amount will lead to unpleasant sickness within hours followed by death within 2 or 3 days from organ failure.

"For many years since the sarin nerve gas attack against the Tokyo subway system in 1995 and the anthrax attacks in America in 2001, governments have feared a large scale chemical or biological attack against their populations. They class abrin as what they call a Category B threat because they believe that any such attack would result in low mortality rates. The reason that they think that it would be ineffective is because they believe that abrin cannot be produced in sufficient quantities to be worthwhile. They are wrong. Abrin is a naturally occurring protein which is found in the seeds of a tropical plant called the rosary pea and, for many years, my client's chemists and biologists have been cultivating the plant and accumulating large quantities of the toxin. The result is contained in the box that you see before you. Your task will be to deliver this box of abrin to England where it will be used for assassination and attacks on public gatherings, military establishments, and public and commercial buildings."

Angelos slowly nodded, already considering how that might be possible.

"I don't have to tell you," said Renard, "that the time, expense, and effort taken to produce this material makes it priceless. My client has more but you must protect this box at all costs. Can you do this?"

Angelos looked at him scornfully, "Of course."

Renard continued, "Apart from the abrin, the box contains a small explosive charge with a timer. We are aware that you are an independent operative, not committed to any particular cause, so we don't expect you to martyr yourself."

On the top of the box was a small spring loaded flap which he pressed and which opened to reveal a small red dial.

"If you are compromised, you are to turn this dial fully to the right, which will give you ten minutes to get away before the charge explodes and disperses the toxin."

Renard carefully pressed the flap closed, hiding the timer switch again.

"You will not be able to use sea ports and airports so you will be travelling through Normandy, as you can see from the addresses. When you reach the third address on the list you will be told how you will travel to England. Once in England you will be met by our people who will take delivery of the package. We have inserted many of our people into Britain along this route so it has been well tested. When the time comes to leave here you will travel via the addresses which you have memorised in the order in which they are listed. When I speak to you on the phone, you will identify yourself by using your existing code name, Angelos."

Renard stood up, "Are you ready for your mission?"

Angelos also stood and stared intently at the box of abrin on the table, "Always."

"Very good. We will meet again before you leave France."

The terrorist closed the door behind Renard who sweated his way out of the room, mopping his face and the back of his neck with the handkerchief as he went. Crossing the room Angelos sat on the bed again, considering the mission: straightforward, routine, and identical to many others already carried out successfully. The only thing unusual about this one was that the package to be carried had the potential to kill half a million people. So what? One person, a million people, what did it matter? The terrorist turned to the vase with the mouse in it and decided to increase its suffering.

Chapter Seven

Lewes Crescent, Brighton - 1040 BST Sunday 29th May

McCabe looked at the note in his hand, "IOU £200. Pay you back when I see you next. x"

During the short walk from the real Caz Knight's flat to Brighton Station and the taxi journey from the station back to his flat, he had been wondering how to deal with Caz's sister, Tricia. Call the police? And tell them what? That he'd brought an attractive woman back to his flat the night before, and that she'd set him up for a bit of burglary on her behalf? He didn't think so.

As it was, the dilemma was solved for him when he arrived at his home because she had already left. The drawer of his bedside table was open, the £200 which he kept in ready cash was missing and the note was in its place. As far as he could tell, nothing else had been taken.

Angry with himself, McCabe showered and tried to put out of his mind what had happened. He dressed in his usual day gear of navy blue cargo pants, brown Henri Lloyd deck shoes worn without socks, a blue denim shirt, and a navy blue Berghaus fleece jacket. Then, still annoyed at his own stupidity, he left the flat and began the twenty minute walk to his boat moored at Brighton Marina. The walk calmed him and, by the time he had reached his boat, he had his mind on the never ending list of maintenance jobs that had to be completed.

Two hours later McCabe had finished rubbing down and varnishing the wheel of his Hillyard 12 Tonner, Honeysuckle Rose, the thirty six foot centre cockpit sailing sloop which he had owned for the last fifteen years. He sat back in the cockpit satisfied that he had at least achieved something today. That wasn't always the case and it never ceased to amaze him how easy it is to potter about on a boat without ever actually doing anything. Not as easy on this one as on a modern boat, of course. If he didn't constantly maintain her oak frames and mahogany hull and panelling with paint and varnish, the weather and the sea would claim her, and he had to be passionate about it. Built just down the coast at Hillyard's Yard on the river at Littlehampton in 1959, a succession of owners had carefully looked after her and he sometimes felt that the boat didn't actually belong to him, but that he just kept her going for the owners who would follow him. She was called Tonyanne when he bought her, and Chad renamed her, performing the Neptune Boat Naming Ceremony with friends and a few bottles of Veuve Clicquot champagne. He chose the name Honeysuckle Rose after the Reinhardt/Grappelli rendition of that tune which contained his favourite Django solo, but usually he just referred to her as Rose. On paper, because of the Lewes Crescent property, McCabe was rich but in reality he didn't have much cash. On the other hand, because of his gigs and the rent from the downstairs flat, he wasn't poor either, and he had the two things that are needed to look after a wooden yacht: time and a willingness to spend however much it took to maintain her. He reached out with his right hand and fondly touched Rose's mahogany cockpit bulkhead with his fingertips and decided that life wasn't bad.

The speaker on the VHF radio suddenly came to life; yet another leisure boat owner asking the Coastguard for a radio check even though it was discouraged. McCabe usually left the VHF on, tuned on dual watch to Channels 16 and 67, to get a feel for what was going on out there, even when he wasn't sailing. There had been routine traffic today, except for some poor sod pulled out of the water earlier this morning. He had listened to the tail end of a conversation between the Coastguard and the fishing boat skipper who had found the casualty, while they confirmed again the position where the body had been pulled out of the sea. Force of habit formed by years of entering distress information into logbooks had made him jot down the position on a notepad, which he kept beside the radio.

Resisting the temptation to sit back and enjoy the sunshine, McCabe got to his feet and stepped down into the main saloon. One of the reasons that he had chosen this boat, in preference to all the others which he had looked at, was that his six foot two inch frame could stand upright inside her with room to spare. As he cleaned the varnish brush in a jar of spirit placed in the galley sink he considered which of the twenty or so small outstanding tasks to perform for Honeysuckle Rose next. He dried the brush with a piece of rag and laid it on the wooden draining board, then he washed and wiped his hands. Picking up his boat guitar, he took a flatpick from his pocket, and sat for a moment on the starboard saloon berth while he played a few notes. Fifteen minutes later he was still there, working the fingers of his left hand smoothly over the fretboard and practising his picking technique with his right. McCabe's D hole Harmsworth and Willis guitar with its solid spruce top, mahogany neck and ebony back and sides, was a modern copy of Django Reinhardt's acoustic Selmer Maccaferri and, as an example of what could be done with wood, it was as impressive as Honeysuckle Rose.

He was part way through a slow rendition of Django's classic tune "Nuages" when his mobile phone rang. He stopped playing and answered it.

"Mr McCabe?"

"Yes."

"Sussex Police here, Mr McCabe. I wonder if we could come and see you?"

"Of course. What for?"

"I'd rather not say over the phone, if you don't mind. Where are you at the moment?"

"I'm at Brighton Marina on my boat."

"OK. We'll be along very shortly. Whereabouts exactly?"

"I'm on Pontoon 16, at the far end on the right, the boat name is Honeysuckle Rose… but…"

"I'll explain when we get there, Mr McCabe. Please stay there. We'll be about twenty minutes."

The line went dead. McCabe put the guitar down then stood, stepped up into the cockpit, sat down again and waited. Was it about his meeting with Caz Knight this morning? He was pretty sure that he hadn't done anything else to interest the police. Nothing illegal. He sat there with anxiety gnawing at him. Had Caz called the police? How did they get his phone number? Yet another distraction and another reason to sit and do nothing on his boat.

They weren't twenty minutes, they were there in fifteen. Two uniformed constables, one in his early twenties and the other ten years older. The older one spoke.

"Mr McCabe?"

"Yes, come aboard. Have a seat."

McCabe waited while the two policemen climbed into his cockpit, with all the clumsiness of people who are not used to boats, and planted their heavy shoes on his decking. The constable who had spoken, and who would be the only one to speak, looked around at the people on nearby boats and said quietly, "Do you mind if we go below Mr McCabe?"

"Of course not."

The three of them sat in the saloon, McCabe looking apprehensive and the two policemen looking awkward. The older policeman made up his mind. There was no easy way to do this.

"I'm sorry to have to tell you this Mr McCabe, but I've got some bad news. A fishing boat discovered a body in the Channel this morning and we think it's your son, Jack."

McCabe stared at him in silence. Did he imagine that? He continued to stare at the policeman.

"Did you understand what I said, Mr McCabe?"

"No."

"I know this is a shock, but we need to confirm his identity with you."

"No."

Both police officers knew that they would never get used to this however many times they had to do it.

"Did you understand what I said Mr McCabe?"

"No."

"Well, we'll just sit here quietly, while you gather your thoughts."

The three of them sat there in silence in the safe world of Honeysuckle Rose's saloon while McCabe considered the absurdity of the situation. Two men he'd never met before had come to tell him that Jack was dead. Ridiculous. Not possible. Everything was normal. It was just another ordinary day in Brighton Marina. But it wasn't an ordinary day. Two strangers had come here to tell him that his son was dead. It must be a mistake.

"Why do you think it was Jack?"

The police officers both felt a surge of relief as the tension was broken. He was talking.

"Credit cards, ID that sort of thing."

"How did you find me?"

"Passport with contact details."

"It could be a mistake," said McCabe.

"That's why we need you to identify the body."

"Yes."

The two police officers waited on the pontoon while McCabe carefully locked up the boat, and then the three of them started towards the security gate. As they walked the interminable length of Pontoon 16, McCabe was aware of other people on the moored boats they passed who carefully avoided staring at him.

"They probably think I've been arrested," he said, for the sake of something to say. Then he realised that his life had just changed forever and there was nothing to joke about.

Chapter Eight

Brighton Marina - 1150 BST Wednesday 1st June

When a drowning victim is retrieved from the sea and taken into a port in Sussex a set procedure must be followed. The police are called and will meet the lifeboat. The ambulance service used to attend but, in most cases, if the casualty is obviously dead, they are no longer required to do so, which allows them to focus their limited resources on the living. If, for example, rigor mortis has set in, as it had with Jack McCabe, the police officer at the scene will follow the guidelines of Sussex Police Policy Document 474/2014 (Section 2: Recognition Of Life Extinct) and will make what is called an assumption of death. The police will call the duty undertaker who transports the body to the public mortuary and, as an inquest is likely, a police officer will attend at the mortuary to ensure continuity of evidence and complete a Form G5 (sudden death) for the Coroner's Officer. The body has to be formally identified. The coroner is informed and will order a post mortem examination to discover the cause of death; then the person who this was originally is no longer a person, no longer a casualty, he is a corpse, male, early twenties in this case.

Following the dissection, after the checking of stomach contents, the weighing of body parts and the examination of internal organs, it was proved beyond reasonable doubt that the cause of death was drowning. The coroner then opened an inquest which was immediately adjourned, and an interim death certificate was issued so that a funeral could take place. The corpse was given into the care of a funeral director and it was taken in a coffin to a chapel of rest where it became a person again. The Coroner's Officer was instructed to gather together witness statements and make enquiries into the circumstances of the death on behalf of the Coroner. Until these enquiries were completed - and it could take months - the full inquest could not be held, which would leave Jack McCabe's family in limbo not knowing what had happened.

Chad McCabe had drunk himself senseless, which is what he always did when life became too difficult. Before that he had done all the right things: identified Jack's body, spoken to the Coroner's Officer, and contacted Jack's mother his ex wife, who normally would hardly deign to speak to him, to tell her what had happened. Then, locked away and grieving on Honeysuckle Rose, he had started on the bottles of cheap wine accumulated during sailing trips to France, and ten year old Laphroaig malt whisky, but anything alcoholic would have done.

Now it was just before midday and, in his sleep, McCabe could hear a persistent knocking on the hull, then it stopped. He turned over and pulled the duvet around his ears and the knocking started again. He turned onto his back and the noise stopped. Opening his eyes he could see that he was in the double berth in Rose's stern cabin, that he hadn't closed the curtains when he had fallen into bed after the drink ran out just before dawn, and that it was now daylight. He looked at his watch. The knocking started again and McCabe pushed back the duvet quietly cursing to himself. At least he was so used to drinking that he didn't suffer from hangovers, but his mouth tasted foul and his brain was only working at half speed. Levering himself out of the bed he saw that he was fully clothed except for his shoes. He stood, slid back the cabin door, stepped up into the cockpit and, squinting against the brightness of the sunlight, he raised the side flap of the cockpit tent. McCabe stopped himself as he was about to voice an angry response to the knocking. Standing on the pontoon and looking at him with a concerned expression was the most beautiful woman he had ever met. She was in her early thirties, tall with thick shoulder length naturally blonde hair, not straight but with a slight wave. She had high cheekbones, and strikingly blue eyes with those wide open enlarged pupils that some women have, which convince every man that they meet that they want him. She smiled a wide dazzling smile and her full lips parted to reveal perfect white teeth, then her expression changed and she looked concerned again. McCabe, unable to prevent himself, looked down and saw that she was barefoot and, as his gaze travelled up her slim but curvaceous body, that she had long bare tanned legs, that she was wearing a tight black mini skirt with a wide black leather belt and a cream silk blouse with the top two buttons undone. He couldn't decide whether she was wearing a bra or not and he tried to put the thought out of his mind. Her left hand was raised, palm upward level with her shoulder, and from the long slim fingers dangled a pair of sling backed stiletto heeled shoes made of black leather. A soft black leather shoulder bag completed the outfit, all of which gave her the look of an expensively groomed fashion model.

"Hello," she said with a seductive smile, a gentle voice and an upper class accent. "My name is Sophie May and I wonder if I could talk to you?"

McCabe was conscious of the fact that he hadn't washed, shaved, or brushed his teeth for two days and that he stank like old bilge water. He smoothed down his hair with his left hand in a vain attempt to improve his appearance.

"Of course," he replied. "Come aboard."

Placing the shoes on the deck she grasped the guardrail with both hands and pulled herself up through the gap in the rail which formed the gate. As she raised her foot to step over the coaming into the cockpit the mini skirt slid up her thighs revealing a flash of white underwear and McCabe looked away to preserve her modesty. She sat on the bench seat looking demure with her ankles and knees together and her hands clasped in her lap.

"I say, you are Mr McCabe, aren't you? How silly of me. I just assumed that you were."

"Yes I am. Chad McCabe."

"I wanted you to know how sorry I am at what happened."

"Well that's very kind of you," replied McCabe, struggling to look normal and escape from the effects of his drinking session. "Did you know my son?"

"I was with him when he went overboard, but you probably know that."

McCabe sat down on the opposite side of the cockpit, "No I don't. I don't know much at all about it. The police won't tell me anything because it all has to wait until there's an inquest, and that could take months. All I know is that Jack was crossing the Channel in a yacht called Tiger Fish and he went overboard."

"You poor man," she said, studying him intently. "You look all in."

McCabe wasn't sure how to answer. Tell her the truth, that he'd been drinking solidly for two days, or lie?

"I had a late night," he replied. Then remembering his manners, "Can I get you anything? Tea? Coffee?"

"Oh, no thank you. I won't keep you. You must have a thousand things to do, but I wanted you to know how awfully sorry I am about Jack."

"It would help me if you could tell me what happened," said McCabe.

There was a sudden bleeping noise and she reached into the shoulder bag, which she had placed on the seat beside her, and took out two mobile phones. She held one in each hand and, after a quick glance at them, put one of them back into the bag. With her thumb she rapidly pressed a succession of buttons on the one in her hand, pressed the send key and put the phone back into her bag.

Sophie smiled her beautiful smile at McCabe, "Sorry about that. Text message. What were we saying?"

"About what happened…"

She looked grave, "Yes. You know we'd crossed the Channel in Tiger Fish two days before? We were in a race from Brighton to Fécamp in Normandy."

"I didn't know," replied McCabe. "I only saw Jack occasionally. We hadn't fallen out, it's just that he had his life, I have mine, you know what I mean…"

"I do know," replied Sophie. "It was the same with my mother and me, we hardly ever saw each other. Then she died four years ago. Everybody's so busy aren't they?"

She waited for a moment but, when he didn't reply went on, "Well, we were coming back from Fécamp in Tiger Fish. Do you know her?"

"No."

"Big yacht. Moored over there on Pontoon 9," she gestured vaguely with her left hand. "We were coming back on Saturday night. It all happened so suddenly. There were just the two of us on watch and the boat was on automatic steering. One minute Jack was having a pee off the back of the boat while I looked ahead and the next minute he'd slipped and was in the water. I wish they wouldn't do that but you know what racing crew are like, anything rather than having to go below."

A common cause of accidents on sailing yachts thought McCabe. It gave rise to an urban myth which says that the US Coastguard refer to it as an FFU, Found Flies Undone.

What did you do?" asked McCabe.

"He was hanging onto the back of the boat with his feet in the water but I couldn't pull him up. I ran below and raised the alarm, and shouted that Jack was hanging onto the back of the boat. I'm not much use in a crisis and I was panicking so Graham and Frik told me to stay below and they went up..."

McCabe interrupted, "Who are Graham and Frik?"

"Sorry," answered Sophie. "Graham Allerton owns Tiger Fish and Frik Benniker is his crew boss when we're racing. Anyway, Graham and Frik went up and it went quiet for a while. Then they shouted down that Jack had gone and between them they got the sails down and got the engine going, and then we went back to look for him."

"But you didn't find him?"

Sophie looked down at her hands and said quietly, "No we didn't."

"How long did you search for?"

"I don't really know. I sort of lost it then. I wasn't much use I'm afraid. We motored up and down for hours I think, and then Graham gave up and we got to Brighton Marina as fast as we could to report it."

"Why didn't they radio for help?" asked McCabe.

"I don't know," she replied looking down at her hands. "I'm not much help to you really am I?"

Sophie looked crestfallen and they were silent for a few moments. Then her face lit up.

"I do know where it happened though, because when we went to the Marina office to report it I heard Graham tell the Coastguard that he wanted to report a man overboard nine miles off of Brighton."

"Did you know Jack well?" asked McCabe.

"Not well. I only met him on these racing trips that we do. He was nice though. I liked him."

"Everybody liked him," said McCabe. "He was one of those people that everyone takes to."

The silence descended between them again until it was broken by Sophie.

"Jack told me that you live aboard here."

"Sometimes I do, yes. All my worldly goods discarded except the essentials. I have a flat as well but I prefer living on the boat."

Sophie reached out and touched the mahogany trim around the saloon door, "She is rather beautiful, isn't she?"

"I think so."

"How do you manage for space?"

"That's easy," replied McCabe. "If I haven't used something for a year I throw it away. It's surprising how little space we actually need. Most people spend a lifetime collecting things that they never use."

"Well I think it's a lovely way to live. Would you take me out in her some time?"

"Of course I will, if you'd like to."

"I'd love to," she smiled at him again and then became serious. "I'd better go and let you get on."

They both stood and she reached out her right hand which felt cool and soft when he shook it.

"It's been so nice to meet you," she said. "And I'm so sorry about Jack."

"Thank you."

Sophie picked up her bag, stepped down onto the pontoon and picked up her shoes from the deck. She smiled her dazzling smile again and said, "Next time we meet will be in happier circumstances, I hope." Then she turned and walked away along the pontoon still carrying the shoes in her left hand, palm up, level with her shoulder.

He watched her until she was out of sight and then went down into the stern cabin. It was time to get his life under control again.

McCabe spent the next half an hour cleaning up the debris of his drinking binge. Then he found some butter and an old loaf in the refrigerator, and toasted a couple of slices which he forced himself to eat although he wasn't hungry. A cafetiere of coffee made him feel almost normal again. As he showered and shaved he thought of Jack and Sophie May, he thought of the meeting he'd had with the Coroner's Officer, and it was while he was dressing in clean clothes that he decided to have a look at Tiger Fish. It could be months before the full inquest into Jack's death so he would carry out his own investigation to discover what had happened.

He locked up, and carrying a black plastic rubbish sack containing his empty bottles he walked the length of the pontoon, pleased to have a purpose again and enjoying the feel of the sun hot on his skin. McCabe unlocked and went through the gate at the end of the pontoon, dumped the sack of bottles in a refuse container as he passed, and crossed the main jetty. As he reached Pontoon 9 he saw that the steel bar security gate was about to opened by a woman coming in the opposite direction. Because his key fob would only unlock the gate to the pontoon that his own boat was moored on, McCabe increased his pace as the woman hurried past him and he caught the gate to Pontoon 9 before it could swing shut and lock itself again. He walked the length of the pontoon reading the boat names on either side of him until, on the hammerhead at the very end, he found her broadside on to him. Neatly sign written in gold lettering on her dark blue hull were the words Tiger Fish of Groombridge.

McCabe stopped and let his eyes wander over her taking in every detail of her spars and rigging, her shape and condition. He recognised her immediately as a Hallberg-Rassy 46: expensive, safe, fast, built of glass reinforced plastic, aluminium spars, teak deck, high quality joinery, centre cockpit with a fixed tempered glass windscreen, large wheel, and a wide binnacle filled with expensive instruments. The overall impression was of a carefully maintained high specification yacht owned by somebody who could afford to look after her. He walked forward to get a closer look and, when he reached her, he stood on the pontoon deep in thought as he studied her stern and tried to picture Jack falling from it into the cold waters of the English Channel. A huge man, moving quickly, suddenly launched himself up the steps from Tiger Fish's saloon and stood firmly in the cockpit, towering above him with his hands balled into fists, and staring at him with menacing steely grey eyes.

He snarled at McCabe with a clipped South African accent, "What do you want?"

Taken aback, McCabe hesitated as he stared up at the man. In the same way that he had surveyed Tiger Fish just now he summed him up quickly: yachtsman, at least six and a half feet tall, late thirties, muscular, tanned rugged face, blonde curly hair, aggressive, violent, dangerous.

"Well? I asked you a question."

"My name is Chad McCabe. I'm Jack McCabe's father."

The man turned and called down into the saloon, "You'd better come up here."

An older man came up the steps into the cockpit. He spoke sternly like someone controlling a dangerous dog, "Alright Frik, there's no need for that." Turning to McCabe, he said pleasantly, "Please come aboard won't you?"

McCabe climbed on board and the three of them stood in the cockpit. The older man held out his right hand which felt limp and clammy when McCabe shook it.

"I'm Graham Allerton. I own Tiger Fish. This is Frik Benniker," he offered, gesturing towards the South African. "He looks after her for me. Won't you sit down Mr McCabe?"

McCabe sat on the starboard side cockpit bench and Benniker and Allerton sat on the opposite side of the cockpit facing him. As he studied Allerton he saw a white haired man in his fifties, wearing thick lensed spectacles, expensively dressed, short in stature and big in confidence. He was well spoken but an occasional lapse indicated that he had probably started from humble beginnings and had consciously worked on his accent.

"What can I do for you, Mr McCabe?" asked Allerton.

"I want to know what happened to Jack."

"Of course you do. What can I tell you? He was on watch at night and he slipped and fell overboard."

"And why couldn't you rescue him?"

"We tried our best Mr McCabe, I promise you."

"Well how did it happen?"

Allerton was silent for a few moments as if he was considering the best way to answer, then he spoke.

"We'd raced to Fécamp on the Normandy coast two days before and we were bringing the boat back to Brighton. There were four of us on board: myself, Frik, Sophie May a friend of mine who was sailing with us, and Jack."

McCabe didn't bother to mention that he'd met Sophie May and commented, "That doesn't sound like enough people to race a boat of this size."

"Ah well, we had a crew of nine on the way over for the race, but the other five came back on the Dieppe Ferry the afternoon before. Jack would have come back with the others on the ferry, but he had a stomach upset and couldn't make the taxi journey to Dieppe."

McCabe interrupted, "Why did they come back on the ferry?"

"We always do it that way. Full racing crew to race and a small crew to deliver her back."

Benniker stirred and looked agitated, "Do we have to explain all this?"

"I think we do Frik," replied Allerton sharply. "Mr McCabe has lost his son."

"Thank you," McCabe said.

Allerton continued, "Well, we left Fécamp at about eight in the evening. That's British Summer Time.

Conditions were very good. A slight swell, wind force four westerly, an easy sail really. Fécamp to Brighton is about sixty five miles on a straight line course so it was a simple overnight trip. I suppose we were averaging about seven knots, so we would easily do it in about nine or ten hours. We weren't racing so we sailed on a constant bearing of 345 degrees true following the rhumb line to Brighton, assuming that the East and West tides would pretty much cancel each other out. We expected to get here at five or six BST the following morning, after a small course adjustment as we made landfall. At midnight we split into watches. Sophie and Jack took the first four hour watch and Frik and I went below to sleep, leaving them in the cockpit to look after the boat. I was woken just before four o'clock by Sophie shouting that Jack had gone overboard. We got the sails down, started the engine, and motored back along our course shining lights on the water, but we couldn't find him."

"Did you radio for assistance?"

"No, the radio wasn't working."

"Did you do anything else to get assistance?"

"Yes. We fired red flares until they ran out, but nobody seems to have seen them."

"Go on," said McCabe.

"We looked for his flares but didn't see him fire any."

"His flares?"

"Yes, I insist that all my crew carry mini flares. I keep them on board and, while they're sailing, they each keep a flare pack in their pockets and hand them in at the end of the trip. They're miniature red flares that fire to a height of eighty metres and burn for about six seconds."

"I know what they are," said McCabe. "I keep them on board myself."

"Do you sail Mr McCabe?" asked Allerton.

"Yes, I own a Hillyard 12 Tonner."

"I see," said Allerton. "So you understand."

"Understand what?"

"You understand how difficult it is to find someone in the sea at night."

"I don't understand why you can't find them if they are firing red flares in a calm sea," replied McCabe.

"But we didn't see any red flares Mr McCabe. We searched until full daylight, and then realised that we weren't going to find him, so we gave up and motored as fast as we could to Brighton. We arrived at about ten o'clock and Sophie and I went straight to the Marina office and raised the alarm. I borrowed their phone to call the Coastguard."

McCabe interrupted again, "Didn't you have mobile phones on board?"

"We did but the batteries had run out while we were in France, and we didn't have any chargers with us. I spoke to the Coastguard on the marina's phone and they told me that Jack had already been found."

"Did that surprise you?"

"It did, but I can only assume that the tide had taken him away from where we were searching."

"And you're telling me that, between the three of you, you didn't have a working phone on board?"

McCabe had suddenly remembered that Sophie had two of them, and presumably Allerton and Benniker each had a mobile phone. Everybody has one.

"That's right," replied Allerton.

"Well I don't believe you."

“I have to get on now Mr McCabe,” said Allerton, visibly annoyed. “I’ve told you everything and I have a meeting to attend.”

“Before I go,” replied McCabe. “I have some more questions to…”

Benniker had sprung to his feet and was standing over him with his huge hands clenched into fists again, “It’s time to leave,” he said quietly.

Shocked at the speed of his dismissal, McCabe stood and climbed down onto the pontoon. He turned and looked past Benniker at Allerton who was now also on his feet.

“I may have more things to ask you,” said McCabe.

“No point, Mr McCabe. We have nothing more to discuss,” Allerton replied.

Chapter Nine

The Cricketers, Brighton - 1316 BST Thursday 2nd June

"It doesn't make sense, Zac," said McCabe.

Zachariah Battersby stared into his pint of Harvey's bitter without answering, while around them the normal clamour of the lunchtime trade carried on hardly aware of the two old friends seated in the pub's only two armchairs by one of the front ground floor windows. When McCabe had suggested that they meet at The Cricketers in the centre of Brighton it had seemed like a good idea but, not being able to deal with other peoples' emotions easily, Zac was finding it difficult to know what to say.

Zac had originally worked for Chad as a handyman and he was now the nearest thing that McCabe had to a close friend. He was a tall, wiry, happy man, well past retirement age, who spoke with a rough Cockney accent, and who never let anything get him down. He had short, fine, white hair with a bald patch on the top always covered by an old faded blue baseball cap. His piercing blue eyes contrasted with his lean face, ruddy because he drank too much although Chad couldn't ever remember seeing him drunk, and when he'd had a few he was inclined to abuse the English language by using long words which he couldn't pronounce and mixing metaphors. Zac was content with his life, having retired from the merchant navy many years ago when he inherited a small house in Guildford Street in Brighton from his sister. McCabe liked his company and was always pleased to see him turn up wearing one of his old checked shirts and baggy brown corduroy trousers. Zac shared McCabe's enthusiasm for wooden yachts, particularly Honeysuckle Rose, and he treated her as if she was his own, putting hundreds of hours into her upkeep for no reward except the chance to sail in her. They had known each other for fifteen years and despite their age difference - Zac was now seventy - they had formed a lasting friendship based on mutual respect and a love of boats and the sea. When he had bought Honeysuckle Rose, at a marina in Portsmouth, McCabe needed help to sail her to her new berth in Brighton, and had enlisted Zac to help him.

On that first trip together, from Portsmouth to Brighton, their relationship was tested to the full. McCabe would have been the first to admit that he had broken all the rules of boat buying. He hadn't haggled, even though the owner had said he was looking for a quick sale because he was trying to relocate himself and his family to France. He hadn't had the engine checked over and he hadn't had the boat surveyed. Instead he had fallen in love with this old run down wooden yacht, which most people would have walked away from, and bought it knowing that, whatever it cost, he would restore it and keep it sailing. Chad and Zac had left Portsmouth harbour on a calm summer evening at the end of July. Because they were enjoying themselves, they ignored the narrow break in the two mile long submerged submarine barrier to the east of Portsmouth, which would have shortened the trip by an hour or so, and followed the channel along the barrier's west side. As they rounded Horse Sand Fort at the end of the barrier the sea was flat, a light northerly breeze was blowing, and the sun was setting behind them. They motored east with just the mainsail up and the ancient BMC Commander 2.2 litre diesel engine, which was actually a marinised London black taxi engine, thudding away. They were heading for the relatively narrow Looe Channel, off the end of the Selsey Peninsula, which you run with the tide behind you, rocks on the port side and shallows to starboard. Once you are through, it makes for an easy passage along the Sussex coast to Brighton.

They were still five miles west of the Looe Channel when the old engine overheated and had to be stopped. Zac proved his worth immediately by getting the cockpit floor up and climbing down into the engine compartment to find out what the problem was. Having checked for the most obvious reasons, it was clear that there was a major blockage in the cooling water system and, without the right tools, they weren't going to be able to fix it. No matter, Rose was a sailing boat so it was just going to take longer. They had some basic provisions: bread, butter, ham slices for sandwiches, tea, sugar and milk that McCabe had bought at a small corner shop earlier in the day and, most important of all, they had water. They hoisted a genoa on the forestay but by that time the tide had turned against them at the Looe, which made the channel impossible. There followed a slow sail against the tide around The Owers, a group of rocks and sandbanks which extends seven miles out to sea from the tip of Selsey Bill.

Shortly after midnight the boat's ancient batteries gave up so the lights went out and, at the same time, the wind dropped completely, but they had rounded The Owers by then and had set a course towards Brighton. The few ships that they saw passed in the distance and only once did a fishing boat come near enough to be a worry. In the dark, without working navigation lights, they were in serious danger of being run down so Zac had shone a torch onto the mainsail, lighting it up sufficiently to be seen, and the fishing boat had changed course to avoid them, no doubt cursing them for amateurs. With the tide again in their favour they drifted slowly towards Brighton, and by mid morning a stiff land breeze had blown up from the north and they sailed the last seventeen miles north easterly at a steady five knots drinking tea, eating sandwiches, and enjoying the sunshine. By early afternoon what little wind there was had backed to the southwest and they ghosted into the Brighton Marina entrance, turned on the engine at the last possible moment and motored up to the visitors pontoon. Dropping the sails as they reached it, and with steam rising from the engine compartment, they landed against the pontoon with a crash. Chad pulled the chord to decompress the engine, which turned it off before it could seize up, and they jumped off to tie the boat up safely.

Chad had tried to apologise for taking Zac to sea in such an unseaworthy boat, but Zac's only reaction had been, "That's alright, matey. It's all water up a duck's arse to me."

Since then, Zac and McCabe between them had completely restored Honeysuckle Rose to her original condition, with McCabe supplying the materials and Zac refusing any form of payment except to be able to crew for McCabe on their numerous sailing trips. An arrangement that suited them both.

McCabe took a sip of his pint of bitter, "It doesn't make sense," he repeated. "There's something not right about it."

"Don't you believe what the people on Tiger Fish said?"

"No I don't. There's something we're not being told. No radio, no mobile phones, sailing up and down firing red flares on a clear night and nobody sees them? It's one of the busiest stretches of water in the world. Not possible. There's more to this than they're saying and I'm going to find out what it is."

They sat in silence for a few minutes longer while they finished their drinks.

"Come on," said McCabe. "As you're going that way, you can drop me at Jack's house, if you would. I've got to sort his things out and there's no point leaving it."

The two friends stood and walked to the door. They went out into Black Lion Street, crossed the road then turned into Bartholomew Square and walked past the Town Hall. Descending the steps to the underground car park they stopped at the payment machine and Zac inserted a ticket into it.

"I'll do it, Zac."

McCabe inserted a credit card into the machine and paid, thankful that he didn't have a car any more and didn't normally have to pay the outrageous parking fees in this town. They descended another flight of steps and walked past the rows of parked cars until they found Zac's old silver Honda Accord. Zac unlocked and they both got into the car and sat in silence for a moment.

"I know this is hard for you, Chad, but it's got to be done sooner or later."

"I know."

"I'll come in with you if you like."

"Thanks. That would help."

Zac started the engine, and they drove out of the car park turning left to join the nose to tail traffic in Kings Road. With the Palace Pier and the sea on their right they negotiated the flow of traffic at the roundabout and continued along Marine Parade, the wide straight clifftop road on the eastern side of Brighton. McCabe gazed at the endless rows of densely packed flats and tall houses on their left as they passed. He usually took pleasure in marvelling at the different styles of architecture along here but today he was deep in thought. Zac drove carefully, keeping within the thirty miles an hour speed limit, aware of the speed camera opposite Marine Square which was waiting to trap him. Chad thought how strange it was that everyone else that he could see was just having a normal day like any other, while for him and Zac it was the strangest day that they'd ever shared.

It started to rain and Zac turned on the windscreen wipers. They turned left into Kemptown, drove along Chichester Place and then turned right into Chesham Road as Zac searched for a parking space, finding one fifty yards from Jack's house. Zac switched off the engine, they both got out and, ignoring the rain, they walked to the house in silence. Chad barely glanced at the white painted render and the bay windows, and he felt for Jack's spare key which he'd had ever since he'd separated from Jack's mother. He slid the key into the Yale lock and as he turned it he had a mental image of his son locking up and leaving here for the last time. Pushing the front door open he stepped over a small heap of post on the doormat and walked the five steps along the hallway to the living room door on the left. Zac closed the front door behind them and followed, thinking how cold and silent the house was. McCabe pressed the brass lever handle down, opened the living room door, and stopped dead in his tracks. The room had been ransacked.

Chapter Ten

Rue de Laborde, Paris - 1201 CEST Friday 3rd June

Angelos went through the apartment fully cleaning it for the second time aware that, however thorough the cleaning, a forensic check would still find fingerprints that had been missed, hairs, DNA, and no amount of washing and wiping would ever remove them completely. It didn't really matter. The terrorist's fingerprints and DNA weren't on file anywhere because no law enforcement agency had ever taken them for their records. The only time that could have happened would have been at border checks and, although often crossing borders, Angelos used routes that never came near any officialdom. Porous borders, especially in Europe, were what allowed terrorists to move freely and any traces of their presence that they left behind could only be cross matched with them if they were caught. In Angelos' case, that wasn't going to happen.

Shouldering the rucksack which contained a change of clothes, wash bag, toothbrush and the precious container of abrin, the terrorist took one long last look at the apartment and picked up a plastic refuse sack. It was tied at the top and contained all of the garbage accumulated since Renard had visited again two days ago and taken the previous sack away with him. Opening the apartment door, Angelos stepped into the hallway and closed the door quietly, glad to be on the move at last. Descending the spiral stone staircase to the lobby, the terrorist opened the street door, stepped out into the sunshine, turned left onto Rue de Laborde busy with cars and pedestrians, and branched right into Rue du Rocher. Near the pharmacy at the end of the street,

Angelos dropped the refuse sack onto a pile of similar ones which had been left on the pavement awaiting collection. Ahead was the huge nineteenth century stone edifice of Saint-Lazare railway station, its French flags and mullioned windows giving it the appearance of a civic office building.

The terrorist crossed the road, passed the huge glass bubble which shelters the entrance to the Metro, and climbed the stone steps into the railway station. The long narrow booking hall was festooned with colourful advertising banners suspended under the low roof light, which stretched the full length of the hall. Joining one of the queues at the booking office Angelos patiently waited and, on reaching the booking clerk's window, asked in heavily accented French for a single ticket to Rouen, paid in cash, and took the ticket and change. At the nearby news stand the terrorist picked up and paid for a copy of Le Figaro, then walked through a high arch onto the station concourse with its twenty seven platforms distributing trains to Northern France. Stopping in front of a large display board the terrorist checked for the time of the train and saw that there were eighteen minutes to wait. Angelos walked to the back of the concourse from where there was a clear view, and stood, back to the wall, appearing to read the newspaper. Two armed soldiers slowly sauntered past, scanning the crowd, and only gave the terrorist a cursory glance. Angelos also watched the crowd and was satisfied that none of the hundreds of people there was in the least bit interested in someone who, to them, was just another student waiting for a train.

Five minutes before the train was due to depart the terrorist folded the newspaper, walked casually to platform twenty seven where the silver and grey SNCF train was waiting, and boarded Coach 10 with two minutes to spare. The carriage was almost full and Angelos edged along the corridor scanning each compartment and found one which had five empty seats. The other three seats were occupied by a woman who was sitting by the window, and two small children who bounced up and down next to her on the green and grey upholstery in anticipation of the journey about to start. Angelos liked children. Closing the sliding door, the terrorist hoisted the rucksack onto the tubular steel rack above the seats, sat facing the woman and, to discourage conversation, immediately opened the newspaper, appearing to be engrossed in its contents. The train began to move.

The compartment door slid open with a bang and a large, sweating, middle aged man dressed in a bright green polo shirt and light blue golfing trousers, barged into the compartment struggling with two large suitcases.

"Damn," he said to his wife in a booming voice. "Nearly missed it."

American - the enemy - thought the terrorist, touching a jeans pocket and feeling the flick knife, its six inch long stiletto blade sharpened on both edges and with a needle point, folded and ready. Old fashioned but as effective as a gun at close quarters and less likely to be a problem if searched by police. Switchblades are illegal in most civilised countries and they wouldn't be happy, but the knife said criminal rather than terrorist. Besides, if it gets to the point where you have to use a gun they'll shoot back which would result in death, and death is only for martyrs.

Angelos considered sticking the knife into the fat American's throat just before the next station and leaving the train.

Chapter Eleven

John Street, Brighton - 1132 BST Friday 3rd June

The young detective constable sat facing McCabe across a table in one of the busy police station's interview rooms. On the table between them were two plastic bags: one large containing Jack McCabe's clothes, and one small containing his personal effects.

The DC patiently repeated what he had already said, "There is nothing to indicate that it was anything more than a routine burglary, Mr McCabe. Your son's death was reported in the local press and there are plenty of villains who would have known that the house was unoccupied."

"Doesn't it seem odd to you that the house was searched so thoroughly?" asked McCabe.

"That is unusual, I must admit, but presumably they felt they had plenty of time to go through the place. Normally burglars are in and out as quickly as possible. You still can't tell me what's missing?"

"That's the problem," McCabe replied. "I don't know what was there in the first place, but I find it strange that they left valuable items behind, even cash. It doesn't look like your average burglary to me. More as though they were looking for something specific."

The policeman looked sympathetic, "I know this is very upsetting for you, Mr McCabe, but we're doing everything we can to find out who it was."

"What does that mean? You fingerprint the place and compare the prints with your database? If that doesn't work you wait until you catch some burglar and he pleads guilty to this one and a hundred other burglaries, so that he gets a lighter sentence. Have you found any fingerprint matches?"

"No we haven't."

"So what are you doing to find out who broke into my son's house?"

"As I said, we're doing everything we can, Mr McCabe."

McCabe gave up. An overworked police force wasn't going to waste time on a burglary which was just one of many that happen in a city like Brighton every day.

"Well you're not doing enough," he gestured at the two bags. "Do I have to sign for these?"

"If you would please."

The policeman turned a clipboard towards McCabe and handed him a pen.

McCabe signed the form on the clipboard and stood up.

"I don't think my son's death was an accident you know, and you should be investigating that as well."

"There's going to be an inquest, Mr McCabe. It will all be examined then."

"But that's going to take months. What do I have to do to get some action now?"

"I realise how difficult this has been for you," replied the detective, "but, unless the Coroner's officer finds some evidence to back up your claim, I'm afraid nothing is going to happen. I think you would be best advised to let it rest."

"Let it rest? There's no way I'm going to let it rest," answered McCabe angrily. "My son drowns in suspicious circumstances. Nobody wants to talk about it and now his house has been searched and you can't see any connection between the two. I'm going to keep digging until I find out what's going on."

"Then all I can say, Mr McCabe, is that if you do come up with any new information, you let us know about it and we'll consider it on its merits."

McCabe picked up the bags, "Don't you worry, I will."

He walked to the door and opened it.

"Mr McCabe, you must be careful not to make any unfounded accusations," warned the policeman.

McCabe paused for a moment, then turned to face him. Barely controlling his anger he spoke slowly and deliberately, "I'll find out what's going on, and when I do you'd better take me seriously."

Fuming with frustration at the attitude of the police, he left the police station and called a taxi which took him to his flat in Lewes Crescent. As the taxi pulled up outside he asked the driver to wait, went up to the flat and put the two bags containing Jack's things into the wardrobe in his bedroom. Returning to the taxi he instructed the driver to take him to the Old Steine and got out of the car at the Palace Pier, not sure where he was going to go next but knowing that it involved drinking. As the green man at the pedestrian crossing by the Royal Albion Hotel showed that it was safe to cross, he stepped out into the road and was met by a tirade of obscenities from a cyclist who jumped the lights and flashed past him at speed, missing him by inches. Furious, McCabe turned and began to run after the cyclist who looked back, then seeing McCabe chasing him the man stuck his middle finger in the air and was gone, pedalling furiously and disappearing along the seafront. McCabe went after him, ignoring the cars, running in the road in a blind rage determined to catch up with the cyclist and then… What? As he reached The Old Ship Hotel he suddenly got a grip on himself, slowed down, got back onto the pavement and, bent double with the exertion, put his hands on his knees and gradually got his breath and his composure back.

What was he doing? Ignorant cyclists abuse pedestrians every day. They're just idiots and not worth bothering about. Calm down, he told himself. Sure he was angry, but angry with whom? The people who had ransacked his son's house? The police who showed no interest in the burglary or Jack's death? Or was he just angry with himself because of his inability to change events? Chad realised where he was so he crossed the road, carefully this time, and walked along Black Lion Street to The Cricketers.

The lunchtime trade hadn't started yet and he easily found a vacant stool at the bar. He ordered a pint of Harvey's bitter and a large Laphroaig whisky, rapidly drank them both and ordered the same again. Gloomily, he sat and stared into the mirror which was almost hidden behind the bottles on the backbar until, like déjà vu, a voice said, "Hi, Chad."

Chapter Twelve

Rouen, Normandy - 1410 CEST Friday 3rd June

Seventy minutes after leaving Paris the train pulled into Rouen-Rive-Droite Station, one hundred and thirty kilometres to the north west. Angelos rose from the seat, removed the rucksack from the overhead rack, went out into the corridor and moved down the train to the exit door. The American was still talking in his loud booming voice and the terrorist was relieved to be free of the temptation to kill him. The train stopped and Angelos stepped down onto the platform into unexpected semi darkness. Looking along the platform the terrorist saw that the railway lines ran underneath the station building and at each end of the platform there was daylight.

A short distance from where the terrorist was standing there was a sign which read Sortie and, beside the sign, there was a stainless steel escalator. For a few moments Angelos was delayed as the throng of people from the Paris train took their turn to filter onto the escalator which took them all to the upper level. Stepping off of the escalator, Angelos followed the mass of passengers as they turned into the enormous art nouveau style booking hall four storeys high with a vaulted roof and a colourful frieze at third storey level composed of modern murals. Angelos walked steadily, not too fast and not too slowly, scanning the booking hall for any sign of police, but it was clear. There was no reason to believe that the French police were aware of the terrorist's movements or even that they would be interested, but it was this sort of caution that had kept Angelos at liberty for the past three years. It was the same caution that had kept the American on the train alive. There was no point in drawing attention to oneself for one fat American, there were much more important targets, but in a different time and place the man would not have survived. The terrorist left the station, walking past the Hotel Astrid and along the Rue Jeanne d'Arc towards the city centre. The street commemorating Joan of Arc, another freedom fighter, who was martyred by the English in fifteenth century Rouen thought Angelos.

Outside of the tabac, at the junction of Rue Jeanne d'Arc and Rue Verte, was a rack of post cards and maps. Selecting a Rouen street map, Angelos entered the tabac, ordered a coffee in perfect French and paid for the map at the same time. In Paris Angelos had spoken with heavily accented French, but had decided to speak in Rouen with perfect French; it was this sort of detail that would confuse an investigation if anybody followed and interviewed people that the terrorist had spoken to. Sitting at a Formica covered table at the rear of the tabac, with the rucksack placed on the floor, Angelos studied the map and sipped the coffee. Seeing that the street with the safe house was no more than two kilometres away, Angelos memorised the route and then folded the map.

The tabac was busy with men who appeared to have finished work for the day: individuals were reading newspapers, and small groups were drinking beer and gossiping. None of them was taking any notice of the terrorist who sat quietly watching them. Angelos wondered what they would do if they knew that in the rucksack was enough toxin to kill everyone in central Rouen? Perhaps it would add excitement to their dreary lives. Something to talk about for years to come, that they had been in the tabac at the same time as the mass killer and international terrorist Angelos who had been sitting amongst them as cool as you like, just drinking coffee and looking as normal as everyone else.

Angelos stood up, pushed the map into the rucksack, walked to the open door and nodded as the patron said, "Au revoir."

In the street the terrorist turned and walked to the next corner, following the memorised route until reaching the Place du Général de Gaulle. Turning south, Angelos picked up the Rue de la République and then turned east along the Rue d'Amiens, realising too late that, one hundred metres ahead, two gendarmes, patrolling on foot with FAMAS assault rifles, were slowly walking in the opposite direction. The terrorist's nerve held, even to the point of keeping to the narrow pavement so that the gendarmes were obliged to step into the road to pass, which they did with a nod and a smile. Angelos walked on for a few seconds then stopped to cross the road and glanced to the right to see the two gendarmes turn right into Rue de la République.

Five minutes later, having reached the Rue Marin Le Pigny, the terrorist was standing opposite a modern concrete apartment block which was painted a bland off yellow colour, nine storeys high and continued along the full length of the street. On the side of the street where Angelos was standing was a similar block and, further along the street, was yet another apartment block at right angles to the others which would have created a cul de sac if it wasn't for the fact that an arch had been formed in it to allow the road to continue underneath and beyond. From the outside, the symmetry of the hundreds of rectangular windows made each apartment look like all the others. It was the first address.

Angelos crossed the street and approached the large glass entrance door with glazed panels on either side of it. One of the keys that Renard had handed over would fit the expensive lock. The second one that Angelos tried opened the door, and the terrorist went in and entered a large empty lobby with a marble floor, a staircase and a lift. The terrorist's footsteps echoed around the stairwell until, on the second floor, there was the door that Angelos was looking for. Trying the keys again, Angelos found the one that fitted, opened the door and entered. Another soulless apartment in another city, and another interminable wait for instructions.

Chapter Thirteen

The Cricketers, Brighton - 1312 BST Friday 3rd June

Whatever else McCabe might have thought about Tricia Knight, he had to admit that she had a lot of nerve.

"I'm sorry I ran out on you, Chad, but my sister phoned me after you left her flat and I knew you'd be pretty upset."

McCabe turned to face her, his anger welling up inside him again, "Well you'd be right about that, but why did you steal my cash?"

"I didn't steal your cash, Chad, I just borrowed it.

Here..." Tricia fished around in the same leather bag that she'd had when he'd met her in Reinhardt's Bar and pulled out a handful of twenty pound notes, "I've been looking for you so that I can give it back."

She counted out ten notes onto the bar, gave them to McCabe and stuffed the rest back into her bag.

"There, sorry about that."

She smiled up at him as if helping yourself to other peoples' cash and returning it later was the most natural thing in the world. McCabe thought that, to her, it most probably was.

Tricia ordered a glass of Prosecco for herself and another pint and Laphroaig for McCabe without asking him whether he wanted one, then paid for the drinks and settled on the vacant bar stool next to him. He felt his anger starting to dissipate. There was something about this woman that made it hard to feel badly about her.

"I was sorry to hear about Jack, Chad."

"You knew him?"

"I used to see him around. I'd talk to him sometimes but I can't say I knew him well. I raced with him a few times when we were both crewing for people. Sometimes, when he was skippering a boat for an owner who didn't really sail, he'd ask me to crew for him as well. The Round The Island Race, Cowes Week, round the cans on a Sunday, stuff like that. He was good company," she paused for a moment. "It's hard to believe that he's gone. There are lots of rumours going around, do you know what happened?"

"He was coming back from Fécamp after a race on a boat called Tiger Fish and he went overboard and drowned."

"I know Tiger Fish, a Hallberg-Rassy. South African crew boss called Frik..." she hesitated. "Not nice people."

"In what way not nice people?"

"They're not friendly," Tricia replied. "They enter races but don't join in the after race parties, which is unusual. People tend to keep away from their boat because of Frik. He's a nasty bit of work and best avoided, especially if you're female. Perhaps I'm speaking out of turn."

"Not at all," said McCabe. "I'm trying to find out what happened and anything you know about the boat is helpful."

"Well, I know that Jack used to crew for them sometimes, which surprised me because he was such a nice guy. He was so in demand that he had the pick of skippers he could crew for, so I never understood what he was doing on Tiger Fish. Sailing's supposed to be fun."

McCabe was gradually realising that he didn't know Jack well, either. They would meet up occasionally for a drink and chat about sailing but not much about what was going on in each other's lives. Perhaps, like most parents who don't want to burden their children with their problems, he didn't reveal much about himself to his son, and Jack in his turn wasn't very forthcoming about what was happening in his world.

"Are you alright, Chad?"

McCabe was suddenly aware of the pub sounds around him and Tricia staring at him with a concerned expression, "Sorry. I drifted a bit there."

"That's alright, you've been having a rough time."

"I suddenly thought that although he's my son, I don't really know much about him."

"Do you want to talk about him?"

"I do."

"Go on then. Tell me what you do know about him. It might help."

And McCabe, for no reason that he could make sense of, decided to talk to this attractive stranger, who he had good reasons not to trust, and he opened up to her about his family. As she said, it might help.

"Did you know that Jack was American?"

"No. I'd never have guessed that," replied Tricia.

"His mother is Hannah Rainbird."

"Hannah Rainbird the model?"

"Yes."

"Wow! I don't think he ever told anybody that."

"Jack was born in New York, but he's been living in England since he was three. That's why he didn't have an American accent. He had American and British citizenship."

"So you're married to Hannah Rainbird?"

"Not any more. We met years ago when I was playing a gig at a restaurant in Putney. She's got a house on the Thames at Richmond. We had one of those relationships that go off like a rocket and then suddenly fizzle out. You know?"

Tricia nodded and smiled.

"She went back to the States after three months, and I didn't see her again for fourteen years. Jack was born seven months after she went back and she never told him about me, or me about him. One weekend I was having a drink in the lounge at the Grand Hotel, listening to the pianist, and suddenly there she was. She was working on a shoot in Brighton and staying at the hotel. Our relationship started up again as if it had never finished. She told me about Jack and we were married two months later. Jack was thrilled that he'd found his father and he changed his name from Rainbird to McCabe and we should have all lived happily ever after."

"But you didn't."

"No, we didn't."

Hannah bought a house in Kemptown and we lived there and at the Richmond house. Jack went to school in Brighton so we were here most of the time. Very quickly, Hannah decided that I was a waste of space - not enough ambition, drank too much, which is probably true. She spent more and more time at Richmond or travelling because of her modelling, so Jack and I lived in the Kemptown house and she turned up when she wasn't working, which wasn't often. Jack got into sailing big time when he was eighteen. He got the bug from me, I think. Anyway, he crewed in races every Wednesday evening in the summer, and on Sunday mornings all year round, took the RYA exams, and became a very competent sailor. Did you know that he used to be in the police?"

“No way! I find that hard to imagine. I would have thought he was much too laid back for that,” exclaimed Tricia looking surprised.

“He was. He joined Sussex Police when he was nineteen. He was full of enthusiasm to start with but after a couple of years he packed it in saying that he was disillusioned with it. He said that he’d joined the police to make a difference, but what was the point of catching villains who got clever lawyers and were released when it got to Court?

“He got a job with a yacht broker and he’s been doing that ever since. Sailing and boats were his main interests really, so it was perfect for him, I suppose. He spent every day at different marinas taking prospective buyers out for test sails and talking about boats. Wherever I sail on the South Coast all of the marina people seem to know him. He’d found his ideal job.”

“But what about you and Hannah Rainbird?”

“We ended up detesting each other and there were endless arguments. The music and gigging lifestyle, which she’d originally loved, she began to hate. She liked the property deals that I did but thought I should be doing them ten at a time rather than in ones and twos. I drove to the Richmond house unannounced one afternoon and found her in bed with a male model. I couldn’t even get angry about it. I just walked. Drove back to Brighton. Cleared my stuff out and moved into the flat you were in the other night. Jack was old enough to look after himself by then so that wasn’t a problem, and he stayed at the house. Two years later we divorced. I didn’t want anything from her so she kept her money and property. She didn’t want anything from me so I kept my business, which was virtually bankrupt anyway, and that was the end of it. Jack and I still saw each other but he always seemed a bit guarded after that. Loyalty to his mother I suppose."

McCabe stopped talking and looked into his beer, lost in thought again. Then he looked at Tricia, "Sorry, I keep thinking that there's no way he could have just fallen off of the back of a boat. He was too experienced."

"I'm surprised at that, too," said Tricia. "When I crewed for him he always spent a lot of time before we sailed talking to us about safety. He was really hot on it."

"What about you?" said McCabe. "I'm sorry to go on about my troubles."

"No, you talk about them all you like," she said. "I'm sorry I added to them."

"You didn't really. As soon as the police came to tell me about Jack I forgot about everything else for a while. I just concentrated on all the formalities and then getting pissed."

She smiled, "Not always the best solution if you want to deal with things."

"What made you send me to burgle your sister's flat, anyway?"

Tricia was quiet for a moment, then, "Have you heard of a local villain called Ricky Bishop?"

"No."

"Well I borrowed some money from him, and he decided that I wasn't going to pay it back, which I was. He wouldn't think twice about making an example of me and I thought that his heavies might be watching my sister's flat, knowing that I'd go there."

"So you sent me instead."

"Sorry, couldn't think of what else to do."

"Why didn't you just ring your sister up and ask her to meet you with the money?"

"Because she wouldn't have done that, Chad. She's rather tired of my escapades."

"Bloody hell, Tricia. I could have been arrested."

"No," she smiled. "Who dares wins and all that. Caz was pretty angry when she phoned me after you left her flat, Chad, and I assumed you would be too. I was so desperate that I had a look through your place for some cash and then cleared out. I was always going to return it."

"It takes a lot to get me angry, Tricia. I get annoyed but I have to be seriously goaded to lose my temper and, when I do, I really lose it."

"It won't happen again, Chad."

He smiled at her, "I'm sure it won't."

"Good, because I still need somewhere to stay for a bit."

At that McCabe laughed out loud. There was something so disarming about this girl that he couldn't help liking her, and the feelings that he'd had when they'd gone back to his flat together all returned. He wanted to look after her.

"OK, but you don't help yourself to any of my stuff."

"I promise."

McCabe went quiet again, the gloom about Jack's death settling over him once more.

"If I can do anything to help you find out what happened to Jack, Chad, you know I will."

"I know, and thank you. Tomorrow I'm going to sail out to where Jack disappeared and retrace what happened. You come as well, if you like."

Chapter Fourteen

English Channel - 1406 BST Saturday 4th June

Honeysuckle Rose was hove to in the English Channel and McCabe was sitting at the mahogany table in her saloon with Zac Battersby and Tricia. It was hot and all of Rose's scuttles and sliding windows were open. From outside came the noise of an occasional slap as a small wave hit the hull, but the sea was relatively calm and Rose, with her long keel, moved gently forward with a small, slow, rocking horse movement as the light north easterly breeze filled in the backed genoa and mainsail.

Zac had made them each a mug of instant soup, which they sipped occasionally, and spread out in front of them was Admiralty Chart No. 2656 English Channel - Central Part. Lying on the chart were an almanac with tidal information, a tidal atlas, dividers, a parallel ruler, a protractor, and a 2B pencil.

"The police weren't interested, Zac," said McCabe. "After you left they took two hours to turn up, had a quick look, established that the intruders had forced an entry through a window at the back and said they'd get a Scene of Crimes Officer to come and dust for fingerprints. Just another Brighton burglary, it happens all the time."

Zac scratched the two days growth of stubble on his chin, "Did they take much?"

"I don't know what Jack had there to start with. They didn't take anything obvious like the DVD player or TV. It seems odd. As if they were looking for something specific. I don't think we'll ever know."

Zac nodded wisely as if all of this just confirmed what he'd always thought. That anything is possible and shit happens.

McCabe looked at the chart in front of him, "Jack was an experienced sailor. He wouldn't have just gone overboard in calm weather and, even if he had, it should have been simple to pick him up."

Tricia sat quietly, listening but being careful not to intrude on the two friends by making pointless conversation.

Chad reached over and picked up the notepad lying by the radio.

"I had the VHF on after Jack was picked up by the fishing boat. I didn't know it was him of course, but I made a note of the position."

He flicked through the pages of the notebook.

"Here it is. Bearing 077 degrees five miles from the Greenwich Meridian Light Vessel. We need to know Tiger Fish's positions as she crossed the Channel."

He put the notebook down and looked at Zac.

"Allerton said that they left Fécamp at 2000 BST, so that's 1900 Greenwich Mean Time, on the evening of Saturday 29th of May, wind westerly force four, averaging seven knots on a bearing following the direct rhumb line to Brighton Marina. What time was high water Dover on that day?"

Zac opened the almanac and found the Dover tide tables, "1923 GMT on the Saturday and 0805 GMT on the Sunday. Neap tide."

McCabe wrote the times down on the notepad.

"Allerton told me that the alarm was raised at 0400 BST, so that means that they would have been sailing at seven knots for eight hours, a distance of 56 miles."

McCabe picked up the ruler and pencil and drew a straight line on the chart linking Fécamp Harbour and Brighton Marina. He took the dividers, opened them, and adjusted them against the scale on the side of the chart until the distance between the two points of the dividers represented seven nautical miles. Then he walked the dividers along the line from Fécamp Harbour eight times, scaling 56 miles on the chart. At the point where the dividers stopped he made a pencil mark. He picked up the tidal atlas and studied it, turning the pages and making notes.

"I calculate that, during the eight hours they sailed, they had 4.6 knots of westerly tide and 0.3 knots of easterly tide. Take the smaller from the larger and that means that the tide pushed them West by 4.3 nautical miles."

McCabe placed the edge of the ruler on the 56 mile pencil mark and drew a short line due west. He picked up the dividers again, and adjusted them against the scale on the side of the chart until they measured 4.3 miles. Then he placed one point of the dividers on the 56 mile pencil mark and, where the other point touched the due west line, he made a dot with the pencil and drew a small triangle around it to denote an estimated position. He stared at it for a few moments.

"That's where they're saying that Jack went overboard, somewhere near where we are now," said McCabe.

He opened the dividers again so that one point was in the centre of the triangle and the other point was touching Brighton Marina, then he placed the two points against the scale on the side of the chart to calculate the distance.

"Nine miles off of Brighton. Just as Allerton reported to the Coastguard."

McCabe looked at the notepad again.

"The fishing boat reported finding Jack at 0704 GMT bearing 077 degrees five miles from the Greenwich Meridian Light Vessel."

He picked up the square transparent plastic protractor and placed it, north up, with the centre of it exactly over the symbol on the chart for the Greenwich Meridian Light Vessel. Taking care to line up the protractor's vertical centre line with the vertical lines on the chart, he made a pencil mark where the edge of the protractor read 077 degrees. Using the parallel rule McCabe drew a pencil line between the Light Vessel symbol and the mark he had made, then measured off five miles along the line with the dividers. He made a dot with the pencil at the five mile point and drew a small circle around it to denote a position fix.

"So this is where he was found," said McCabe quietly. "Between the east and west shipping lanes."

Finally, he drew a straight line between the circle where Jack was found and the triangle where Allerton said he went overboard, and measured the distance with the dividers. Eighteen miles.

McCabe sat back and breathed out heavily.

"So what they're saying, Zac, is that Jack went overboard here," - he pointed at the triangle - "at 0300 GMT, and was found four hours later eighteen miles away here." He tapped the circle with his index finger. "Even if we add in some leeway, that's not possible, is it?"

"No it's not," replied Zac. "The tide would have carried him, but not that sort of distance. A couple of miles at the most." He looked indignant, "That means they've given the Coastguard a false position, but why would they do that?"

"Because they're hiding something Zac, and I'm going to find out what it is. Let's get back to Brighton."

The three of them finished their soup and went back to the cockpit. Together, with Tricia at the wheel, they gybed Honeysuckle Rose around and hardened up the sails, adjusting them until she settled down, chuckling along at three knots as the breeze strengthened, on the northerly heading which would take her back to Brighton.

Chad listened to the water gurgling along the hull and watched a gannet, fifty yards away, hurtle streamlined into the sea like a falling arrow and then reappear with the fish which it had targetted. The sound of the water and the spectacular dive of the bird would have been a joy to him normally, but there was no joy today. This had been a pilgrimage to the place where Jack had been lost, but it was a lie. He wasn't there.

Chapter Fifteen

John Street, Brighton - 1020 BST Monday 6th June

McCabe sat in the same police station interview room as before and waited. He was uncomfortably aware of the CCTV camera, fixed in the corner at ceiling level, which was staring at him with its single blank eye. Whether it was switched on or not he had no idea. In front of him on the table were the chart, almanac and tide tables. Already he had been waiting for twenty minutes and he impatiently drummed his fingers on the table. Suddenly the door opened and an overweight, untidy man in a baggy grey suit entered the room and closed the door behind him. He was of medium height, in his mid forties, and had short black hair which was parted on the left and slicked down above a puffy round face. The collar of his white shirt was frayed and his light blue tie had a grease stain on it. The only attractive feature about him were his eyes, which were deep brown, kindly and alert. Under his left arm was a manila folder and he was wiping his nose with a grubby off white handkerchief.

"Mr McCabe?"

"Yes."

"Sorry to keep you. I'm Detective Sergeant Arthur Barnard."

Barnard moved to the other side of the table, sat down, blew his nose heavily into the handkerchief, examined the contents and then shoved it into his right trouser pocket. He leaned forward and held out his right hand to McCabe who overcame his sense of disgust and shook it.

“Now,” said Barnard, sitting forward in the chair and placing the folder on the table in front of him. “I understand you have further information about your son’s death.”

“I do,” replied McCabe. “They’re lying about it.”

“Who’s lying?”

“Graham Allerton.”

Barnard opened the folder to reveal a sheaf of loose A4 papers and turned over a couple of them, studying them carefully for a few moments.

“Ah, the yacht owner. What is it that you think he’s lying about?”

“He’s lying about the whole thing,” answered McCabe, opening the chart and spreading it out on the table between them. “I’ve been studying the tide tables for the night that Jack went overboard, and none of it agrees with what Allerton says happened.”

“Really?” said Barnard, suddenly full of interest. He pulled his chair closer to the table eagerly, “Show me.”

For the next ten minutes McCabe explained in detail the positions, the fact that Jack couldn’t have gone overboard where Allerton said he did, that even if it was true that the VHF radio wasn’t working, it was unlikely that none of their mobile phones were working. He explained that it was hard to believe that they didn’t see Jack’s mini distress flares and impossible that nobody saw Tiger Fish’s red parachute flares.

When McCabe had finished there was silence for a moment. Then Barnard sat back and looked at him.

“I see what you’re getting at,” he said, “but it’s not evidence.”

McCabe was stunned. Barnard pulled out his handkerchief and blew his nose again.

"Aren't you going to do anything about it?" asked McCabe.

"Nothing I can do, Mr McCabe. It's just supposition. If you put all that to Allerton he'll just say that he must have got the position wrong."

"What about the flares then?" asked McCabe getting agitated.

"Well I suppose nobody saw them and that's the end of it."

McCabe felt his anger welling up in him. This man wasn't listening.

"Look," he said angrily, leaning forward and pointing his finger at Barnard. "I've been sailing out there for more than thirty years and you can't fire a red parachute flare at night without somebody spotting it and calling the Coastguard. There are too many people out there."

"Perhaps they were all looking the other way at the time. It was just an accident Mr McCabe. You've got to accept it."

McCabe slapped his hand on the table and shouted, "It was not an accident. You people are not in the least bit interested in finding out the truth are you?"

Barnard stood up, "Alright Mr McCabe, that's enough. I'm sorry that you've lost your son, and if you have any proper evidence to show us I'll be pleased to consider it. Until then I suggest that you stop looking for mysteries that aren't there and see what the inquest comes up with."

Chad looked at Barnard and said quietly, "I'm wasting my time here, aren't I?"

"I'm afraid you are, Mr McCabe."

McCabe stood, gathered up the chart and books, and walked out.

Chapter Sixteen

Dyke Road Avenue, Hove - 1405 BST Monday 6th June

McCabe's taxi drove slowly along Dyke Road Avenue, the driver ignoring the impatience of the drivers of the cars behind him. On both sides of the road were detached houses which stank of money, larger than average but not big enough to be palatial. McCabe wondered why people so apparently wealthy would choose to spend huge sums to live side by side with their neighbours instead of buying some privacy out of town. On the left he spotted a ceramic plaque with the number of Allerton's house, which he had found on 192.com, and called out to the driver to stop. The driver, indicating too late, earned himself a long warning horn blast from the car behind him as he turned between two sand coloured brick entrance pillars onto the short tarmac drive and stopped the car. The drive curved out onto the road again through two more brick pillars thirty yards from the first. McCabe paid the driver, got out of the car and closed the door. The taxi drove out to the road, stopped briefly then turned right and headed back towards the centre of Brighton.

McCabe stood back in the late spring heat for a moment and studied the house. It was modern, built on two floors in a pseudo Georgian style with cheap looking bricks which matched the entrance pillars. It had two wide PVC windows on the ground floor with fake leaded lights, three identical windows on the first floor, and a tiled, hipped roof above. On his left and attached to the house was a double garage and adjoining that was a high fence with a tall oak gate which, presumably, provided access to the rear. There were five brick built steps up to the front door, which was sheltered by a portico supported by two white, circular, fibreglass columns. The property made a statement but probably not the one which the owner intended; money but no style, which was exactly the impression that McCabe had formed of Allerton when he had first met him at Brighton Marina. McCabe walked up the steps to the glossy black, imitation antique, panelled front door and pressed the doorbell which was a brass button with a white china surround screwed onto the brickwork. From inside the house he heard the sound of chimes and, after a short wait, the door was opened by Frik Benniker.

"Yes?"

This close up he looked enormous as he filled the door opening, barefoot, wearing a pair of faded blue denim shorts and a white tee shirt which emphasised every muscle on his upper body.

"I've come to speak to Mr Allerton."

"Is he expecting you?"

"No."

"Wait there."

Benniker closed the door again and McCabe waited.

Two minutes passed until suddenly the door opened wide and Benniker said brusquely, "Follow me."

McCabe stepped into the hallway, and Benniker closed the door then led the way with McCabe trailing obediently behind him. Benniker ducked under the door opening as they turned right into a large living room, which was furnished with three armchairs, and a four seater sofa all upholstered in expensive cream leather. On one wall was a huge plasma television screen and on the other walls were a few cheap prints. In the corner was a small bar with a collection of bottles on it, and underfoot was a thick white carpet. They crossed the room and stepped through a wide glass patio door, which was already open, into the garden.

The garden consisted of a paved patio with steps down to a large swimming pool, which took up most of the remaining area, and was fringed with a narrow strip of well kept grass and a high Leylandii hedge on three sides. On the patio was a circular teak garden table with an umbrella and four teak chairs. In one of the chairs sat Allerton wearing a white towelling robe and looking as though he had just had a swim. In front of Allerton and ten feet away were two teak sun loungers in the steamer style, and reclining on her back on one of them was Sophie May. Her eyes were closed as she soaked up the sun. Her blonde hair contrasted with her tanned and oiled body, and she was wearing only a scarlet bikini bottom so tiny that McCabe, although he tried not to think about it, was sure that she must have shaved off all of her pubic hair. The bikini was tied with bows at the sides.

"Mr McCabe, how nice to see you," said Allerton. He remained in his seat and, this time, there was no attempt to shake hands.

"Would you like a drink?"

"No thank you."

"Well I would. Sophie, get me a vodka and tonic would you? There's a good girl."

"But I'm comfortable," she complained, without opening her eyes.

"Just do it would you?" said Allerton sharply.

What was it in his voice wondered McCabe? Cruelty? Anger? Had he just walked in on an argument or did Allerton always speak to her like that?

Sophie opened her eyes and stood up, a resigned expression on her beautiful face. She turned towards McCabe and smiled.

"Are you sure I can't interest you in anything Mr McCabe?"

"Quite sure, thank you." He smiled at her, and forced himself to look her in the eyes rather than let his gaze stray over her perfect naked breasts.

She turned, padded across the patio, and entered the house through the patio door.

Benniker stood impassively by the door with his arms folded and stared at McCabe with what appeared to be a sneer on his face.

"What can I do for you, Mr McCabe? Or may I call you Chad?" asked Allerton.

"Mr McCabe will do fine."

"Ah, so I can conclude that this is not a social visit."

"Correct," said McCabe.

"Well let's get on with it then shall we? I'm a very busy man."

All pretence at friendliness had now disappeared.

"What do you want?"

"I want to know why you lied to the Coastguard about the position where my son went overboard?"

"And what makes you think I lied?"

"I don't just think you lied, I know you did. I worked out the positions and I know that what you told the Coastguard can't be true."

Allerton looked at him without answering for a few moments, then, "I can understand you being upset, McCabe, but coming here and making ridiculous accusations is hardly sensible, is it?"

McCabe moved towards the table and Benniker immediately crossed the patio and grabbed him, forcing his right arm up his back, while Allerton looked on passively.

"Not sensible at all," said Benniker, the Afrikaans accent adding aggression to his words.

Teeth gritted from the pain and forced to bend forwards McCabe struggled, "Let go of me you bastard or I'll get the police here and have you arrested."

"Self defence," sneered Benniker.

Allerton waved his hand, "Alright Frik that's enough, let him go."

"No way, he was going to attack you."

"Were you going to attack me, Mr McCabe?"

"Of course not."

"Of course you weren't. Let him go Frik."

Benniker shrugged and reluctantly released him, shoving him forward at the same time so that McCabe collided with one of the garden chairs.

"Sit down, Mr McCabe," said Allerton, more as a command than an invitation.

McCabe, attempting to recover his dignity, sat in the chair which had just bruised his shins and glared at Benniker. Benniker glared back and towered over him.

Allerton studied McCabe thoughtfully, "Now, explain to me what the problem is."

"I've studied the charts and tides for that night. My son's body was found eighteen miles away from where you say you were searching. So you lied Allerton, and I want to know why?"

"So you thought you would turn up here uninvited, walk in and accuse me and then I would admit that I made a false report. Is that it?"

"Something like that," said McCabe.

"And then what?"

"And then I'll get the police to question you, and you can explain yourself."

"Well I'm sorry to disappoint you, McCabe, but I'm not going to admit anything of the sort, so I think it's time that you left."

"I'm not leaving until…"

"Alright Frik," said Allerton, and Benniker reached out a huge hand, grabbed McCabe's shirt collar, and hoisted him out of his chair, once more forcing his arm up his back. McCabe, forced to bend double as if he was bowing to Allerton, protested.

Benniker swung him towards the house, "Be quiet monkey, or I'll kick the kak out of you."

Allerton stared at him coldly, "Goodbye Mr McCabe. Don't come back."

McCabe gave up the struggle as Benniker pulled him upright and frog marched him across the patio. From the corner of his eye he saw the beautiful, nearly naked Sophie May appear at the patio doors with a drinks tray in her hands and a frightened expression on her face. Then he was being forced around the side of the house and marched down a narrow pathway beside the garage. At the end of the path his face was forced into the wooden gate while Benniker released a bolt so that he could open it. That done, Benniker violently pulled him back, wrenched the gate open and, without a word, forced McCabe's arm further up his back so that he again had to adopt a bending position. With his free hand he grabbed McCabe by the seat of his pants and launched him headlong onto the tarmac drive. McCabe heard the gate slam shut behind him and curled into a ball as he waited for the kicking to start, but he was alone and he heard the sound of the bolt as Benniker secured the gate again from the other side.

For a few moments McCabe lay still, then he got to his feet and brushed himself off with his hands. His left knee hurt, his shins ached and his cheek was grazed. Limping to the road he leaned against one of the entrance pillars, found his mobile phone, relieved to see that it was still working, and called for a taxi. He continued to lean against the pillar while he waited for his breathing to slow down and his heart to stop racing, then he limped away from the house wincing at the pain in his knee.

Chapter Seventeen

Rue de Laborde, Paris - 1541 CEST Monday 6th June

The door to Angelos' Paris apartment exploded inwards and was followed immediately by an M84 stun grenade which rolled across the carpet and exploded one second later with a blinding flash, 170 decibels of sound, and a violent shock wave, all designed to confuse and disorientate anyone in the room. The grenade was immediately followed into the apartment by two members of the GIGN (Groupe d'Intervention de la Gendarmerie Nationale) dressed completely in black, wearing body armour, and gas masks. Each man carried a French manufactured Manurhin MR73 revolver and trained it from side to side as he sighted along the barrel ready to fire.

One of the men shouted, "Clear!"

Two more GIGN quickly entered the room and took up positions on either side of the bathroom door with their backs to the wall and guns raised, while the first two aimed their weapons at the door. The man to the left of the door turned and kicked it in and, in the same movement, returned to his back to the wall position. As the door flew open, the lock torn completely off, the man to the right of the door turned and, with his left hand, threw in another stun grenade which exploded immediately. The man who had kicked in the door turned again and stood in the doorway aiming his gun into the bathroom.

"Clear!"

All four men relaxed.

The leader of the group, who had been first into the apartment, removed his gas mask and turned back to the entrance door calling out loudly, "You can come in now Monsieur. The apartment is empty."

Jean-Louis Gravier, tall and elegant, dressed in a black tailored business suit, white shirt, plain light grey tie and polished black shoes, stood in the doorway with his hands in his pockets and peered through the smoke and fumes.

"Nice job gentlemen, but disappointing. I thought we had him. Thank you for your trouble."

The afternoon sunlight filtered through the smoke being drawn outwards through the shattered glass of the balcony doors, and one of the team stamped out the sparks in the smouldering carpet where the grenade had exploded.

"Will you need us any more Monsieur?" asked the leader.

"Thank you, no," replied Gravier, glancing at the empty wardrobe, its door blown open by the force of the blast. "There is nothing here. Our man has gone."

He noticed, lying on the floor by the bed, a shattered glass vase and a dead mouse with its feet missing.

Henri Girard, Gravier's assistant, stepped back from the doorway to allow the GIGN men to leave the apartment, and then crossed to the bathroom and looked through the doorway, careful not to touch anything. He surveyed the damage caused by the stun grenade in the confined space.

"Nothing in here either, Monsieur," he said, a note of gloom in his voice. "Unless the forensic people come up with something."

Girard, wearing the same unpressed dark brown suit, which he had worn to work for as long as Gravier had known him, was a short, morose, thuggish man with cropped grey hair and small bright brown eyes. They had worked together for three years, during which time a professional bond had formed between them which made them a formidable partnership.

Gravier could hear the uniformed police in the hallway calming down anxious neighbours and keeping them away from the apartment. In due course they would all be interviewed.

"Where has he gone?" asked Gravier thoughtfully.

"Wherever it is Monsieur," replied Girard, "he has the whole of France to hide in, and we don't even know who he is or what he looks like."

Chapter Eighteen

Lewes Crescent, Brighton - 1524 BST Monday 6th June

Clinging to the handrail, McCabe limped up the last few steps and crossed the landing to the front door of his flat. Turning the key and opening the door, he hopped inside and closed the door behind him. The radio was blaring out a music station, which meant that Tricia was in. He hopped over to the breakfast bar, turned off the radio, then struggled to the sofa and threw himself down onto it. Tricia skipped down the stairs and greeted him with her usual, "Hi, Chad."

He didn't answer and she stopped at the bottom of the stairs, "You OK?"

"Not really. I went to Allerton's house and that South African of his threw me out. Literally. I think I've got a busted knee."

"Well I warned you about him. Can you stand on it?"

"A little bit but it hurts like hell."

"Probably just bruised then. You need to rest it and it'll be fine in a day or two. Have you had any lunch?"

"No."

"Why don't you go upstairs and soak in a bath? I'll make us a meal and then you can tell me what happened. I've been out and got some provisions in. Your fridge hardly had anything in it."

McCabe dragged himself upstairs, soaked for half an hour and changed into a pair of light beige chinos, a blue denim shirt, and his least worn brown deck shoes. When he came down again he was feeling better about life and Tricia was waiting for him.

Places had been laid on opposite sides of the breakfast bar, and between them was a large bowl of salad containing chunks of boiled potato, green beans, green pepper, black olives, wedges of tomato, small cubes of cucumber, and sliced spring onions. On each plate was a generous serving of shelled crayfish. Tricia drizzled the salad with a dressing she had prepared by whisking olive oil, lemon juice and crushed garlic together, and they both sat down to eat.

"I'm not the world's greatest chef, Chad, but I try," said Tricia while pouring two glasses of chilled Chablis.

"Wow, thank you. Looks good to me."

Tricia helped him to a portion of the Nicoise salad, then she served herself and they ate in silence for a minute until she said, "Tell me then."

"Tell you what?"

"Tell me what happened at Graham Allerton's house."

Now that he'd had time to relax and calm down, McCabe's main emotion was one of embarrassment at the ease with which Benniker had manhandled him off the premises, and the way in which Allerton had dismissed him, but he gave Tricia a précis of what had happened that afternoon.

"Rough lot, aren't they?" was her only comment.

"They sure are. Unnecessarily so, which just confirms what I thought before, that they're hiding something. What do you know about Allerton, Tricia?"

"Only what I hear from gossip, and there's a lot of that about him. Local boy made good. A working class lad who made a lot of money buying houses and flats, and letting them. Supposed to be the landlord from hell who despises his tenants. He used to be a well known face on the Brighton club circuit but not any more. Getting older, I suppose. He must be in his fifties now, I should think. He was never very pleasant. Treats everybody as if they're beneath him unless they have more money than he does."

"Do you know Sophie May?" asked Chad. "She was sailing with them the night Jack went overboard."

Tricia looked thoughtful, "I know she always sails with them on cross channel races but that's about it. I see her in wine bars occasionally but she's not really part of the Brighton social scene. Not the social scene that I'm in, anyway. She's Allerton's latest trophy girlfriend. It's all for show though. Everyone knows that he's not interested in women. Apparently, he's not interested in men either, come to that. He gets turned on by making money."

Tricia took a sip of her wine and looked over the glass at him, "What turns you on?"

He looked at her and smiled, ignoring her obvious flirting, "Making music, sailing, stuff like that..." He wasn't going to fall for that again and he carried on eating.

"Have you always lived in Brighton, Chad?"

"No, I was born in Maida Vale in London. Well off parents. Father a solicitor, mother a nervous wreck. She was going to kill herself, apparently, when she was six months pregnant with me, but she got talked out of it by The Samaritans. That's why I was called Chad, after Chad Varah who'd founded The Samaritans sixteen years earlier. She eventually committed suicide when I was four, so I was brought up by my father and a succession of nannies and housekeepers, and then boarding school. He didn't have much time for me. He used to tell me that I was as dim as a TocH lamp, which was another reference to Chad Varah who was also TocH's padre. Their logo looked like an Aladdin's lamp."

"Who are TocH?"

"An organisation formed in the First World War to promote Christianity amongst soldiers. Very well known by people of my father's age, but not so well known now."

"Did you and your father get closer as you got older?"

"No. He strongly disapproved of my musical ambitions so, when I was 16 years old, I left school, left home and hardly spoke to him again. I lived on my wits playing my guitar in bars and busking in London and Brighton. Had a relationship with a girl in Brighton and stayed. My father died when I was thirty and left me the property in Maida Vale, which I sold and used the money to start buying and selling property in Brighton."

He stopped, wondering if he was disclosing too much about himself, " What about you?"

"There's not much to tell about me, Chad. I've lived in Brighton all my life. My parents are quite elderly now and they don't want much to do with me. I've got a sister, who you've met, and they want even less to do with her. I've had lots of relationships, never married, no children."

"What do you live on?" asked Chad.

"Oh, this and that. I work in bars sometimes, and clothes shops. I help people out when they need temporary staff."

Chad was thinking that she sounded very vague about her life, and asked, "So, where do you live?"

"I don't live anywhere, Chad. I just move around. My clothes and stuff are all at a girlfriend's house in Hove. I stay there sometimes but I can't go there at the moment."

Chad put his knife and fork down still unsure how much of what she told him he could believe, "Are you still avoiding this Rick…?"

"Yes, Ricky Bishop. But he won't know I'm here, so you needn't worry."

"I'm not worried," said Chad. "I don't even know who he is."

"He's a drug dealer. Very big locally. He supplies smaller dealers, and they supply even smaller dealers, who supply the end user."

"Do you take drugs, Tricia?"

"I used to but I don't any more. I was a recreational user rather than a junkie and I stopped before it got out of control. How about you?"

"No," replied Chad, "apart from a bit of puff at parties when I was young and stupid. I've never taken any hard drugs. I figure I'd have two choices if I did. One, I'd like them in which case I'd have a problem, or two, I wouldn't like them so there's no point trying them. I have enough problems pouring alcohol down my throat, without stuffing things up my nose or injecting."

"Do you drink a lot, Chad?"

"Much more than is good for me. I tend to binge sometimes. That's how I know that if I got hooked on drugs I'd only have two chances of giving them up. One would be fat and the other one would be slim."

He picked up the glass and raised it to her, "Cheers! Can I do anything to help you with this Bishop character?"

"No thanks, Chad. I can deal with it. I just need to lie low for a bit."

"Well, if you need me to talk to him or anything like that…"

"You don't want to talk to Ricky Bishop, Chad. In fact you don't want to go anywhere near him. If you upset him, he'd kill you as quick as look at you."

Chapter Nineteen

Rue Nélaton, Paris - 1900 CEST Monday 6th June

Rue Nélaton, near the Eiffel Tower in the Fifteenth Arrondissement of Paris, is the site of the old Vélodrome d'Hiver, France's first permanent indoor cycle track which was destroyed by fire in 1959. It is a site with unhappy connotations. During the Second World War the Vel' d'Hiv, as it was known, was used to accommodate thousands of Jews, rounded up by French police, before they were transported to extermination camps. The street is short. At one end is the Bir Hakeim Metro Station, named after the battle in 1942 when the Free French Army helped to delay Rommel's Afrika Korps for sixteen days, allowing the British time to regroup before defeating him at El Alamein. At the other end of the street, forming a tee junction, is the Rue du Docteur Finlay.

On the east side of Rue Nélaton is a white concrete office block ten storeys high with single paned windows, set back from the pavement and partly screened by trees. In front of the building a huge French tricolour flies from a tall flagpole. The main entrance, guarded by armed police, is constructed of black marble, and above the entrance set into and contrasting with the marble are the words "Ministère de L'Intérieur" in gold lettering. Amongst other things, the building is used by the Direction Général de la Sécurité Intérieure, usually referred to as the DGSI, the French equivalent of the British MI5 or American FBI. The DGSI's function is to protect France's internal security, and the central administration is divided into five sub directorates: counter terrorism, the protection of the

French economy, general administration, technical administration, and counter espionage.

Jean-Louis Gravier's speciality was the hunting of terrorists and, in a windowless eighth floor lecture room at Rue Nélaton, he was addressing a group of twelve DGSI operatives who had been assigned to work this case with him. On the desk beside him was a laptop computer connected to a projector which would cast images onto a screen at the front of the room. The operatives, seated in two rows in front of him, were a mixture of Case Officers, and Watchers trained in surveillance techniques. They all listened attentively as Gravier spoke.

"Good evening gentlemen… and ladies," said Gravier with a slight nod of his head to the two female operatives who were seated together in the back row, looking as charming as ever he thought. "We have a target running, but we don't know who he is or where he is."

He turned to the laptop, "Lights please."

As the overhead lights were extinguished, "We know who his handler is."

Gravier pressed the enter key on the laptop and the first slide of a short PowerPoint presentation was projected onto the screen. In colour, it was a picture of the fat man which showed him exiting the street door of the terrorist's Paris apartment eight days previously, taken with a long lens from the building opposite.

"His name is Morad Mediene. He is of Algerian extraction, and he has lived in France since he was a small child, although he travels outside of the country extensively. He uses the code name Renard, and he is believed to be a terrorist organiser for any group who will pay him enough. He has been back in France for the past five weeks. We know this because we have had him under twenty four hour surveillance since he returned to the country. Nine days ago he visited a phone shop in Paris. He bought two mobile phones complete with sim cards and set up two pay as you go accounts. One of the surveillance team entered the shop as soon as he had left, identified himself to the shop assistant and, after a little persuasion including the threat of arrest, he obtained the mobile phone numbers of each of the two accounts.

Gravier pressed the enter key on the laptop again displaying a wider view of the same apartment building.

"The day after he purchased the mobile phones, Renard visited this building. One of our Watchers followed him in and identified the apartment which he went to. He was there for no more than twenty minutes. Since then, as well as watching Renard, we have also been watching the apartment.

"The mobile phones were used for the first time at noon today - one of them to make a call and the other to receive it. The conversation was in English and they used voice distorting software. The call was placed in Paris and was received in Rouen."

Gravier pressed the enter key, and as the recording of the two distorted, deep sounding electronic voices was played, a translation was displayed on the screen.

Phone 1 (receiver): "Angelos".
Phone 2 (caller): "Have you arrived?"
Phone 1: "Yes."
Phone 2: "Proceed as instructed."

Gravier turned and pointed at the words on the screen,

"Angelos. It could be a coded message or the target's code name."

He pointed at the next line, "Have you arrived? It could be a coded instruction or it could be exactly what it says, a question."

Gravier turned back to the room, "With no other information, for the time being, we will assume that it's what it appears to be. We will refer to the target as Angelos and assume that he has arrived at an address unknown to us which might be in Rouen. We will also assume that the caller is Renard."

He pressed the laptop key again and another photograph of Renard leaving the same building with a refuse sack appeared on the screen.

"Renard was photographed again last week visiting and leaving the same building. We believe that he gave the phone to Angelos when he visited the apartment. Would you switch the lights on please, Henri?"

Henri Girard was standing by the door and he flicked the switches as instructed, bathing the room in hard fluorescent light. Gravier sat on the corner of the desk and looked at his team.

"This afternoon, with myself and Monsieur Girard in attendance, the GIGN raided the apartment but it was empty, so our man is on the move. The building is owned by a property company which rents out the apartments furnished, on short lets. They let this one for a month to a man whose identity turns out to be false and who paid the rent in advance plus the same amount as a deposit, all in cash. We believe that it was Renard and, after the damage that the GIGN did, we don't expect that he'll get his deposit back."

The team laughed politely.

"The forensic people are doing a detailed examination of the place but, with so many tenants passing through, we don't expect to get much from it and that sort of study could take weeks. All of the neighbours have been interviewed and nobody admits to having seen Angelos or heard him. The only thing we know about with any certainty at the moment is who his handler is, that is to say Renard. We also know the number of the mobile phone, which he may or may not still be carrying. We're monitoring that and we have to hope that he uses it again. It's not much to go on, is it?"

Some of the group shook their heads.

"We are particularly interested in this one," continued Gravier. "Renard has been associated for the last year with a group which has been trying to accumulate the components for a chemical attack. We don't know who Angelos is or what he looks like. We don't know where he is, and we've no idea where he's going."

He paused while he looked at each of his operatives in turn, and they all knew what he was about to say.

"Now I want you to find him."

Chapter Twenty

Woodingdean - 1240 BST Wednesday 8th June

Two days later, on a bright, windless afternoon, McCabe stood by Jack's graveside at the Lawn Memorial Cemetery in Woodingdean on the eastern edge of Brighton. At his side was Zac Battersby looking uncomfortable in his old black double breasted suit, white shirt and black tie. On the other side of the grave, facing him, was his ex wife Hannah Rainbird. Around them were the relatives, like Zac's suit, not seen since the last wedding or funeral. They watched in silence as the coffin was slowly lowered into the ground, while McCabe looked over the heads of the mourners at the cemetery itself, with its well kept graves in acres of green grass, high up on the Sussex Downs and sloping gently towards the sea a mile and a half away. Each grave was marked with a plaque set into the ground, and the complete absence of headstones and the flowers planted on the graves gave the impression that it was a huge garden and each burial plot was a small flowerbed. Not a bad place to spend eternity he thought. He could hear the faint noise of traffic passing on Warren Road behind him a quarter of a mile away. The sun still shone in a blue sky with a few small puffs of white cloud and the rest of the world carried on as if nothing unusual was happening.

The burial ceremony over, McCabe glanced down at the coffin, said a last silent goodbye, and he and the other mourners turned and walked towards their cars, leaving the gravediggers to finish their work.

A man in his early twenties, smartly dressed in a dark grey suit, stepped forward, "Excuse me, Mr McCabe."

Chad and Zac stopped as the young man held out his hand and McCabe shook it automatically.

"My name is David Anderson. Jack and I were friends and I just wanted to say how sorry I am…" He stopped and looked awkward.

"Thank you David. Did you know him well?"

"Pretty well. We raced on Tiger Fish and socialised together. I was his lodger for a while. It's been a bit of a shock."

"It's been a shock for all of us David."

"I'm sorry to bring it up here," said David, "but I heard a rumour that Jack's house was burgled. Is that right?"

McCabe studied him, "How did you hear that?"

"Oh, I don't know," he replied vaguely. "Just people talking."

McCabe tried to remember who he had told about the burglary: the police, Zac, nobody else. It wasn't important enough to make the local news.

"Do you have any idea why his house might have been burgled, David?"

"No idea at all, but it happens all the time in Brighton. Do you think there's some connection with his accident?"

"I don't know," replied McCabe. "It seems odd that they don't appear to have stolen anything. As if they were looking for something specific. Whether they found it we've no idea."

David shook his head slowly, "That would be strange, but I can't think what they might be looking for, I'm afraid."

They were silent for a few moments until David said, "Well I just wanted to speak to you and let you know that he'll be sadly missed. I've lost a good friend."

"We're going to the hotel along the road for a buffet and drinks David," said Chad. "Will you join us?"

"Thank you, I'd like that. I'll see you there."

As David turned away and walked towards his car, Zac spoke, "I won't come to that if you don't mind. You know me, not really much good at these functions with a lot of people. I'll go home and change, and then spend the rest of the day on Honeysuckle Rose doing a few jobs, if that's alright with you, Chad."

"Of course, Zac. You go ahead. I'll see you there later."

As Chad turned away, he saw Arthur Barnard walking towards the road and went after him, catching up with him and calling as the police officer was about to get into his car, "Wait a minute please."

Barnard turned, "I'm sorry, Mr McCabe, I didn't mean to intrude. Just paying my respects."

"Thank you for coming. I was wondering if you've got any further with your investigation."

"What investigation is that, Mr McCabe?"

"The investigation into my son's death, of course."

"We're not investigating your son's death, Mr McCabe. There'll be an inquest and the Coroner will decide what happened, but it could be some time yet before that takes place. I realise that it's difficult for you, but you must be patient."

"But aren't you doing anything? Interviewing Allerton and Benniker? Surely you…"

"Sorry, Mr McCabe, I have to attend an urgent meeting. Goodbye."

Barnard waved his hand, got into his car and drove off.

***

It was dark by the time McCabe arrived at Honeysuckle Rose. He had spent three hours at the buffet listening to his relatives while they reminisced about better times, ate sandwiches and drank large quantities of sherry, spirits, wine, and beer. A lot of them were so distantly related that he didn't recognise them, and it was obvious that they had only come to meet the famous Hannah Rainbird. In that they were to be disappointed, and they said so. After completely ignoring Chad and then cold shouldering him when he approached her, Hannah had left with her three person entourage immediately after the graveside ceremony and didn't show up at the reception afterwards.

As the relatives gradually drifted away, they all agreed that they should meet more often and why didn't they? McCabe knew why they didn't. It was because so many years had passed that they had absolutely nothing in common, and it was with some relief that he watched the last of them leave. He had phoned for a taxi, taken his tie off, and gone on a pub crawl in Brighton and Hove knocking back as much white wine and whisky as he could in the shortest space of time. But even McCabe had limits and he knew that it was time to stop and get his head straight. He had decided to spend the night on his boat and, apart from that, he'd told Zac that he'd meet him there, although that was hours ago.

A taxi had brought him to Brighton Marina, and he was now walking the length of Pontoon 16 past the yachts and motor cruisers moored shoulder to shoulder on either side of him in the gloom. It was unusually quiet and still in the marina, and the water was a smooth black mirror reflecting the dim low level lighting, designed not for full illumination but just adequate enough to outline the edges of the pontoon. As he neared Honeysuckle Rose he could see a chink of light escaping past the drawn curtains in her saloon. The side panel of the canvas cockpit tent was already unzipped and hanging loose, and he stepped up onto the side deck and then into the cockpit, bending as he pushed the panel aside. The stern cabin and saloon doors were both open. The stern cabin was in darkness and light streamed out from the saloon.

Resting his hands on either side of the low doorway and stooping to peer down into the saloon, he called out, "Still here, Zac?"

There was no reply.

McCabe crouched to see further into the saloon and heard movement behind him followed in the same instant by a flash of light. He saw and felt nothing more as his body dropped from the cockpit into the saloon and thudded onto the cabin sole in a heap, nor did he hear the shot which had been fired from close range at the back of his head.

Chapter Twenty One

Rouen - 1000 CEST Thursday 9th June

As most people know, when a mobile phone is switched on it emits a signal even when not being used for a call. The signal is picked up by the cellular phone network, which is constantly scanning for such signals, and this is how the network can route calls to and from a mobile phone as soon as they are attempted. Angelos knew this and was careful to only switch on the mobile phone at the appointed time each day and to switch it off no more than two minutes later, which included removing the battery to ensure that the phone couldn't transmit.

In France, The Internal Safety Law known as Loi sur la Sécurité Intérieure or LSI, which was enacted in 2003 as a reaction to the attacks on the World Trade Centre in New York, allows immediate access on demand by the Authorities to the computer data of telecom companies. Using this law, the DGSI had secured the cooperation of the mobile phone service provider, and had monitored Renard's and Angelos' phone use for the past twelve days. If required by the Authorities, and using a process of triangulation, a network provider can establish, with reasonable accuracy, where a phone is by monitoring its signal with the three nearest phone masts, and establishing the phone's signal strength at each mast.

In Rouen, in a large meeting room on the third floor of an anonymous office building on the Rue Bourg l'Abbé, discreetly owned by the Ministry of the Interior, Gravier was briefing his team again.

"Every day Angelos switches on the mobile phone at exactly midday for two minutes, each time in a different location. He hasn't made any calls and, so far, he's only received the one call, which I played for you at the briefing on Monday. We know from this that he was in Rouen at noon every day this week, and we anticipate that he will activate the phone again today at 1200 hours."

He stopped for a few moments to sip at a cup of coffee.

"By the time we reach the place where the phone was being used it's been switched off and, even if he's there, we don't know who we're looking for. Apart from the first time, he's used the phone in places where there are large numbers of people, presumably to blend into the crowd. The locations where he's used it so far are all in central Rouen, which is why we are here."

Henri Girard stood up and began handing out printed sheets of paper to each of the operatives.

"The information that you've just been given," continued Gravier, "contains the street names and location maps showing where the phone was used."

He waited for a few moments while they all studied the maps.

"The first location, three days ago, was in the Rue André Gide, the second was at the Place de la Calende by the Cathedral. The third, yesterday, was at the junction of Rue de La Champmeslé and Rue du Général Leclerc.

"Although he moves around so that the phone can't be traced to wherever he's staying, he still thinks that it's secure and doesn't believe that we'll be tracking it. If he did he wouldn't be using it, so he's made his first mistake. It's possible that we may have him on security cameras. That's our break gentlemen and ladies. Your job now is to find the cameras around the places where he's been using the phone, then we'll get the police to gather as many disks as they can, and let's see if we can have a look at him."

Chapter Twenty Two

Brighton - 1147 BST Thursday 9th June

McCabe was floating face up, horizontal underwater, but slowly rising to the surface where it was brighter. As he turned his head, pain seared through his brain and, as everything went black, he decided not to move again. Seconds, minutes, or hours later he was floating to the surface again and this time he kept still. He could hear noise in the distance. What was it? A buzzing, like flies on a window pane, which slowly became clearer until he realised that it was people speaking close to him. Tricia's voice. He opened his eyes and the light and the pain in his head made him screw them up again. Squinting for a moment he could see that he was lying on his back in a room. Then he passed out.

Later the same day he surfaced again and this time he kept his eyes shut and listened, but the close voices had gone. In the distance a clattering noise, muffled voices now rising and then falling as if they were walking past but behind a wall. He opened his eyes slowly, squinting until he became accustomed to the light, then he opened them fully ignoring the pain in his head. The same room. He stared at the white ceiling and waited for the nausea to pass.

"You're with us then?" Tricia's voice again, this time smiling.

"Hospital?" asked McCabe.

"Yes."

McCabe closed his eyes and slept.

The next time he woke Tricia was still there and a middle aged doctor was standing over him.

"How are you feeling?"

"Headache."
The doctor pulled a pencil torch from his pocket, "I'm not surprised, old chap. I'm just going to look into your eyes."
He gently lifted each of McCabe's eyelids and shone the torch into the pupils, "Good."
"Why am I here?"
"You have concussion old chap. You got shot in the head last night but, fortunately for you, the bullet glanced off of your skull. According to the police they dug a deformed small calibre bullet out of the woodwork of your boat, probably a .22 they said. I'm not a firearms expert, but if your skull is thick enough and the angle is right that can happen."
McCabe suddenly remembered, "Where's Zac. Needs help."
"You just relax old chap. We're going to keep you here under observation for a few days, but I think you'll be OK. Get some rest and you'll be fine. I'll come back and see you later."
As the doctor left the room McCabe tried to raise himself on his elbows but fell back with the effort, and the pain was worse.
"Wait. Zac…"
"You've got to rest," said Tricia. "That was last night. Everything's fine."
"Got to find Zac," said McCabe, and then he fell into a deep sleep.

Chapter Twenty Three

Rue Massacre, Rouen - 1202 CEST Thursday 9th June

Angelos switched off the mobile phone and discreetly removed the battery. Four days had passed and there was still no contact from Renard. The terrorist pocketed the phone, shifted the weight of the rucksack slung over one shoulder, and walked quickly away from where a phone trace might bring the police. Angelos had no reason to believe that the police had any knowledge of the phone but it always paid to be careful. The terrorist had come out for provisions and then to listen for a call from Renard. Each day, when leaving the apartment, all of Angelos' possessions and the precious abrin powder were packed into the rucksack and carried, in case it was necessary to move on suddenly.

The terrorist turned and merged with the shoppers and tourists who were strolling along the narrow Rue Massacre in the medieval centre of Rouen, and turned right at the end into the Rue aux Juifs. Suddenly, the deafening clatter of a police helicopter echoed around the street as it appeared just above rooftop level hovering directly above the terrorist, and the street was full of armed police. Angelos turned, backed up against the plate glass window of a jewellery shop, and frantically looked up and down the street searching desperately for a way out. Apart from the knife the terrorist was unarmed. Seconds later, a large white police van and four police motor cyclists swept into the street at high speed from Rue Jeanne d'Arc and roared across the cobbles towards the terrorist, adding to the clamour of the helicopter. Angelos felt a sudden surge of panic and realised that there could be no escape.

Unshouldering and reaching into the rucksack, Angelos fumbled for the container of abrin, ready to set the delayed timer that would detonate the charge and disperse the deadly toxin into the air. At the same time the vehicles surged past at speed and, a hundred metres further on, swung left through the open gates of the Palais de Justice which were immediately closed behind them. The helicopter rose high above the street, turned away and disappeared from view, and the only sound was the excited buzz of conversation from the tourists. Angelos' adrenaline fuelled heart thudded and then began to slow with the realisation that it had been a transfer of high security prisoners to the Law Courts. The gendarmes on foot, spaced at fifty metre intervals along the street, relaxed and none of them paid any attention to the terrorist standing there still gazing upward at where the helicopter had been.

Angelos leaned against the shopfront, and stared across the street at the freshly cleaned stonework of the Normandie Parliament building, thankful not to have been carrying a firearm. Without doubt, it would have been used when the terrorist instinctively started shooting. Turning and threading a way through the groups of unsuspecting onlookers filling the narrow pavement, Angelos walked back to the apartment. In the rucksack, the lethal powder remained secure. It could so easily have been spreading now in an ever expanding cloud of chemical death across the densely populated city of Rouen.

Chapter Twenty Four

Brighton - 1107 BST Friday 10th June

When McCabe woke he was alone. He lay still and tried to think. Hospital. He was hungry and thirsty. It was daylight. Too much effort and he gave up. He dozed for a few minutes and then woke again. He lay there for several minutes trying to remember what had happened. Honeysuckle Rose, saloon lights on. He'd heard somebody moving behind him then seen a flash of light. Tricia was here, and a doctor. The doctor said he'd been shot in the head. Rose, Tricia, doctor, when was that? Rose was night time after Jack's funeral. Tricia and the doctor day time. Today? All too difficult.

He raised his arms then moved his legs; they seemed to be working. With an effort he raised himself onto his left elbow and his head throbbed as he stayed in that position for a minute until, ignoring the pain in his head, he swung his feet out of the bed and sat on the edge. There was a jug of water on the bedside locker and he poured some into the glass which was beside it and drank it greedily. His right shoulder ached. He replaced the glass, put his feet on the floor and carefully stood up.

On the other side of the small room was a washbasin with a mirror above it, and McCabe slowly limped over to it. Why was he limping? He flexed the muscles in his right leg and realised that it was aching. He steadied himself with both hands on the washbasin and looked into the mirror. There was at least two days growth of beard on his face, his eyes were bloodshot, and around his head was a bandage which was holding in place a pad at the back. It reminded him of the old black and white photographs of wounded soldiers in the trenches. To his left was a door. With a hand against the wall for support McCabe staggered over to the door and opened it. Inside were a shower cubicle and a toilet. McCabe lurched into the room, lifted the front of his hospital gown and relieved himself, pushing down the flush handle afterwards. He stood for a moment trying to collect his thoughts. Rose. He had to find out what had happened to his boat.

McCabe lurched back into the next room and sat on the bed. For the first time he noticed a narrow hanging locker. He roused himself again, crossed the room and opened the locker door. Inside on hangers were the clothes he was wearing when he was brought in. His black funeral suit and white shirt. On a shelf were his black tie, shoes, socks and underpants. McCabe emptied the locker and, with more energy now that he had a plan, he placed the contents on the bed. He went into the shower room, and with difficulty undid the ties at the back of the hospital gown and dropped it on the floor. He turned on the shower and stood under it for five minutes allowing the hot water to wash over and revive him, while keeping the water away from his bandaged head. He stepped out of the shower and rubbed the steam from a long mirror on the wall and looked at his naked body. His right shoulder and hip were black with bruising. Now he knew why they ached. McCabe limped into the bedroom, found a towel in the bedside locker and dried himself.

He dressed with effort, wincing as he put his underwear, shirt and suit on. His shirt collar and the back of the suit had dried blood on them, presumably his. The tie he shoved into the inside jacket pocket and, at the same time, he realised that all of his pockets were empty. They must have taken his keys, wallet and comb for safekeeping. Then he realised that they had also taken his watch. What time was it? What day was it? McCabe looked into the mirror over the washbasin and saw a wild man staring back at him, unshaven and dressed in a creased suit with a bandage around his head. He turned, crossed the room, opened the door, and stepped out into the corridor closing the door behind him.

To his left the corridor extended fifty feet with doors on either side. At the end was a door marked Fire Exit. To the right the corridor carried on into the distance and, at the end of it, a white-coated doctor was conversing with a nurse and a uniformed policeman, all three with their backs to him. He turned left and limped towards the fire door. McCabe pushed the door open and, as it swung shut behind him, he found himself in a stairwell. He steadied himself on the handrail and slowly edged his way down the concrete stairs, moving his feet so that they were both on the same step before he moved down to the next one. Wincing with the pain, it took him five minutes to descend the four storeys to ground level and, when he reached the bottom of the stairwell, he was confronted by two more doors.

On one side of the stairwell was another fire escape door, presumably leading to the outside world, with a sign on it reading "This Door Is Alarmed". Not that way unless he wanted the whole hospital alerted to the fact that he was trying to get out. On the other side of the stairwell was a door which led back into the hospital. McCabe rested for a few moments grateful that, so far, nobody else had used the stairs and asked him if he was alright, or worse, raised a hue and cry that one of the patients was trying to escape. Escape? Was that what he was doing? Was he a prisoner? He thought not but was sure that anyone seeing him in his current state would attempt to stop him leaving. He stood up straight and, ignoring his aching leg and shoulder, buttoned his jacket. Gritting his teeth, he pulled the door open with his left hand and in as straight a line as possible walked through it limping only slightly. To his left was a corridor, ahead of him was another corridor, to his right was what appeared to be a reception desk, and beyond the reception desk was a revolving door with a glass swing door on either side of it leading to the outside world.

McCabe walked steadily past the reception desk ignored by three people who were queuing there and the two receptionists, who had their heads down as they searched for papers. He headed for one of the swing doors, thinking clearly enough to know that he would not have the strength to push through the revolving door, or the speed to get through it if someone came through in the other direction at the same time. He was ten feet from the door when a man brushed past him, nearly causing him to stumble, and pushed his way through it. As McCabe reached it the door swung back in his face and he stopped. He pushed but with the pain in his shoulder and hip could not get enough leverage to open the door against its powerful floor spring. Feeling a sense of panic, he tried again without success, and then once more, closing his eyes and wincing with the effort. He began to fall forward, opened his eyes, and realised that the door was opening as he stumbled through it. He mumbled a thank you to the slightly built young woman who had pulled it from the outside and was waiting to get in. She looked at him curiously without speaking and McCabe continued on his way; no time to be the gentleman now.

His momentum carried him forward as he staggered and caught himself, then negotiated three parked cars, and realised that he was in a service road behind the hospital. Deliberately straightening his back, he turned right and carried on walking as normally as he could, although each movement was agony. He continued along the pavement counting another fifty paces and then stopped, leaning with his back to a brick wall, clenching his teeth and gasping with the pain. He opened his eyes as a woman hurried past gathering her two small children to her and avoiding eye contact. Carrying on for another hundred yards down a brick paved slope and past a row of parked ambulances, McCabe reached a public road and felt the late morning sun strong on his aching head and bright in his eyes. He knew where he was now, still in Brighton and on a road called Bristol Gate. Brighton Marina was only a mile away and he could get back to Honeysuckle Rose and see what was happening. In his muddled state, he determined that he would walk there regardless of the punishment that his body was feeling. McCabe turned right and began to weave his way down the steep hill. In the distance ahead of him he could see the rooftops of Kemptown and the sea beyond. Reaching Eastern Road he turned left and carried on stumbling and limping along the pavement. He ignored the undisguised disgust on the faces of passing pedestrians who saw him as just another Brighton drunk who had been on a bender, then been in a fight, and had a bandaged head and dried blood on his crumpled suit to show for it.

Every few minutes McCabe would stop and rest, leaning against the long flint wall bordering the huge tract of land on the left belonging to Brighton College. After a minute or so he would limp on again. Twenty minutes later he was still in Eastern Road and not even a quarter of the way to the marina. He stopped again and, this time, instead of leaning against the wall he put his back to it and sank down onto his haunches, incapable of carrying on. As McCabe squatted there, gasping with pain and exhaustion, he took no notice of the car that pulled into the kerb and stopped in front of him.

"Are you alright, Mr McCabe?"

He opened his eyes and focussed on the car, then on the driver leaning across the passenger seat and calling to him through the open window.

"Mr McCabe. Are you alright?"

Realisation came slowly. Calling to him from the car was Detective Sergeant Barnard.

"Do I look alright? I've been shot in the head."

Chapter Twenty Five

Rue Bourg l'Abbé, Rouen - 1223 CEST Friday 10th June

At the locations which Gravier's DGSI team had been instructed to visit there was a distinct lack of security cameras. In the first two, the Rue André Gide and the Place de la Calende, there were no cameras at all. In the third location, at the junction of Rue de La Champmeslé and Rue du Général Leclerc, they identified three cameras, two in shops and one in the lobby of the Crédit Industriel et Commercial Bank in Place Jacques Leliéur. They also had a fourth location from yesterday when Angelos had switched on the mobile phone near the Gros-Horloge, the huge ornamental clock at the end of Rue Massacre in the centre of Rouen. At this new location they had only been able to find one camera, which was in the lobby of the LCL bank. The Police had obtained the stored data from all of the cameras, and a technician had copied the ten minute segment between 11.55 am and 12.05 pm from each recording onto a single disk for the appropriate day. The result was a disk with thirty minutes of recordings from the three cameras for day three, showing pedestrian activity from different viewpoints for the crucial ten minutes that the target was believed to have been in the area. For day four they had a disk with only ten minutes of recording showing the cobbled street in front of the LCL Bank.

In a small room, on the first floor of the offices on the Rue Bourg l'Abbé, Henri Girard was seated at the only desk. In front of him were two desktop computers side by side, each one set up to run the images from one of the disks: day three on the left hand computer, day four on the right. Gravier was standing behind him, looking over Girard's shoulder and drinking coffee. They were the only people in the room.

They were examining the data on the day three computer, and they had already discounted the twenty minute sequence taken in the two shops on the assumption that if the target was waiting for a call he wouldn't answer it where he could be overheard. This left them concentrating on the ten minute segment recorded by the camera in the lobby of the Crédit Industriel et Commercial Bank. The camera was placed in such a way that it recorded anyone entering or leaving the bank through the glass doors at the front of the lobby, and it also showed the view through the doors and into the pedestrianised Square in front of the bank. Girard studied the screen carefully as a steady stream of people entered and left the bank, but he was more interested in the activity in the Square behind them. A young man with a rucksack over his shoulder stood at the pavement edge on the far side of the Square with his back to the camera, then he turned and walked left until he was out of vision. At the same time, a woman and a child holding hands walked past from right to left. An elderly, well dressed man with a walking stick moved slowly past from left to right in the middle distance. A young woman with a rucksack walked past from right to left close to the front of the building glancing into the bank doorway as she went. Two teenage girls sharing a joke passed from left to right. Children, old women, young women, old men, young men; for ten minutes they watched the procession of people passing or coming and going through the doors. When the day three recording had finished playing Girard turned his attention to the day four computer, and Gravier pulled up a chair and sat beside him. Neither of them spoke.

Girard clicked the left mouse button and started the ten minute recording running. The view was from the entrance to the LCL Bank, angled from the left side of the lobby into the Rue du Gros-Horloge. This time there were no glass doors but an unobscured view into the street. In the top right of the picture they could see the beginning of the Rue Massacre at its junction with Rue du Gros-Horloge, its half timbered buildings disappearing away from them. In the lower right of the screen were six tables with a dozen cane chairs belonging to the tabac next door to the bank; people were sitting there au terrace as they drank and chatted to each other. Filling the left side of the screen, directly in front of the bank, was a clear view of the street, and ten metres away on the opposite side was an opticians shop bearing the sign Les Opticiens Conseils. For over five minutes, not sure what they were looking for, Girard and Gravier watched the recording of a throng of people passing the camera. As the clock on the bottom left corner of the screen read 12.01.52 a woman with a rucksack over her shoulder walked into view from the left and stopped outside the optician's shop. She took a mobile phone from her jacket pocket, looked at its screen for a few seconds, then pressed one of the buttons. The woman removed the phone's battery, put the phone and battery back into her pocket, then walked along Rue Massacre and quickly disappeared from view. Girard clicked the left mouse button and stopped the recording, then rewound it until they had a clear view, face on, of the woman with the phone and rucksack. Girard paused the recording, freezing the image on the screen. He turned to the other computer and fast forwarded the recording of the day three locations until he reached the point where Angelos had walked past and glanced into the bank doorway. He froze that image as well. Girard and Gravier looked from one screen to the other comparing the two images of the woman with the rucksack, hardly able to believe their luck.

"It's a woman, sir," said Girard quietly, "and we have her."

"I think we do," replied Gravier.

They both sat back in their chairs and studied her. Early twenties, jeans, trainers, open necked shirt, casual jacket, tall, dark hair, tanned complexion, attractive.

"Well done Henri," said Gravier. "Circulate her picture to the police with instructions not to apprehend her but to report back to us if she's spotted. Tomorrow at noon I want our watchers spread out through the centre of Rouen looking for her."

Chapter Twenty Six

John Street, Brighton - 1209 BST Friday 10th June

McCabe was in the same chair, in the same room at Brighton Police Station, listening to the same Detective Constable he had seen when he was given Jack's belongings. His head was throbbing, his body was aching, and he was still trying to take in what had happened.

When Barnard had picked him up and insisted that they go back to the hospital McCabe had refused and, in turn, insisted that they go to Honeysuckle Rose. Barnard had told him that he couldn't go to his boat as it was a crime scene and was still being examined. In the event, Barnard had brought him here, on the basis that if he was strong enough to refuse hospital treatment, he was strong enough to help the police with their enquiries.

McCabe stared at the half finished cup of tea in front of him, which had made him feel sick, "What day is it?"

The policeman looked surprised, "Friday."

Friday. The funeral was on Wednesday, so he had been in the hospital for thirty six hours and lost a day.

McCabe pulled himself together and tried to concentrate.

The policeman watched him.

"How long have I been here?"

"About twenty minutes."

McCabe stared at the table for a few moments, "Do you think I can go now?" he asked.

"You're not under arrest. You can go whenever you like, but it would help us if you would tell us what you know."

"I don't know anything. I don't even know what happened. Why don't you tell me?"

The policeman considered that for a moment, then replied, "Alright."

He pulled a notebook from his inside jacket pocket, flicked through a few pages, and then, as if he was making a statement in Court, droned, "On Wednesday the 8th of June, at about 10.30pm, a berth holder on Pontoon 16 at Brighton Marina saw that the lights of the yacht Honeysuckle Rose were on and that the boat was open, but nobody appeared to be on board. He decided to check that everything was in order. He knocked on the side of the boat and got no reply. When he looked in he saw a man, yourself," - the detective paused and looked at McCabe pointedly - "slumped on the floor at the bottom of the saloon steps. He raised the alarm and police and an ambulance were called. It was discovered that the man had been shot."

McCabe tried to focus his mind on Wednesday night. He had been to Jack's funeral. He remembered going on a pub crawl.

"I got a taxi … I got a taxi from Hove."

The policeman made a note, "When?"

"On Wednesday night."

"Why were you in Hove?"

"I was having a drink."

The policeman made another note.

"Where did you get the taxi to?"

"From Hove to the marina."

"What time was that?"

There was a long silence while McCabe tried to work it out.

"About ten o'clock."

Another note.

"What did you do then?"

"Walked to Honeysuckle Rose. The lights were on. I went on board."

"Was anyone else there?"

McCabe thought about that for a few seconds.

"I didn't see anyone else."

"What happened then?"

A long silence while McCabe stared at the table with a look of concentration on his face, then said, "There was someone else there. I heard a noise behind me. Someone was in the stern cabin."

The policeman was staring at him intently.

"Then?"

"Nothing," replied McCabe. "I don't remember anything after that. The doctor said I was shot."

"It's not much of a story, Mr McCabe, is it?"

McCabe was suddenly exhausted and he'd had enough. He wanted to leave.

"Alright," he said. "I'll tell you what really happened."

The young detective eagerly held his pen poised to write in the notebook.

"I got back to Honeysuckle Rose, hadn't had a very good day, so I pulled a gun out of my pocket and shot myself in the back of the head, threw the gun overboard, and fell down the steps."

The door opened as the detective finished writing it down verbatim, and DS Barnard walked in wiping his nose.

"How are we doing Constable?"

He turned towards Barnard, "Got it, Sarge. He just admitted it was attempted suicide. Says he threw the gun overboard."

Barnard stuffed the handkerchief into his pocket, pulled a chair up to the table and sat down opposite McCabe looking quizzical.

"Did you say that, Mr McCabe?"

"Yes, I did. Your Constable's an idiot."

"Can I see your notes please, Constable?" asked

Barnard, and held out his hand as the policeman passed

the notebook to him.

He scanned it for a few seconds and said, "Thank you, Constable. Why don't you take a break now? Get yourself a cup of tea. I'll take over."

Barnard gave the notebook back to the detective who stood up looking pleased with himself, shot a smug look at McCabe and left the room.

Barnard looked at McCabe and smiled a grim smile.

"A good young officer that. Just a bit too keen sometimes. Fast track university graduate; very bright but not much common sense yet."

Wearily McCabe replied, "I've had enough of this. I'd like to go."

"Of course, you must be tired after all this excitement. I'll get a car to take you. We've finished examining your boat. You can have it back now."

"Thank you" said McCabe.

"Would you like to know our conclusions?"

"As long as you give me a lift home afterwards."

"We've done all the obvious things. Fingerprints, lots of those, most of them yours I should think. If you don't mind, before you leave we'd like to take your fingerprints so that we can eliminate them. I suspect that the intruder won't have left any prints of his own.

"You were shot from behind from a few feet away. We recovered the bullet so we know that it was a .22

but the round glanced off, probably because you were bending forward. The bullet lodged in the deck beam over the hatchway. It was enough to knock you out, but not enough to kill you. It doesn't look like a professional job. Small calibre weapon, a bit too hit and miss, literally.

" All of the boat contents have been pulled out, so it looks as if somebody was searching for something. We don't know what, so I'd be grateful if you'd let us know if anything is missing.

"You were probably shot because you turned up at the wrong time and would have been able to identify the intruder.

"You've been under armed guard in the hospital since Wednesday night, and the uniform who let you get out is in a lot of trouble, but we don't think that you are likely to be targeted again."

Barnard stopped talking.

"Is that it?" asked McCabe.

"That's all we have at the moment."

"But why were they searching my boat?"

"I don't know, Mr McCabe."

"My son drowns and his flat is burgled, but you don't seem to have done anything about it. I'm shot and my boat is searched, and you can't tell me why. What the hell are you going to do about it?"

"We're doing what we can, Mr McCabe, I promise you."

McCabe gave up. He was too worn out to pursue it and he slumped back into the chair.

"Come on," said Barnard gently. "Let's get you fingerprinted and then I'll find you a ride home. You've had enough for one day."

***

Fifty minutes later, the unmarked police car dropped McCabe off at the landward end of the West Jetty at Brighton Marina, and he trudged wearily towards the steel security gate. He tried to ignore the noise being made by the lunchtime diners on the Boardwalk to his right, all seated at tables in front of the string of busy restaurants. How pleasant everything was for them on this warm afternoon as they ate and drank, looking out at the acres of expensive boats laid out in front of them. For McCabe the world was anything but pleasant. He put his hand into his pocket to find his key ring which, apart from normal keys, held the small key fob proximity card which would identify him to the Access Control System and open the security gate. Then he remembered that all of his belongings, including his keys, were still at the hospital.

Two smartly dressed middle aged couples were approaching from the other side of the gate which one of the men opened by pressing the rocker switch on their side. McCabe stood back as they passed through the gate, and he lurched through before it could close again. Fifty yards further on he reached the steel gate to Pontoon 16, which was also locked electronically. No proximity card, no entry, and he put his hands on the bars and leaned forward, his forehead against the gate, worn out.

Behind him an elderly man dressed in a tracksuit and carrying a towel and wash bag came out of the shower block.

"You alright there?"

"Yes I'm fine thanks," McCabe lied as he straightened up. "I've left my keys behind and I'm wondering how to get in."

"Allow me."

McCabe stood back as the man waved his own small black plastic fob in front of the keypad and, with a beep, the lock was released. The stranger pulled the gate fully open and stood back to let McCabe through, then he let the gate swing shut behind them and marched away down the pontoon, boarding a motor cruiser about half way along. McCabe followed at a much slower pace. He was exhausted and all but staggered as he took the long walk to Honeysuckle Rose at the far end of the pontoon. When he reached her he heaved himself aboard and stood swaying in the cockpit.

Tricia was looking up at him from the saloon with a startled look on her face and her right hand to her throat.

"God, you made me jump."

"Sorry," McCabe mumbled, as he sat down heavily on the cockpit cushions. "I didn't know you'd be here."

"I've been cleaning up," she said. "You wouldn't believe the mess. Blood, fingerprint dust, all your things everywhere."

She climbed the steps into the cockpit and stood over him, "Let me have a look at your head."

He felt her fingers in his hair and, for the first time in years, started to sob. The tension that had been slowly building since Jack's death broke and, as his shoulders heaved, she stood there with her arms around him and held him against her until he regained his composure.

"You've got to sleep, Chad. I'll make up your bunk and you can get straight into it. I'll change the dressing on your head in the morning."

She went down the steps to the stern cabin, and McCabe sat and stared out at the marina, wondering why his life was in such a mess.

"Come on," she called.

He looked down into the cabin and Tricia was beckoning, "Come on."

He stood and gingerly descended the steps into the cabin, hanging on to the grab handles as he lurched towards the port berth and sat on it. Tricia removed his jacket, and as he lay down she swung his feet onto the bunk. She removed his shoes, covered him with a duvet, and closed the curtains to keep out the sunlight.

"I'll be here when you wake up," she said, but McCabe was already asleep.

Chapter Twenty Seven

Rouen - 1200 CEST Saturday 11th June

Nicolette Garnier looked younger than her age and was known as Mimi to her DGSI colleagues; a reference to the opera La Bohème because she was always complaining that her hands were cold. She was a twenty four year old university graduate and one of the most popular members of Gravier's team of watchers. The watchers, instead of working in their usual groups, had been spread thinly across Rouen in the hope that one of them would spot Angelos, and Mimi was on her own seated at a table in front of a half timbered restaurant at the junction of Place Barthélemy and Rue de Martainville. She had bright blue eyes, was petite with shoulder length straight black hair, and was wearing a grey knee length skirt, a white cotton blouse, a grey jacket and buff coloured high heeled shoes. On the ground beside her was a grey leather shoulder bag. She was sipping a glass of tonic water complete with ice and a twist of lemon and she looked like any other pretty French girl, not cold today, enjoying the sunshine on this Saturday morning while she waited for someone to join her, perhaps. To her right, on the other side of the cobbled Square, stood Angelos although Mimi appeared not to notice her.

Five days had passed since the DGSI had begun their search for her, and yesterday they had seen her on the CCTV pictures. An extensive search of images on their databases, and those of friendly foreign security services, indicated that she was a "cleanskin" terrorist, unknown to them, at least by sight. Yesterday she had not been recorded on any CCTV images but she had used the mobile phone in Rue Saint-Patrice in Rouen, and Gravier was hoping that she was still in the city. Mimi was not yet completely convinced that it was her. She was dressed in a similar way to the target in the CCTV images and she had a rucksack, but Mimi was still not sure.

The target had just turned on her mobile phone. She waited and within a minute the phone rang. She pressed the answer button, put the phone to her ear and said quietly, “Angelos,” although Mimi could not hear that.

She listened and heard Renard’s voice say, “You will go to the next address and I will not contact you for at least five days.”

Angelos replied with the single word, “Yes,” pressed the disconnect button, switched the phone off, took the battery out of it, and pushed it into the pocket of her jacket. Turning, she crossed the Square towards Mimi, passing in front of her as she walked away along Rue de Martainville.

Mimi, now certain that she had found Angelos, reached for her shoulder bag, took some Euros from the bag’s side pocket, left them on the table, and followed her.

Chapter Twenty Eight

Brighton Marina - 1104 BST Saturday 11th June

He came to, slowly. A ray of sunlight beamed through a chink in the curtain above his head on the starboard side of the cabin, and McCabe, staying warm under the duvet, took several minutes to work out that, as Honeysuckle Rose was moored facing north, the sun was shining from the east so it must be morning. When he moved his limbs he realised that his whole body still ached. Ignoring the pain, and with a lot of effort, he sat up, and turning, swung his feet to the floor. He sat there for a few moments looking at the contents of the drawers which had been strewn around the cabin when it was searched by his attacker. McCabe stood, opened the door to the heads, went in, relieved himself, pumped the bowl out into the holding tank, and pumped seawater back into the bowl. Leaning against the bulkhead he stared down at the original Blake brass handled pump and, not for the first time, thought that it was time he replaced it with something more modern which took less effort to use. McCabe went back into the cabin, removed the clothes that he had slept in then returned to the heads where, standing naked, he pumped some water into the wash basin and splashed it onto his face and washed his hands. He pulled the plug from the washbasin and dried himself. In the cabin, he raked through the pile of clothes on the floor, found a clean pair of underpants and put them on. From the hanging locker he took a clean denim shirt and a pair of blue cotton trousers, and put those on as well. Finally, he slipped his feet into a pair of brown deck shoes. McCabe slid back the door and, across the cockpit through the open door of the saloon, he could see Tricia in the galley.

She smiled at him, "Good morning. How are you feeling?"

"Like I've been run over."

"Well you've got a bit more colour in your face. Come on. I heard you moving about and I've just made some coffee."

McCabe hauled himself up the steps from the stern cabin and sat in the cockpit as she passed a cup of coffee up to him. He sipped it carefully, black with two sugars. She had remembered his preference.

"No point offering you breakfast, is there?

"No thanks."

Hard to break the habit which he'd had all of his adult life, he thought. He had never eaten breakfast because coffee and three cigarettes had always been the way he started the day. Since he had given up smoking and was only left with the coffee he still couldn't face the thought of eating as soon as he had woken up.

"Have you been here all night?"

"Yes," she replied. "I found a sleeping bag and pillow in the forward cabin and slept in there."

McCabe sipped his coffee, staring blankly at the gash in the deck beam where the bullet had struck. He was slowly coming to life.

"It's good of you to be here, Tricia."

"Well someone needs to keep an eye on you," she said. "You must have had a rough day yesterday. You caused quite a panic when the hospital discovered that you'd disappeared. I'd given them my number so they called me and I went up there, but by the time I arrived the police had found you. I've got your things by the way," and she picked up a plastic bag which was lying on the table and passed it to him.

"Thanks," said McCabe, opening the bag and taking out his wallet, keys, and small change, which he put into his pockets. In the bottom of the bag was his thirty year old steel Rolex Oysterdate watch which he clipped around his left wrist.

"Any better?" asked Tricia.

"Better than I was. My head has stopped throbbing. I just ache all over now."

"On the subject of your head, let's have a look at it."

Tricia came up into the cockpit and stood next to him as she removed the dressing from his head wound.

"OK," she said. "We'll leave the dressing off and let the air get to it. The hospital said that you'll have to have the stitches taken out in ten days or so. It could have been a lot worse. You're lucky to be here at all. Do the police have any idea who did it?"

"They're not interested, Tricia. The idiot who interviewed me thinks that I tried to commit suicide by shooting myself. Fortunately his boss seems to have more sense, but they're not doing much to find out what's going on. They've asked me to let them know if anything's missing."

"You'd better check then. I've cleaned up but left things pretty much where they were so that you can see if anything's been taken. I phoned Zac, by the way, to let him know what had happened and that you're OK. He said he left here a couple of hours before you arrived the other evening and didn't see anything suspicious."

McCabe finished his coffee and then went down the steps into the saloon. He looked around. Tricia had cleaned up all traces of the police activity, and had picked up the things that had been strewn around the floor and stacked them on the saloon seating. He checked that his guitar was undamaged and then, for the next hour, he slowly and carefully put his possessions back in their original places in lockers and drawers as he tried to discover what, if anything, was missing. He repeated the process in the forward cabin, and then in the stern cabin. When he had finished he went back into the saloon and sat on the starboard berth deep in thought.

"Well?" asked Tricia, who had been patiently sitting in the cockpit reading her Kindle.

McCabe looked up at her.

"My flare packs are missing."

"Flare packs?"

"Mini distress flares. They're missing," said McCabe.

"Why would anyone commit attempted murder to steal your flare packs?"

"I don't know, Tricia. I had four packs of mini flares and they've gone."

"Have they taken anything else?"

"Not that I can see. It's bizarre. Why would they do that? There's nothing special about them, you can buy them in any yacht chandlery."

"Well at least you can let the police know."

"No," exclaimed McCabe, firmly. "I'm not telling them anything. They're just looking for an excuse to implicate me in all this and the less I have to do with them the better."

Tricia already knew him well enough to realise that, if he was that emphatic, there was no point in arguing with him.

He looked up at her.

"I've got to thank you for everything you've done, Tricia."

"I want to help you, Chad. I like being around you."

McCabe wondered what message she was sending him and looked into her eyes for longer than he should have done.

Tricia looked away, her face flushed, "Can I go back to the flat now, please?"

Chapter Twenty Nine

Rouen - 1219 CEST Saturday 11th June

Angelos was a hundred metres ahead of her as Mimi, matching her pace, followed her along the Rue de Martainville. There were half a dozen pedestrians between them but Mimi would have preferred more. Suddenly Angelos turned, reversed direction and began walking towards her. Mimi entered the nearest shop, a boulangerie and, ignoring the astonished queue of customers waiting to buy the last of the morning's bread, she took off her jacket, turned it inside out and put it back on again. The black lining of the jacket was now on the outside complete with pockets and lapels. She took a circle of elastic from her wrist, twisted it, gathered up her hair at the back and pushed it quickly through the elastic pulling the band tight to the back of her head. She removed her shoes, exchanging them for a pair of black low heeled court shoes which were in her shoulder bag, and quickly unclipped the shoulder strap from the bag. As she glanced up, Angelos passed the shop window. Mimi pushed the shoulder strap into the bag, pulled out two short carrying handles which remained attached to the bag from the inside, and clipped it shut. Opening the door of the shop she stepped out and continued to follow. Mimi was now a young woman with a ponytail, wearing flat shoes, a black jacket, and carrying a handbag.

Angelos stopped to look in a shop window, and Mimi did the same. The terrorist started to walk again and Mimi followed fifty metres behind her as she passed the place where Mimi had first seen her, crossed the Rue de la République, and continued along the Rue

Saint-Romain, narrow and deserted with high mediaeval buildings on either side. Now there were no pedestrians between Mimi and her target, and she felt exposed. After seventy metres Angelos suddenly turned right and disappeared into one of the buildings. Without increasing her pace Mimi continued until she reached the place where Angelos had vanished and, as she reached it, she saw a square arch the size of a large door opening which led through a half timbered building into an alleyway. A plaque on the wall inside the arch read Rue Des Chanoines. She continued walking and glanced down the alleyway as she passed. It was long, about two metres wide, and beyond the arch Mimi could see daylight and more half timbered buildings on either side of the path. She could also see that the deserted alley appeared to narrow after a few metres and that her target was already out of sight. Mimi turned back and hurried purposefully through the arch, her footsteps echoing from the walls as she ignored her training in her eagerness to catch up with the target. Halfway along, the alley suddenly doubled in width as it formed a sudden dogleg then narrowed again as it continued in its original direction.

When Mimi reached the point where the alley widened, Angelos stepped out behind her from a recessed doorway. Her left hand grasped Mimi under the chin and she pulled the petite girl towards her, choking her and stifling her protests, at the same time lifting her so that only her toes were touching the ground. Angelos felt a surge of pleasure as Mimi dropped her bag and, rapidly weakening, grabbed feebly at the terrorist's left arm with both hands as the strength drained away from her. Holding the flick knife in her right hand, Angelos sniffed at Mimi's hair as she gently felt for the pulse in the girl's neck with her little finger while Mimi made weak, unsuccessful attempts to rake her attacker's shins with her heels. Angelos took her time examining Mimi's neck then, having found the pulse, she turned the terrified girl's head to the left and studied the spot closely as she probed slowly and carefully with the point of the knife, gently pushing it into the girl's flesh until it reached the carotid artery. With a slow movement she twisted the knife and pushed deeper, piercing and destroying the artery and surrounding muscle. At the same time, she turned her victim so that the resulting jet of blood spurted away from her and sliced Mimi's jugular vein open for good measure. Angelos released her and, as Mimi's feet touched the ground, the terrorist stepped back, raised her right knee, lifted her foot and booted the helpless girl in the small of her back. The force of the kick sent her flying across the alley, smashing her into the stone wall opposite and knocking her unconscious. Taking care to avoid the blood pumping from the girl's neck, the terrorist bent over her, wiped the knife on Mimi's jacket, closed it and returned it to her pocket. She had been followed and from now on she must be doubly cautious. Angelos picked up the rucksack, then turned and continued along the alleyway leaving Mimi to haemorrhage her life away. She turned right into Rue Saint-Nicolas and gave the girl no further thought.

Chapter Thirty

Brighton - 1246 BST Saturday 11th June

Tricia's old blue Citroen 2CV drew up outside McCabe's flat and she switched off the engine. They had stopped for a quick lunch at a restaurant on the Boardwalk at Brighton Marina, where they discussed the events of the past two weeks while they tried to make sense of them, and continued the conversation throughout the five minute drive to the flat. Now they sat in silence for a few seconds, both deep in thought until McCabe spoke.

"There's too much happening, Tricia. Too much going on for all of this to be unrelated. Jack's death, two burglaries - Jack's house and Honeysuckle Rose - both searched, nothing stolen from the house that we can see but flare packs stolen from Honeysuckle Rose. What's the thing that links them?"

She was quiet for a few moments then replied, "The flare packs."

"Why the flare packs?"

"Because flare packs were stolen from Honeysuckle Rose but not from Jack's flat."

"Because Jack wouldn't have had any flare packs."

"Yes he did," said Tricia. "Allerton told you that Jack had a flare pack but they didn't see any flares fired by him."

McCabe thought for a moment, trying to recall what Allerton had said.

He remembered, "That's right. He said that he kept mini flares on board and insisted that his crew all carry them while they're sailing. So if Jack had a flare pack where is it now?"

"Perhaps it's with his things that the police gave you."

"Let's have a look."

They got out of the car and went into McCabes's flat. Tricia waited in the kitchen while he disappeared upstairs and quickly returned holding the two plastic bags which the police had given to him.

"I've been keeping them in the wardrobe," he said. "I couldn't bring myself to open them."

He put both bags on the breakfast bar. The larger one contained Jack's clothes. McCabe picked up the smaller bag, unsealed it and tipped it slightly, sliding the contents onto the bar. A wallet and a passport both still damp, a set of keys, some loose change, a sailing knife, and a mini flare pack.

The flare pack was red in colour and made from a soft rubbery plastic. It measured approximately six inches along its length, was two and a half inches wide and three quarters of an inch thick, small enough to be held comfortably in one hand. It had a looped string through one end so that it could be attached to the user's wrist. Clipped into the length of the base of the pack was a yellow tube, the firing device, about the size of a ballpoint pen and known as a penjector. Along the top edge of the pack was a plastic strip which, when pulled back, would reveal eight miniature flares half an inch in diameter, only the bases of which would be visible, looking like tiny missiles waiting in their silos. At one end of the penjector was a bayonet fitting. When the bayonet fitting was pushed into the base of a flare then turned clockwise and withdrawn, it would pull the small metal projectile out of the pack with it. The penjector was fitted with a spring loaded lever which could be pulled back three quarters of an inch with the thumb and then released, hammering a pin into the flare and firing it.

McCabe picked up the flare pack and pulled back the plastic strip. It had already been opened. Four of the flares had been removed and only four remained.

"So, Jack did fire distress flares, but those bastards claimed they didn't see them," he said.

Tricia sat on one of the barstools.

"Perhaps they didn't work."

"I can accept that one might misfire Tricia, even two, but not four of them."

He weighed the flare pack in his hand, deep in thought.

"Four mini flares on a calm clear night fired to a height of 70 or 80 metres like it was firework night, and they say they didn't see them? They turned around and started searching as soon as the alarm was raised, according to Allerton, so they must have been clearly visible."

Tricia continued to play Devil's advocate, "Perhaps it was a faulty batch."

McCabe slipped the flare pack into his trouser pocket, "Do you think so?"

He put the other items back into the plastic bag, "Let's find out. We'll go and fire one."

They returned to Tricia's car and she drove them in silence, west along the seafront avoiding the town centre, and then north out of Hove, passing Allerton's house which McCabe pointed out to her. Within twenty minutes they were on the Sussex Downs and she turned the car towards Devils Dyke, a local beauty spot.

The sun shone hot from a clear blue sky, there was not a breath of wind, and Devils Dyke was busy on this Saturday afternoon with hundreds of people taking in the views of the Sussex Weald which lay spread out in front of them as if seen from a plane. They stood and lay around on the grass in groups, children ran about shouting and their parents shouted back.

As Tricia parked the car in the only remaining space in front of the Devils Dyke Hotel, McCabe wondered why so many people came to this particular place at the top of the South Downs, which stretch a distance of over a hundred miles from Beachy Head to Winchester, and all stayed together in a huge mass.

"We'll have to get away from this lot, Tricia. If I start firing flares here we'll have the police on our backs."

She locked the car and they walked west across the turf passing through a group of grounded hang gliders, their owners lounging around while they waited for the wind to come. Following the ancient South Downs Way, within ten minutes they were half a mile from the crowds and they turned right, leaving the path and walking until they were screened from view by clumps of scrubby looking thorn bushes. Far below them lay Fulking set out like a model village in the sunshine, and McCabe could see the roof of The Shepherd and Dog, the pub where he and Hannah had so often had leisurely lunches in happier times. They stopped and he took the flare pack from his pocket.

McCabe removed the penjector, inserted it into the flare pack and pulled out a flare.

"Stand well away, Tricia."

He raised his arm above his head, pulled back the firing pin with his thumb and released it. There was a loud pop. The small metal flare casing rocketed into the air and, at the top of its arc, released a small dust cloud which gradually spread out and drifted to the ground 50 yards away.

"It's a dud," exclaimed Tricia. "No flare, just smoke. Try another one."

McCabe pulled the base of the spent flare from the penjector, extracted another one and repeated the process. Again there was a loud pop and a cloud of dust.

McCabe looked thoughtful, "Well they weren't flares, that's for sure."

He sat back on the grass and picked up the flare pack. There were two left.

"Let's have a look shall we?"

He used the penjector to remove another flare from the pack and took a folded sailing knife from his pocket. After studying the flare briefly he opened the knife and, conscious that he might be about to lose his fingers if it exploded, he carefully began to dig at the grey metal casing where it was joined to the detonator.

"I should keep away Tricia if I were you, in case it goes off."

"Please be careful," she replied anxiously as she moved away, but he was concentrating too hard to notice what she said.

After ten minutes of careful work he had managed to break the seal between the flare and detonator. He put the knife on the grass, held the metal case between the fingers of his left hand, and slowly withdrew the black metal detonator putting it on the ground next to the knife. He was left with only the metal casing nearly two inches long, half an inch in diameter and closed at one end. Peering into the casing he could see that it was full and, tipping it up, he poured the contents into the cupped palm of his right hand.

Tricia came back and sat on the grass next to him, and they both stared at the white powder which he had removed from the flare, not sure what they had been expecting to see.

"Well it's not a flare is it?" said McCabe.

Tricia slowly leaned forward and touched the powder with the tip of her index finger. Then, putting her finger to her mouth and touching the small residue of powder on it to her tongue, she suddenly spat several times onto the grass, a grimace on her face.

"I know what that is," she said. "It's heroin."

"How do you know that?"

"I've seen it before when I knew someone who was hooked on the stuff. It's white heroin powder. Very pure."

McCabe looked stunned.

"Are you saying that Jack was carrying a flare pack full of heroin?"

"It looks that way," she replied.

They sat in silence for a few moments while they absorbed the implications of what they'd just said.

"So now we know why somebody burgled Jack's house, searched Honeysuckle Rose, and shot me," he gestured at the flare pack. "They were looking for this, and couldn't find it."

"We should tell the police," replied Tricia.

McCabe tipped the heroin onto the grass and rubbed his palms together in an attempt to completely get rid of the residue.

"No way." He thought of his last meeting with the police, "They'll find a way of implicating me in this… and do you think I want Jack to be remembered as a drug smuggler? Because that's what they'll say. There must have been enough heroin in that pack to keep half the druggies in Brighton going for a week."

"Well we can't just forget it Chad. What are you saying? We should pretend it never happened?"

"No, I'm not saying that. I can't believe that these drugs were anything to do with Jack. Don't you remember? Allerton told me that he insisted that all of his crew carry mini flares in their pockets? He said he kept them on board and issued them to the crew while they were sailing. If that's true then this pack was part of the equipment on Tiger Fish. Not Jack's at all."

"So should we tell the police that Allerton is carrying drugs on board?" asked Tricia.

McCabe was pensive for a moment, wondering whether Jack would have known about the heroin.

"That won't do any good. Even if they took us seriously, you can bet your life that if the police search his boat now they won't find anything. If somebody believes that the drugs could be discovered with Jack's things he wouldn't be stupid enough to leave any on Tiger Fish."

"So we just forget about it, do we?"

"No we don't forget about it, Tricia. I'm going to find out what's going on. When I've got something cast iron to tell the police then I'll talk to them again. Until then we keep this to ourselves. Come on. Let's get back."

McCabe picked up the knife and the flare pack with its single remaining flare, and put them into his pocket. Then he picked up the detonator and casing, stood up, and threw them deep into the bushes. He reached out a hand, which Tricia took, and he helped her to her feet. She wiped her hand on her jeans, and resolved to put them and the shirt she was wearing through a washing machine before she went near any police drug dogs. In silence, they retraced their steps to the car and McCabe waited by the passenger door as she unlocked. They got in, he pulled the door shut, sat back, and put on his seat belt as Tricia started the engine. She also buckled her seat belt and, as she reversed out of the parking space, he voiced what they had both been thinking.

"Keep your wits about you, Tricia. Somebody wants this flare pack badly and it looks as though they're prepared to do anything to get it."

Chapter Thirty One

Rouen - 0900 CEST Sunday 12th June

The following morning, Gravier's DGSI team was being updated again in the meeting room on the Rue Bourg l'Abbé. The atmosphere in the room was grim. All of them knew about Mimi's murder.

"We have a recording of the phone intercept from yesterday and Renard has told her that he won't make contact for at least five days. That would take us to the 16th, so we don't expect her to use the mobile phone again until then," explained Gravier.

"We have Angelos on CCTV yesterday being followed by Mimi, so we can be sure that she was responsible for her death. We are still watching Renard in Paris and he hasn't moved."

Gravier scanned the faces looking back at him. Some visibly upset, others determined and angry.

"We've considered picking Renard up and sweating him until he tells us where she is but he would be more frightened of the people who are paying him than he is of us, so he's unlikely to tell us. In that case we would lose her completely. Let's agree that, between us, we will find this woman and make sure that she's dealt with."

The team murmured their agreement.

"When this operation began we believed that we were tracking a small time courier who was being used to carry information from one terrorist cell to another. Since then, we have received intelligence from the DGSE which suggests that it is something much bigger than that. If their information is correct, then the terrorist that we know as Angelos is carrying a quantity of a toxin called abrin. You are all familiar with ricin. Well abrin is far more deadly and there is no antidote for it. If released in a public place, even a small quantity has the potential to kill thousands of people after they inhale or swallow it. If they are exposed to abrin they probably won't even be aware of it for twenty four hours but the toxin will slowly kill them by turning their vital organs to mush. It will attack the cells in their bodies, gradually destroying them over two or three days. I'll repeat, that once ingested there is no known cure and we believe that Angelos has enough abrin to kill half a million people. Does anyone have any questions about that?"

Gravier paused, but the room was silent while the watchers considered the enormity of what they had just been told.

"Because of Mimi's death," continued Gravier, "this is now a murder enquiry, so the police are also searching for her and we've supplied them with a photograph of Angelos taken from the CCTV images. We haven't told them why we are interested in her and they have orders not to approach her.

"It's now even more important than before that you find Angelos and you will all stay out there looking for her, but I don't want anyone to get too close. If you see her, call the information in and we'll get a GIGN unit to you. The GIGN have already been briefed on this and three teams are on round the clock standby ready to neutralise Angelos when we find her.

We know from the instructions given to her yesterday that she's moved on to a new address and she could be anywhere. We are hoping that she is still in Rouen."

But Angelos was not in Rouen, she was forty five miles away in Le Havre.

Chapter Thirty Two

North Laine, Brighton - 1254 BST Sunday 12th June

McCabe was standing by the bar in Reinhardt's. The place was half full and there was a buzz of conversation as the lunchtime drinkers and diners waited for the music to start. More people were arriving.

He sipped a glass of Chablis and was deep in thought. For want of a better place to hide it, he'd put the flare pack containing the heroin in his guitar case which was leaning against the wall by the stage. It played on his mind. Why did Jack have a flare pack full of heroin on him when he died? Who put it there? Allerton or his gorilla Benniker? Or neither of them? Perhaps someone else who intended to recover it after Tiger Fish had arrived at Brighton. A yacht of that size could have as many as a dozen crew when it was racing. Allerton had said that five of the crew had returned from France by ferry. Any one of them could have stashed a flare pack full of drugs on board to be collected when Tiger Fish was back in Brighton. Or was Jack smuggling drugs himself? He was suddenly aware that somebody was speaking to him and he looked up to see Jack's friend who he'd met at the funeral.

"I'm sorry. I was miles away."

"That's alright, Mr McCabe. How are you."

"I'm OK thanks. David isn't it?"

David Anderson shook McCabe's hand, "Spot on, Mr McCabe. What a surprise to see you here."

"You're obviously not a regular, David. I play this gig once a fortnight on a Sunday lunchtime."

"Cool. I didn't know you were a musician."

“I’m not sure that I am,” replied McCabe. “I’ve never had any formal training but I’ve been playing for more than thirty years and getting away with it. Three of us today - two guitars and a bass. I play guitar. What brings you here?”

“Oh you know, Sunday, loose end. Thought I’d come in and see what goes on.”

“There’s something you can help me with David. Would you like a drink?”

“Thanks. I’ll have a Bud, please.”

McCabe ordered a Budweiser, paid for it, and carrying David’s beer and his own glass of wine, he led David to a table in the corner where they wouldn’t be overheard. When they were both seated he raised his glass, “Cheers!” They both drank.

“How long did you know Jack for?” asked McCabe.

“A good few years I should think. Let’s see. We were the same age. I’m 27, I met him when he was 18. Nine years. We met at a party and just hit it off. I miss him.”

McCabe studied the other man and wondered whether there was more to his relationship with Jack than just friendship. He had come to terms with his son’s sexuality years ago and decided not to ask.

“I’ve got a question for you, David, and the answer’s important.”

“I’ll do what I can, Mr McCabe.”

“Please, call me Chad.”

“OK.”

“Did Jack ever take drugs?”

David put his glass back on the table and looked flustered.

“I’m not sure I can help you there. Erm…”

“It’s important David, or I wouldn’t be asking.”

David paused for a moment, “Well, you know, I expect he might have tried a spliff once or twice. Most people have I expect. Does it matter now?”

“David, this isn’t just curiosity. I need to know.”

He was silent for a few moments, then he looked McCabe in the eye.

“OK. Sometimes he did.”

“Heroin?”

“Bloody hell no! Nobody in their right mind touches that stuff. A bit of coke perhaps, very occasionally. E at parties maybe. A lot of people do it you know.”

“Any idea where he got it from? Did he have a regular supplier?”

“Not that I know of. He wasn’t a regular user. If people want that stuff they score it in a bar somewhere. There are plenty of people around Brighton who’ll sell it to you.”

Somebody called his name from the stage and McCabe looked up. Andy and Stewart were tuning up and waiting to start the gig.

He stood up and smiled, “I’ve got to go David. You’ve been very helpful.”

They shook hands and McCabe said, “Let’s keep this conversation between ourselves can we?”

David looked relieved to be off the hook, “Of course.”

McCabe made his way to the stage, picked up his guitar and sat on the cane chair that was waiting for him. He checked the tuning on the guitar, nodded that he was ready, waited as Andy played the four bar intro, and then launched into “Sweet Georgia Brown”, pumping out the chords in a four four rhythm on autopilot while Andy on the other guitar took the solo. Four bars of E7, four bars of A7, four bars of D7, three bars of G6/9, one bar of B7, and start again. The audience were nodding their heads in time with the music, which was a good sign.

McCabe had a mental image of his son snorting cocaine which was difficult to get out of his mind, but now he knew that Jack had contacts in the drug business. Was he smuggling drugs for them? The only way to find out was to ask around but, for now, he had to concentrate on the gig.

So he concentrated, and it was a good gig. Over two hours of solid music with a half hour break in the middle, then the usual two tune encore finishing with Rose Room, a happy foot tapper of a number in G with McCabe, unusually, playing the solo. Thunderous applause from a full house, and the trio left them wanting more. Everyone in the room began to talk at the same time. McCabe switched off his amp, stood up, leaned his guitar against the chair, and stepped off of the stage to make his way between the tables to the bar where a bottle of Chablis was waiting for him. The wine, Jimmy the barman told him, had been paid for by the expensively dressed, overweight stranger with coiffured white hair, who was sharing a table on the other side of the room with two men who wouldn't look out of place working on the door of one of Brighton's nightclubs. McCabe poured a glass of wine and, smiling, raised it to his benefactor. The coiffured man raised his own wine glass and, without smiling, nodded. The two bouncers, who weren't drinking, stared blankly at McCabe until the man, who looked to be in his mid thirties, spoke to them and all three turned away.

McCabe scanned the rest of the room, noting that David Anderson had left, and Andy and Stewart joined him at the bar. For the next hour, they drank their free drinks and yarned about music and musicians, all the time being interrupted by people leaving who wanted to congratulate them on the gig. When it went well it was a real buzz.

By the time McCabe was ready to leave, Reinhardt's was virtually empty. He coiled up the amplifier leads and packed them into a compartment in the guitar case, next to the flare pack, which started him thinking about Jack and the heroin again. Then he packed the guitar and walked to the door, turning to make his goodbyes. With the amplifier in his left hand and the guitar case over his right shoulder, he backed unsteadily out of the door into the street as Stewart called out to him, "See you in a fortnight."

McCabe nodded and smiled, "Sure, see you then."

What he couldn't know was that two weeks from today he wouldn't be available to play.

Chapter Thirty Three

Lewes Crescent, Brighton - 1811 BST Sunday 12th June

"I don't want to get involved with those sort of people any more, Chad."

"I'm not asking you to get involved with them. I just need help to find out what involvement Jack had with them. You must know who to ask."

McCabe had returned after the gig at Reinhardt's to find Tricia curled up on the sofa watching a film on TV. He'd watched it to the end with her and then, when she'd switched off the TV, asked her to help him.

"They're dangerous, Chad. Keep away from them."

"I don't have that option, Tricia. I need to find out whether Jack was involved in drugs. I don't know if he was a user, a dealer, or whether he was completely innocent. I can't go to the police with it so the only way I can find out is to ask around. You know who to ask."

"I don't know who to ask."

"I think you do."

She was silent for a while, obviously thinking.

"I owe you, Chad, but you've no idea what these people are like. They don't want any light shone on what they're doing. Anyone from outside who takes an interest in them is going to end up badly messed up or even dead. Sure I know who they are, everybody on the club scene does, but it's all rumours. You never see what they're up to. They're just names that people hardly mention. Local characters with such a reputation for violence and lawlessness that people are afraid to even talk about them."

"Ricky Bishop?"

She looked startled, "What about him?"

"You mentioned Ricky Bishop when we were at The Cricketers. You borrowed some money from him. Could he be involved in drug supply?"

"He's involved in all sorts of things drugs included. I only know him vaguely. If I hadn't been desperate I wouldn't have asked him for help."

"How did you meet him?"

"He's just someone you see in clubs. A local face. Perfectly nice if he doesn't feel threatened by you. That's why he helped me out with a loan, because he likes me, but I've no wish to meet him again."

"How can I find him, Tricia? It's a starting point. If he knew Jack I might be able to find out more about why Jack was meeting dealers in bars. That's what his friend told me anyway."

"Keep away from him, Chad. He's too dangerous. Why do you think he would have known your son?"

"I don't, but I've got to start somewhere. If he's involved in drugs he must know people I could talk to."

Tricia began to laugh and then stopped herself, "You're serious, aren't you?"

"Of course I am."

"How long have you lived in Brighton, Chad?"

"Thirty years on and off."

"Well how come you don't know about people like Bishop?"

"I've never spent much time socialising, Tricia. I do my gigs and go home. If I go out at all it's usually to a pub. I don't know what goes on in the clubs. I went to the old Kings Club a couple of times when I was first here but I didn't like it much. I'm not into dancing the night away. Not my thing."

She looked at him aghast, amazed to hear someone say that they didn't like the club scene.

"So, how do I find Bishop?"

"You don't, Chad. You don't go anywhere near him. He's not a local pusher. It's rumoured that he's one of the top distributors in the South of England. You don't get to do that unless you're ruthless. He's not just a villain, he's a gangster. If he thinks you're taking an interest in his business he won't like it and, trust me, he has no respect for people he doesn't like. Besides, there are lots of small dealers in Brighton. I'll ask around for you, but I'm not going near Ricky Bishop.

"Thanks, Tricia. I really appreciate it. David said that Jack got drugs in bars sometimes. I'll do that. I'll go around the pubs and bars with his photograph and ask if anyone remembers him. Between the two of us we should be able to find something out."

She took his hands in hers.

"Be careful, Chad. I don't think you understand what these people will do to you if you upset them."

Chapter Thirty Four

The Lanes, Brighton - 2132 BST Wednesday 15th June

McCabe closed the door of the pub behind him and stood in the street wondering where to go next. It was the ninth pub that he had been into that evening; wandering in, talking to customers, and showing them Jack's photograph. Around him The Lanes were teeming with trendy young people enjoying a midweek evening out. He watched as a group of girls passed him making their noisy way from one bar to the next, excited and half off their heads on shots. When the pubs chucked out, they would choose one of Brighton's clubs where they could dance all night and keep going by taking MDMA, sometimes known as Ecstasy, and drinking bottled water. It was a warm evening, their clothing was minimal, and one of the girls caught McCabe staring at them and gave him a withering dirty old man look.

So far, he hadn't met anyone who admitted to recognising Jack, and he only had a vague plan as to what he would say if somebody did. He thought that, once he had made contact, he would be able to question them about how deeply his son was involved in drugs, and find the supplier. It was the third evening that he had been searching and, so far, the reception had been distinctly unfriendly. He had quickly discovered that people enjoying an evening out didn't take kindly to being approached by a weirdo with a photograph asking meaningless questions. He had started upmarket and was gradually working his way down. The pub he had just been in was rough, and the clientele clearly didn't take kindly to strangers interrupting their social life.

Neither did the landlord, and McCabe had left just a few seconds before being thrown out.

He walked along Market Street deep in thought, trying to piece together all the events of the last two weeks. Jack's drowning, the flare pack full of heroin, Jack's funeral, Jack's house burgled, Honeysuckle Rose ransacked, Tiger Fish, Allerton and his South African thug Benniker. The whole business had taken over McCabe's life. He stopped in front of a pub which he hadn't visited yet and waited as a group of happy smiling people came out. Then he went through the doorway into the crowded bar, already reaching for the photograph in his jacket pocket.

That was how it would continue. In the evenings he toured the pubs and bars, and each night he returned to his flat, played his guitar, drank, and got maudlin. Each day he became increasingly depressed at his inability to make any progress, but he was wrong. The people he was looking for had noticed him.

Chapter Thirty Five

Le Havre - 1358 CEST Thursday 16th June

Le Havre, situated on the estuary of the River Seine, is the largest port in Normandy and the largest container port in France. Destroyed by the RAF and Royal Navy during Operation Astonia in September 1944, the centre of Le Havre was rapidly rebuilt with reinforced concrete, creating a modern, open feel combined with the false impression of a lack of history.

In a first floor apartment on the Boulevard de Strasbourg in Le Havre, Angelos was eating an apple. Five days had elapsed since she had received her last instructions from Renard, and she had once again had to risk her safety by going to a public place and switching on the mobile phone. Since she had been followed by the girl in Rouen, Angelos was convinced that each time she left the apartment she risked being caught, although by whom she couldn't be sure. Police? Security services? It didn't matter who. What she was sure of was that the mobile phone had been compromised.

There had been no call from Renard again today so she had found the emergency number which was programmed into the phone and dialled it. In a matter of seconds it was answered and she had heard Renard's distorted but familiar voice.

"Yes?"

"Angelos."

"Yes?"

"This phone is no longer secure."

There was a slight pause and then Renard spoke again, "You will stay where you are and travel to the final address in eight days time."

“I understand,” replied Angelos and switched the phone off, removed the battery, and dropped the phone and battery into a pocket on the rucksack.

In Paris, Renard destroyed his phone and bagged it for disposal later.

Being careful to check that she wasn’t being followed, Angelos had returned to the apartment, walking via the Boulevard Clemenceau to pick up a Le Havre street map and a bus timetable from the Tourist Information office. Taking a chance, she had left the rucksack containing the abrin at the apartment and then gone out again to a small supermarket, 300 metres further along the Boulevard de Strasbourg, where she had purchased enough provisions for eight days. Now she would be confined to this room until it was time to move on. She was bored.

Finishing the apple, Angelos threw the core into the sink, then she took the container of abrin from the rucksack and turned it over in her hands, playing with it and feeling the smoothness of the metal casing. She put it on the coffee table and stared at it imagining the sickness and death it would cause when its contents were released.

She looked around the room, not dissimilar to the apartment in Paris, an L shaped bedsitter with a separate bathroom, identical to more than a hundred other anonymous apartments and hotel rooms that she had lived in for the past four years. Constantly moving, constantly changing employers, bombing, killing, discreetly carrying and delivering anything to anyone, anywhere; a professional terrorist for hire by any group which could use her talents. Angelos slumped into an armchair and gazed through the single window, thinking of the circumstances that had brought her to this place.

Originally, when she had been drawn into extremist politics as a teenager at university she had believed, but she soon became disillusioned with her contemporaries who talked and agitated but took no direct action. Then for the first and only time in her life she had fallen in love and the student that she was in love with had drawn her into a small terrorist cell which was financed and armed. Operating as a four person unit, they trained her to handle weapons, to make improvised explosive devices, and she found that she was able to kill and maim for a cause without conscience or compunction. For a while she worked with the group that had trained her, but she soon realised that if she ignored the ideology there was a great deal of money to be made by working for other groups with different causes and she began to freelance. So they came for her one night and she killed all three of them including her lover.

She was no longer committed to any political creed, and for three years she had earned huge amounts of money by selling her services to anyone who would pay. She only spoke when she really had to and, when she did, she spoke in French, German, Italian, Arabic, or perfect English with an American accent. She had used many names and been involved in major security incidents in various parts of the world, and although Angelos had been the subject of security operations in several countries she had never been identified by the Authorities. After this job, at the age of twenty two, she would retire.

Angelos turned on the television using the remote control and flicked through the channels until she found CNN. For a few minutes she watched their news broadcast in English. On the screen was a report detailing a meeting between the American President, the

British Prime Minister, and the King of Saudi Arabia. As the three leaders shook hands for the cameras Angelos' face contorted into a sneer and, cursing, she hurled the remote at the television and was furious as it bounced off leaving only a mark and a depression in the screen. She rose to her feet, crossed the room and, with all her strength, ripped the television from the wall, flinging it to the ground and then stamping on it as it crashed to the floor. The television was silenced as the picture disappeared. Now she didn't even have TV to watch and for the next eight days, in her isolation, she would become more and more consumed with hatred against the world as her thoughts turned inward.

Chapter Thirty Six

Brighton - 1426 BST Friday 17th June

Tricia and McCabe left the sushi restaurant and walked to the steps in the corner of Bartholomew Square, which lead to the underground car park. The same steps that Chad had walked to with Zac two weeks before, on the day they had discovered that Jack's house had been burgled. Chad and Tricia were continuing the conversation that they had been having over lunch. Both of them had been asking around for nearly a week about Jack and, as they had found nobody who had come up with anything to link him to any drug buying or selling, he was either completely innocent or it was something that people weren't going to talk about. Either way, they had decided to give up. It was pointless.

As they reached the entrance to the car park a tall, tough looking man with short ginger hair hurried out of it and barged his way between them, shouldering McCabe aside as he went. McCabe staggered and then spun round to challenge the man who was, by now, halfway across the Square. Tricia put a hand on his arm.

"Don't, Chad. There's no point."

Fuming, McCabe paid the parking fee at the machine, and they descended the steps to parking level 1. He gradually calmed down as they crossed the well lit but deserted and silent car park, passing row after row of cars until they reached Tricia's 2CV when his anger returned with a vengeance. They both stopped, speechless. All four of the car's tyres had been cut and punctured, and across the bonnet of the little blue car were sprayed the words "Nosey Bitch" in red aerosol paint.

Tricia began to cry, and McCabe put his arms around her and waited. Graffiti and random acts of destruction are commonplace in a city like Brighton but he knew that this wasn't random. Tricia's car had been targetted and it was because of him.

"I'm sorry, Tricia."

"It's not your fault," she sobbed.

"It is my fault. I shouldn't have involved you in any of this."

A minute passed without either of them speaking until she drew away from him, wiping her eyes and cheeks on her sleeve. McCabe passed her a clean handkerchief, which he kept in reserve for occasions like this. She sniffed, and half smiled and stood straighter.

"It's only a car. I can get it fixed."

"No," he reacted quickly. "You won't pay for it, I will. It wouldn't have happened if it hadn't been for me."

McCabe put an arm around her and pulled her into him, "Come on. We'll get a taxi back to the flat."

They retraced their steps out of the car park and, when they got back to the Square, they turned right and descended the broad concrete staircase which fans out like a waterfall into Bartholomews; a short, wide, cul de sac at the back of the Town Hall. There was no moving traffic in the street, only a few parked cars, and neither of them took any notice of the stationary Renault van as they passed it. They walked diagonally across the road towards its junction with East Street about fifty yards away, with Tricia a few feet ahead. In a corner of his consciousness McCabe heard the van start up, and if it hadn't been for the fact that the driver had revved the engine so noisily he wouldn't have turned around to see it hurtling in their direction. He had a second to see that the driver was the ginger haired man who had jostled them earlier, and that he was aiming the van directly at Tricia. McCabe sprinted and cannoned into her, hurling them both between two parked cars as the van swept past, the name of a hire company painted along its side disappearing in a blur. By the time that McCabe had got to his feet it had rounded the corner into East Street. He knelt beside Tricia expecting her to admonish him, but at the last moment she had seen the van driving at her, and she realised that he had probably saved her from death or serious injury. As it was, her only injuries were grazes to her hands. Tricia looked at him and he could see the fear in her eyes.

"What's happening, Chad? First my car, now this. Somebody's trying to kill me."

Chapter Thirty Seven

North Laine, Brighton - 2020 BST Friday 17th June

The wine bar in the North Laine was buzzing, full to the doors with excited teenagers trying to look cool and twenty somethings trying to look sophisticated, all starting their evening there before they spread out across the city in search of pleasure. McCabe was seated on a barstool, staring into an overpriced glass of Chablis and wondering where to go from here. Tricia had reported the damaged car to the police and to her insurance company. McCabe had called Zac who, using some of his numerous contacts in the car trade, had arranged collection of the car and transport to the insurance company's preferred repairer.

Neither Tricia nor McCabe thought that there was any point in informing the police about the attempt to run her down, and she had decided to stay out of harm's way at his flat for the time being. Having resolved over lunch with Tricia that there was no point in making any further investigations into his son's disappearance, after the attack on them this afternoon McCabe was now more determined than ever to discover what Jack had been up to. Someone was speaking to him.

"Mr McCabe?"

He turned to see Sophie May standing next to him, looking as stunning as ever, dressed in expensively cut jeans, high heels, and a tight low cut halter necked top.

"I thought it was you. Do you mind if I join you?"

Before he could answer she had pulled a vacant bar stool closer to him and was seated next to him.

He felt sensuality emanating from her as if it was a tangible thing like heat. She gazed into his eyes intently and for a moment he was aware of her body language, reading signals that she could not possibly mean to send. Or could she? Sophie smiled at him, a beautiful radiant smile, and he suddenly felt his pulse quicken and his spirits lift.

"May I call you Chad?"

McCabe mentally shook himself and told himself not to be so stupid.

"Of course you can. Would you like a drink?"

"No I won't, Chad, thank you. I was just leaving when I saw you here."

McCabe couldn't understand how he hadn't noticed her. Even in a crowded bar she stood out as if she had a spotlight on her. Sophie moved her barstool even closer to him until she was almost touching him. She smiled again and then her expression changed to a look of concern.

"I'm so sorry about what happened the last time we met," she said. "Benniker is a complete bastard. I can't stand him."

McCabe suddenly had a mental picture of Sophie, topless with a tray of drinks and a shocked look on her face, as he had endured the humiliation of being frog marched out of Allerton's garden.

"I suppose it was a bit stupid of me to walk in and expect them to answer my questions."

"Well, they didn't have to treat you like that. I was furious with them. When I asked them what you'd done they wouldn't tell me. Just said you'd been asking too many questions. I would have told you what you wanted to know."

"Perhaps you could help me now then?"

"I will if I can."

"I worked out that the position Allerton gave where Jack went overboard was wrong. It didn't correspond with where he was found. If Allerton's position was correct, the tide would have carried him to a point miles away from where the fishing boat actually picked him up."

Sophie looked thoughtful.

"I don't know about tides, but I don't see why they would lie. What would be the point?"

"What happened after you raised the alarm?" asked McCabe, unable to answer her question.

"Frik and Graham came up and turned the boat round and they went back to search. I wasn't much use, I'm afraid. I go to pieces in a crisis like that. Graham was shouting at me and telling me not to get hysterical so I went to my cabin and just cried. When I came up later they'd given up the search and we were on our way to Brighton again."

"My cabin," thought McCabe, not "Our cabin".

"Do you mind if I ask you a personal question?" he said.

She smiled again seductively, "You can ask me anything you like."

"What's your relationship with Allerton?"

"He's a friend. Just platonic. I've known him for years. You know how it works. Wealthy men like that want to have attractive women around, like trophies. In return I get to go sailing in a fantastic yacht. I like sailing even though I don't know much about it, and I get frightened sometimes because I can't swim."

"You could wear a life jacket," observed McCabe.

"Oh please," she replied, laughing. "What do you think that would do to my figure?"

McCabe smiled, “So do you have a man in your life? I mean…” he stopped, wishing that his question hadn’t sounded so direct.

She laughed again. A beautiful, happy laugh.

“I know what you mean Chad. No, there’s no man in my life.” She stared into his eyes again, “Would you like to volunteer?”

It had been a long time since McCabe had been in the situation where he was genuinely propositioned, and he’d forgotten the rules. Slightly flustered, he smiled again, “Can I get back to you on that?”

She put her hand on his thigh, “Whenever you want to Chad.”

Neither of them spoke for a few moments, then an outburst of raucous laughter from a group on the other side of the room broke the spell and she took her hand away.

“Shall we swap phone numbers?” she asked, and fished around in her handbag finally producing two mobile phones. She held one in each hand, glanced at both and put one back into the handbag.

McCabe pulled his phone from his pocket, and they exchanged numbers, programming them into their respective phones.

“I must go,” Sophie said, putting the phone into her bag as she stood up.

McCabe also stood, “Why do you carry two phones?”

“One for personal, one for business. I’m a PR Consultant,” she replied. “Never know when a client might want me.”

McCabe held out his hand and she ignored it. Instead, leaning forward, she put her right hand on his shoulder and kissed him on the cheek.

"Call me if you want me Chad."

Sophie turned and walked to the door. As she reached it she looked back, smiled, and blew him a kiss.

McCabe gazed after her as she stepped into the street, then he sat on the barstool again and picked up his glass of wine.

"What a beautiful girl. You're a lucky man."

He turned to see who had spoken and saw, making herself comfortable on the seat which Sophie had just vacated, a woman well into her sixties who had clearly seen better days. She was short, slim to the point of skinny, heavily made up, had long wavy grey hair, and her face looked as though it had once been beautiful but a lifetime of hard living had finally caught up with it. The woman wore black leather calf length boots, tight blue jeans, an open necked denim shirt which partly covered her huge bust, and a black imitation leather jacket. She seemed to have drunk more than was good for her and her speech was slightly slurred.

McCabe grinned, "It's not like that. She's just somebody I know vaguely."

"Well I could see she liked you. I'm Grace by the way. Sometimes known as Amazing Grace because I drink so much it's amazing that I don't collapse." She let out a loud cackle, pleased with the joke which she had probably told a hundred times before. "Would you like to buy me a drink? I've got something to tell you. I'll have a large brandy."

Intrigued, McCabe decided to go along with it and ordered the drink for her. When the barman placed it in front of her she picked it up eagerly with her long bony fingers and drank half of it straight away.

"What's your name, darling?"

"Chad McCabe. What is it you've got to tell me?"

She put the glass on the bar and suddenly became conspiratorial, leaning forward and speaking more quietly.

"Well Chad, you've been asking around about your son haven't you?"

"Yes."

"I can help you. I know everybody in this town, but it'll have a price."

McCabe suddenly decided to take her seriously.

"How much?" he asked.

"Fifty quid. I can introduce you to somebody and he'll tell you what you want to know."

"OK," replied McCabe. "When can I meet him? Now?"

"Not now. Tomorrow night." She gestured towards the window, "Meet me at the pub over the road at ten o'clock. I'll bring him with me."

"You're on," said McCabe and stood up to go.

"What about the fifty quid?"

"Tomorrow when I see you," he replied.

Grace looked disgruntled.

"What about another drink then?"

McCabe took out his wallet, pulled out a ten pound note and put it on the bar in front of her.

"Thanks," she chortled. "I could tell you were my kind of man. Would you like to come home with me?"

McCabe grinned, "Not tonight thanks, Grace. I'll see you tomorrow."

For the first time in over two weeks he was smiling as he left the bar.

Chapter Thirty Eight

North Laine, Brighton - 2216 BST Saturday 18th June

McCabe was early for the meeting and Grace was late. Hemmed into a corner of the scruffy pub he felt his age as he stood shoulder to shoulder with the Saturday night crowd. The oldest of them was at least twenty years younger than he was, and they appeared to be mostly groups of students all talking at once in loud voices to make themselves heard. A good place for a meeting if you didn't want to be overheard, assuming that the other party could understand what you were saying in the din. By the time Grace arrived he was already on his second pint of Harvey's.

The front door of the pub opened and Grace breezed into the bar still wearing the same outfit which she'd had on the night before. With her was a short man of about forty with a shaved head and a weasel face, wearing ragged jeans, grimy trainers, an equally grimy tee shirt, and a camouflage jacket. He was unshaven, unkempt and might have been sleeping rough but he didn't look any worse than a lot of the other customers in the bar. Spotting McCabe on the far side of the room, Grace forced her way through the crowd with her grubby companion in tow, roughly shouldering people aside until she reached him.

"Hello darling," she shouted, putting her arm through McCabe's and making him slosh beer onto the floor. She was drunk and clung to him for support.

"I brought him you see. I said I would, didn't I?"

She turned to the other man and vaguely waved her free hand, "This is Harry the Swish. Harry, this is Chad McCabe."

Then to McCabe again, "That'll be fifty quid, thank you."

McCabe put his glass on the table next to him, gently extricated himself from her grip, and reached for his wallet. He counted out five ten pound notes and passed them to Grace as Harry looked on with greed showing on his face.

"Are you stopping, Grace?" shouted McCabe, as she counted the notes and then pushed them deep into her cleavage.

She gave out her cackling laugh, "No thanks darling, I've got an appointment somewhere else. You never know, maybe I'll get lucky tonight."

McCabe wondered whether getting lucky referred to sex or an endless supply of free drinks.

"Bye darling. Come and find me if you need help with anything else," she shouted, and then she was gone, pushing people aside again to get out of the pub.

Raising his voice, McCabe asked, "Would you like a drink Harry?" and, with his right hand, he did the universal drink in the hand mime.

Harry wiped his streaming nose with his sleeve and mumbled, but McCabe thought that he could lip read the words, "A pint of bitter."

He turned towards the bar, quickly finishing the rest of his pint, and ordered two more. He passed one to Harry when they arrived.

"Come on," shouted McCabe. "Let's go outside."

The two men worked their way through the crowd, eventually escaping out of the door to where three white metal tables, taking up half of the pavement, were pressed up against the front wall of the pub. None of them were in use so McCabe chose the centre one and they sat on scruffy, white plastic garden chairs facing each other across the table. It was almost dark but the street lights had not been switched on yet, and McCabe could sense rain in the air as the long spell of still, hot weather finally came to an end. Thunder rumbled in the distance.

"Cheers," said McCabe, raising his glass.

"Yeah," said Harry and took a swig of his pint.

McCabe attempted to get a conversation going, "Unusual name, Harry the Swish."

"Yeah," mumbled Harry.

"Why do they call you that?"

"Well, the real name's Harry Cratch but it's what I used to do, see," replied Harry suddenly animated. "Scenery painter. Six inch brush, swish, swish, one of the best. Didn't look like anything close up, but from a distance it looked like the real thing."

"Why did you stop?"

"Did my 'ead in with drugs, didn't I? Couldn't do it any more," he looked wistful. "All the top theatres I did."

"Couldn't you do rehab or something? Get back into it?"

Harry snorted and wiped his nose with his sleeve again, "No chance. Look, you didn't come 'ere to get me into re'ab, what you wanna see me for?"

"Didn't Grace tell you what I wanted?"

Harry looked shifty and glanced up and down the street as if he was being followed, then he leaned towards McCabe and lowered his voice as he spoke.

"She says you're looking for someone."

McCabe took the thumbed photograph of Jack from his jacket pocket and passed it to across the table, "Do you recognise him?"

Harry picked it up and held it between his forefinger and thumb, squinting at it in the twilight, holding it close to his eyes.

"Is this who you're looking for?"

"No, that's my son. His name is Jack McCabe. He died. I'm looking for whoever supplied him with drugs."

"What you wanna find 'em for?"

"I want to ask them some questions."

"I dunno," said Harry. "It's dangerous. Those sort of people don't take kindly to questions. You could get your 'ead kicked in, or worse."

"You can't help me then?"

"No, I didn't say that. Just that it could get me in a lot of trouble. It'll cost you."

"How much?" asked McCabe.

"A lot. Well it's dangerous see. My mate talked too much, and instead of selling 'im smack they sold 'im a wrap of that white powdery stuff that grows round car battery terminals. Died in agony after injecting that he did. Then they set light to 'im."

"So it's dangerous. How much?"

"Hundred quid."

"Alright," McCabe said.

"In advance."

McCabe laughed, "No way, Harry. I don't even know you. Let's forget it shall we?" and he sat back in his chair and drank some of his beer.

The little man adopted a whiny, wheedling tone as he saw the chance of some easy money disappearing, "No. No need to forget it. I need to score, Mr McCabe. How's about something in advance?"

"I'll give you twenty now and the rest when you come up with the information."

"Let's see it then."

McCabe took out his wallet and passed Harry a twenty pound note which he snatched and hastily shoved into his trouser pocket.

"I'll need the photo" said Harry and pushed that into his pocket as well.

"When can you let me know something?"

"Tomorrow. I'll do some asking and meet you tomorrow, but not here. Do you know the old churchyard off Church Street?"

"Yes, Saint Nicholas church."

"That's the one. I'll meet you there tomorrow night, same time, ten o'clock," said Harry.

"You'll have the money with you, won't you?"

"Definitely," replied McCabe. "Thanks Harry. Would you like another drink?"

"I would, Mr McCabe."

"OK. I've got a couple more things to ask you."

McCabe went back into the pub, fought his way through the crowd again and ordered two more pints. Five minutes had passed before he got back to the pavement, and Harry had gone. He sat down at the table again with the two beers and wondered if he would ever see Harry the Swish again, or whether he had just been conned out of twenty pounds for Harry's next fix. He drank one of the beers and then decided that he'd had enough for one night. Leaving the second beer on the table, he stood and began to walk towards the taxi rank in East Street. It was starting to rain.

As he turned into Jubilee Street, two men and a woman hurried past him as they headed for shelter. Apart from a silver Mercedes, which cruised slowly towards him, the street was deserted. McCabe walked steadily with his head down and the collar of his fleece turned up, holding it together at his throat in an attempt to stop the rain from running down his neck. Still with his head down McCabe saw the feet and then the legs of three men walking towards him and he moved to the inside of the pavement to let them pass. As he drew close to them the man nearest to McCabe stepped in front of him and pushed him hard against the wall and the three of them formed a semi circle around him. One man on each side of him held him by an arm, and the one in the centre had a knife in his right hand which he held up to McCabe's face, the tip of the knife inserted into McCabe's left nostril.

McCabe pressed his head back hard against the wall, and looked into the watery blue eyes and puffy face of the stranger with coiffured white hair who had bought him the bottle of Chablis in Reinhardt's Bar after the Sunday gig. The man smelled of perfume, not aftershave, and he was wearing make up which was beginning to run in the rain. The men who were holding McCabe were the bouncer lookalikes who had been sitting at the table with the knife man, and the ginger one on McCabe's left, he now recognised, was the van driver who had tried to run down Tricia.

"What have we got here, Tom?" said the knife man in a camp voice.

"A nosey bugger, Mr Bishop," replied the thug on McCabe's left. He was the same height as McCabe and breathed halitosis that he could have shut doors with.

"And what shall we do with him boys?"

"Teach him a lesson, Mr Bishop," replied the thug holding McCabe's right arm. He was a foot shorter than McCabe but strong, and the menace in his voice seemed to make him even more dangerous than Ginger Tom on McCabe's left.

"I think you're right Chancey," said Bishop, applying pressure to the knife. "We should teach him a lesson."

McCabe pressed himself against the wall raising his head as far as he could in a vain attempt to avoid the blade in his nostril.

"Go on then Chancey," ordered Bishop, and he stepped back, removing the knife as Chancey released McCabe's arm, turned, then with the force of a professional boxer punched him a sharp jab in the pit of his stomach.

Ginger Tom released him as McCabe dropped to his knees with his head bent forward, retching as he brought up the beer he'd drunk, projectile vomiting it across the pavement.

"Oh for goodness sake," said Bishop. "Now look what you've done to my shoes."

Ginger Tom on McCabe's left took a half step back and swung his right foot into McCabe's backside with as much force as he could. McCabe was launched forward, vomiting again and bringing up more beer as he lay with his face in the mess on the pavement.

"Alright boys, pick him up."

The thugs took an arm each and hauled McCabe upright so that he was facing Bishop in a kneeling position.

"You've been asking too many questions, haven't you?" shouted Bishop, seizing a handful of McCabe's hair and forcing his head back.

McCabe looked at the make up running down Bishop's face, and thought how bizarre it was to be beaten up in the rain by a fat raving queen.

"Well remember my name, dear. It's Ricky Bishop and I don't like inquisitive pricks like you. Got it?"

McCabe grunted.

"Good," said Bishop, releasing McCabe's hair. "So don't do it again," and he stepped back and gestured to the other two to let him go.

McCabe fell forward into the vomit clutching his stomach and groaning.

"You're disgusting you are," said Bishop, staring down at him.

The three of them turned and walked away towards the silver Mercedes-AMG parked half on the pavement further along the street. When they reached it, Chancey found a cloth and wiped Bishop's shoes, then all three got into the car and drove off.

McCabe waited for a minute and then slowly got to his knees. He fell back and dragged himself until he was half sitting, half lying, against the wall with the rain pouring down on him, looking like a Brighton down and out. A passing couple crossed the road to avoid him and hurried on their way. Reaching into his jacket pocket, he pulled out his mobile phone and dialled Tricia's number. At last, he was getting somewhere.

Chapter Thirty Nine

Le Havre - 1311 CEST Sunday 19th June

From the railway station in the east of Le Havre to the Hotel De Ville in the centre, a distance of over a kilometre, the Boulevard de Strasbourg runs, tree lined and wide with a mixture of old and modern apartments, offices, restaurants and shops.

Near the corner of Boulevard de Strasbourg and the Rue Maréchal Gallieni is Le Cardinal Restaurant. Its black and red frontage with its tables and chairs au terrace, projects across the full width of the pavement in a semi circle, forcing pedestrians to step into a line of parked cars to bypass it, seemingly contrary to any logic of urban design. It is only four hundred metres from the apartment where Angelos was holed up. The interior of Le Cardinal repeats the colour scheme of the frontage with plum coloured carpet and black furniture, the whole reminiscent of a bygone era. Along one mirrored wall are booths which afford a small element of privacy, and in one of these booths Gravier and his assistant Henri Girard were enjoying a lunch of steak frites.

"We know she's here somewhere, Henri, because of the phone intercept, and we have her on CCTV arriving at Platform 4 of Le Havre Gare on the train from Rouen."

"Yes sir, but where is she now? It's a big city."

"She must be in a safe house somewhere and she won't move until she has to. We know from the phone call to Renard that she was told to move in eight days. That was three days ago, so she'll surface in five days' time. That's when we'll get her, but how will she leave Le Havre?"

Girard picked up four french fries with his thumb and two stubby fingers, dipped them into some mayonnaise, popped them into his mouth and, as he chewed, he listed the possibilities.

"By car, by train, by bus or by ship."

Gravier sipped at a glass of Bordeaux and considered what Girard had said.

"She knows that the mobile phone is no longer secure, Henri, so she won't use it again. If she knows that the phone was being tracked then she also knows that we've followed her to Le Havre. We assume that she travels alone so, if she leaves by car, she'll have to go to a rental office and hire one. By train and we catch her at the railway station. By bus and we have her at the bus station. She's been moving towards the coast so perhaps she intends to cross La Manche to England. If she does that we'll get her at the ferry port."

"She's boxed herself in, sir," said Girard. "We cover all of those places and we'll catch her."

"So," said Gravier, "the police are watching the streets for her. Our team will watch the train station, the bus station, car hire offices and the ferry terminal. When she moves we'll see her."

He was quiet for a moment.

"There is a flaw in this plan, Henri, but I can't see what it is."

Chapter Forty

Queens Road, Brighton - 2155 BST Sunday 19th June

McCabe walked along Queens Road still feeling sore from the beating of the previous night. Tricia had responded to his call and arrived in a taxi within thirty minutes, during which time he had sat in the street, shivering and soaking wet, and ignoring the repulsed looks of people walking past. She had gathered him up and, after bribing the driver with extra cash and convincing him that McCabe wouldn't be sick in the cab, she had taken Chad back to his flat and done her best to make him comfortable. He had spent today at the flat slowly recovering, not fully but enough to get moving again. A taxi had dropped him off at the Clock Tower in the town centre five minutes ago and now he was heading for his meeting with Harry the Swish, not really expecting him to be there.

He turned left into Church Street and began to make his way up the steep hill. The sky was overcast and the glow of the street lights reflected from the pavement which was wet from the rain earlier in the evening. On McCabe's left was a long rendered wall topped by chain link fencing and on his immediate right was a line of parked cars. On the other side of the street stood a row of small attractive houses all with their curtains drawn against the night. No traffic passed and the street ahead was deserted. He followed the wall until he reached an opening in it and stopped. Looking back, he saw that a man in a raincoat was walking up the hill fifty yards behind him. He was too far away to see any detail, but it wasn't Harry. McCabe turned left between the two brick piers which formed the opening in the wall, and stopped while he waited for his eyes to adjust to the sudden gloom. The man walked past the opening and continued up the hill.

McCabe was standing in the old churchyard. On his immediate right was the dark bulk of St Nicholas Church, clinging to the top of the hill and still with the appearance of the small country church that it had been when it was constructed in the 14th century. To his left the grass disappeared into the shadows with the occasional shapes of trees, ancient tombs and gravestones scattered seemingly at random over it. In front of him a brick path led along the side of the church and stopped where it met a lamp post which cast a small circle of yellow light onto the ground. McCabe walked slowly along the path towards the light as the rain dripped onto him from an overhanging tree. The churchyard was brooding and silent, and a more macabre place to arrange a meeting at night he could not have imagined.

He reached the lamp post and stopped. McCabe could see now that the path continued down the hill from where he was standing and there was another path off to the right which led to the front door of the church. He paused for a moment and then, feeling exposed under the light, he stepped off of the path and into the shadows. He listened but all he could hear was the faint sound of water dripping from the trees onto the grass and path. There was no movement in the churchyard and no sign of Harry. He stood there motionless and waited.

After half an hour, during which time nobody had entered or left the churchyard, McCabe gave up, stretched his limbs, and decided that he had been taken for a ride and Harry had cheated him out of twenty pounds. While he was waiting, he had noticed that a grave, ten feet away from him on his right, was surrounded by iron railings. He wondered why. It was on the edge of the pool of light from the lamp post and he walked over to it, unconcerned now whether he could be seen or heard. He stooped to read the inscription on the gravestone in the dim light.

In
memory of
STEPHEN GUNN
who died 4th. of September 1813.
Age 79 Years.
Also MARTHA. Wife of
STEPHEN GUNN,
who was Peculiarly Distinguished as a
bather in this Town nearly 70 Years.
She died 2nd. of May. 1815.
Aged 88 Years

McCabe straightened up, suddenly intrigued. He was standing by the grave of Martha Gunn, the famous Brighton Dipper. In the 18th and 19th centuries people didn't just launch themselves into the sea as they do now. They would descend with as much dignity as possible from a bathing machine and employ people like Martha Gunn to shove or dip them under the waves. Curious, McCabe skirted the railings to take a look at a smaller stone, which he could dimly make out at the other end of the grave. His foot caught against something soft and he pitched headlong onto the wet grass. Instantly he forced himself to his feet again, a feeling of fear clutching at his stomach as the adrenaline started to pump through his body. Looking back he could only see black shadows on the ground. He waited until he had recovered from the shock then, holding on to the railing with his left hand, he slowly edged his way back feeling with his right foot until, again, he encountered something soft. His heart thudded as he leaned forward until he could make out a human form lying face down on the grass. He prodded it twice with his foot but got no response, then, in spite of the horror of the situation, he could not stop himself from reaching out with his hand and touching. He felt a shoulder, and taking hold of the clothing he pulled, rolling the form over until it was face upwards. Staring up at him, faintly illuminated by the yellow light from the lamp, was Harry the Swish with a stupid look on his face and a .22 sized hole in the middle of his forehead.

McCabe ran, intent on getting as far away as he could. Across the grass, stumbling over graves, falling twice, careering down the hill in his panic waiting for a shot to ring out from the darkness. He reached another path and, still running, he followed it out of the graveyard and emerged in Dyke Road. A bus went past. Further down the hill were people. He slowed to a fast walking pace. He was sure that nobody had seen him come out of the graveyard. If he could get away without being noticed he should be in the clear. Or should he call the police? He dismissed the idea as soon as he had thought of it. It wouldn't help Harry, who would be found soon enough anyway, and McCabe, if he did call them, would be in a great deal of trouble. The police seemed to have difficulty believing anything he told them anyway. He crossed North Street at the Clock Tower, carried on down West Street, turned left along Duke Street and kept walking. Where to? Away. Away from the horror story that his life had turned into. He was heading for The Lanes and he needed a drink. Duke Street led him into Ship Street and he hurriedly followed the road round into Prince Albert Street, turned right into Black Lion Street and went into The Cricketers Pub.

It was Sunday evening and there were twenty or so people in the bar; couples mostly engrossed in each other and chatting quietly. McCabe ordered a large Laphroaig whisky, knocked it back in ten seconds and then ordered another one ignoring the barman's look of surprise. He took it to the table by the window and sat in an armchair with the drink in his hand, staring into space while he tried to make sense of what he had just seen. Why? Why had Harry been shot? Obvious. To stop him talking. To stop him talking to whom? To me! McCabe suddenly realised that he had got too close and, if he continued, he would probably end up dead himself. Who did it? Benniker? Bishop and his thugs? Who was Jack's supplier?

"Do you mind if I join you?"

He was suddenly snapped out of his contemplation and realised that DS Barnard was standing over him with a pint in his hand. McCabe gestured to the empty chair opposite. Had Barnard been standing at the bar watching him?

"Of course I don't," he lied. In reality, he couldn't think of anybody he would less like to speak to at the moment.

Barnard put his drink on the table and eased his untidy bulk into the armchair.

"How have you been, Mr McCabe? I've been worried about you."

"Oh, you know. Minding my own business."

"That's not what I've heard," said Barnard.

"Really? And what have you heard?" replied McCabe, trying not to look like someone who recently discovered a fresh corpse and didn't report it to the police.

Barnard watched him intently for a moment.

"Apparently you've been trawling all of the low life bars, and a lot of the better ones, in Brighton, flashing a photo of your son and asking people if they know who supplied him with drugs."

McCabe was silent.

"Why do you want to know, Mr McCabe?"

"Because I want to find out why he died."

"We've discussed this before, Mr McCabe. It will all come out at the inquest but it was probably an accident."

"And I've told you that it couldn't have been an accident. I've even shown you that Jack couldn't have gone overboard where they said he did."

"I know it's difficult for you, Mr McCabe, but if you ask questions in the wrong places you'll attract the attention of some pretty dangerous characters. You could even put your life at risk."

McCabe was ahead of him and had already come to the same conclusion, so was not inclined to argue.

"I know," he said. "I've already decided the same thing. I wasn't getting anywhere anyway. Time to give up I think."

Barnard looked pleased, "Very sensible. Don't think I'm not interested in what you've told me but I can't start a murder investigation into a case where all the evidence says that it was an accident. We don't have the resources for it."

"What about me getting shot then?" said McCabe. "You agree that was attempted murder."

"I agree with you on that one and we're doing what we can to find out who was responsible."

"But you're not getting very far, I take it."

"I wouldn't say that Mr McCabe, but I'm afraid I can't tell you anything at the moment. Let's just say that we're making progress."

Barnard pulled out his handkerchief and noisily blew his nose.

"Sodding hay fever. I hate this time of year," he said, examining the contents of the handkerchief. Then he heaved himself to his feet, finished the rest of his pint and put the empty glass on the table.

"Try and stay out of trouble, Mr McCabe, and leave it to us." He turned towards the door and went out into the street still blowing his nose.

McCabe couldn't make up his mind about DS Barnard. Was he a complete idiot or extremely clever? What did it matter? It didn't seem to him as though Sussex Police were going to find out anything about all of this. It was up to him. He stood up, put his glass on the bar and ordered another large Laphroaig.

Chapter Forty One

Brighton - 2030 BST Tuesday 21st June

It was two days since he'd discovered Harry's body and McCabe was sitting on a barstool in Reinhardt's listening to the regular Tuesday evening band; a guitar, bass, and violin trio. He had brought his guitar, which was in its case leaning against the wall by the stage, in case the evening turned into a jam session, which it often did.

According to the BBC Radio News, which he had been listening to while doing jobs on Honeysuckle Rose earlier that day, a jogger had found Harry shortly after dawn the previous morning and the police had opened another murder enquiry. So far, they hadn't been in touch with McCabe, but he was in no doubt that they would be when they discovered that the bullet that killed Harry matched the one that had lodged in the woodwork of his boat after bouncing off of his skull, or when they spoke to Amazing Grace. Brighton was becoming more and more dangerous for him.

Everyone in the bar turned to watch as Sophie May walked in through the front door. She was dressed in a mini skirt and stiletto heels again, and moved towards him smiling. McCabe stood up as she reached him, and she put her hand on his arm as she leaned forward to kiss him on the cheek. He detected the delicate apple fragrance of her perfume as she settled herself onto the stool next to him and crossed her long bare legs, allowing the mini skirt to ride up. The other drinkers in the bar turned back to their companions and continued with their conversations, only the men sneaking a surreptitious glance at Sophie from time to time.

"It's good of you to come," McCabe said.

"Any time," she replied, smiling again and maintaining eye contact with him for a few seconds longer than was necessary. "I was hoping you'd phone me and you did."

McCabe asked Jimmy the barman for another glass, and showed her the bottle which he had already started.

"Is this ok for you?" he asked.

"Anything," she replied.

"I was wondering if you could help me answer a few questions?"

She stopped smiling.

"Oh, Chad. You disappoint me. I thought it was my body you were after."

She looked seriously at him for a few moments and then giggled and gave him her beautiful smile again.

"Only teasing."

McCabe smiled back, eager to please.

Sophie uncrossed her legs, sat up straight facing him, placed both hands on her knees, and adopted a mock serious expression.

"You have my full attention."

"It was about Jack," said McCabe. "Did you know he took drugs?"

"No I didn't, but I didn't know him very well, Chad. I only met him on sailing trips."

"Does it surprise you?"

She thought for a moment.

"Not really. Lots of people take drugs. I assume it was recreational, he didn't strike me as any sort of addict."

"Oh, I think it was just an occasional thing," answered McCabe. "I've been trying to find out where he got them from. Do you have any idea where he would find a supplier?"

"Why do you need to know?"

McCabe needed to make a decision. He'd reached a dead end and, if he was going to get any further, he needed help.

"If I tell you something can we keep it between ourselves? You might be shocked."

She leaned towards him, reached out, took his right hand and, holding it with both of her hands, cradled it in her lap.

"You can tell me anything Chad. I want to help."

The decision was made.

"When the police gave me Jack's effects they included the flare pack that he'd had in his pocket when he went overboard. The flares didn't work because they had powder in them. Heroin."

She was silent for a moment, then, wide eyed, she replied, "My God. What did you do with them?"

"I kept them."

"Have you still got them?"

"Yes. I've got them with me."

She looked stunned.

"You're crazy. You can't carry heroin about. You'll get arrested."

"I hadn't thought about that," said McCabe. "I've been too busy trying to find out why he had the drugs on him when he died."

"Have you told the police?"

"No, not yet. I want to keep them out of it. The last thing I want is for Jack to be remembered as someone who was involved with drugs."

"You don't think it was for his own use?" she asked.

"I don't think so. Too large a quantity. I think he might have been delivering it for somebody."

"My God," she said again. "A courier."

"It looks that way."

"What are you going to do?"

"I don't know. A friend of Jack's told me that he used cocaine sometimes. I've been showing his photograph around the bars to see if I could find out where he got it from, but I haven't got very far."

She crossed her legs again still holding his hand, the back of which was now resting on the bare skin of her thigh, and he felt a sudden erotic pleasure at the contact.

"Chad, nobody is going to admit to that are they? You silly boy, you'll end up getting hurt if you go around asking questions like that."

"I've already come to that conclusion myself," he replied. "I got roughed up three nights ago. That's why I've stopped asking around."

"What happened?"

"I got warned off by somebody called Bishop."

"Ricky Bishop?"

"That's right. Do you know him?"

"Chad, everybody in Brighton knows him, except you obviously. Don't you read the papers? He's dangerous. Drugs, prostitution, anything illegal that makes money. He's very rich, never gets caught and he's a complete psycho. Occasionally the police get him into Court but they can never get a conviction."

"Why not?" asked McCabe.

"Because the witnesses either refuse to give evidence or they disappear."

"Do you think he could be the supplier I've been looking for?"

"No. Somebody like Bishop would be too big to deal at street level. If Jack had a large quantity of heroin on him, it would be more likely that he was bringing it in for a dealer who would wholesale it to smaller dealers. Whoever it was for, give it up. Those people are killers."

The band had stopped playing and a voice interrupted them.

"Sorry to bother you Chad."

The guitarist had stepped down from the stage and was standing beside him.

McCabe turned, "That's OK, Roy. What can I do for you?"

"Would you mind standing in for me for a couple of numbers? I've got to make a phone call."

"No problem," replied McCabe. This was an opportunity to show Sophie what he could do.

"Thanks, mate," said Roy, and he disappeared out into the street.

McCabe turned back to Sophie.

"You don't mind do you?"

"Of course not. I didn't know you played."

McCabe removed his hand from hers and drained his wine glass, "Stay and listen."

"I will," she replied, and gave him her fabulous smile again.

"I'll leave the bottle with you," said McCabe. "We'll talk after."

He made his way to the small stage concentrating only on jazz now. Taking a flatpick from his pocket, he removed his guitar from its case, checked the tuning and waited for the cue to start playing. The bass player counted them in, the violinist played the intro Grappelli style, then McCabe joined in with the rhythm and they swung through three verses of "Honeysuckle Rose". When they had finished, the audience applauded and McCabe glanced across to Sophie to see what her reaction was, but she was no longer sitting at the bar. She had left while he was playing. Too bad. Perhaps it just wasn't her kind of music. He carried on playing until Roy returned and then sat at the bar again, drinking and listening to the rest of the set. Occasionally he wondered if Sophie would come back, but she didn't. He would phone her and invite her out to dinner.

The remainder of the evening passed rapidly, as it always did when he was listening to Manouche Jazz, and it was after midnight when McCabe left Reinhardt's. The streets were quiet, and still thinking about Sophie he walked along Bond Street heading for the taxi rank. As he passed the stage door of the Theatre Royal he heard footsteps behind him and felt a violent punch to his kidneys. He fell forward over a car that was parked by the kerb, his left arm was forced up his back and he realised that he was lying across the bonnet of Bishop's silver Mercedes. His guitar case was snatched from his right hand and he was dragged to the car's rear door, which was being held open by Chancey, the smaller of Bishop's thugs. Whoever was holding him - and the halitosis was a big clue - forced him through the door and onto the floor of the car, then Chancey climbed in behind him, kneeling on his back to keep him face down. McCabe heard the car door close then he heard the boot lid being opened and shut. The other rear door was opened, and someone got in and sat with their foot on his head forcing his face into the carpet. He heard the driver's door open and then close again. The engine started and the car was moving. Nobody spoke, and McCabe decided that if he protested the only result would be more pain. There was no doubt in his mind that he was taking his last car journey and that after a great deal of suffering he would be dead.

Chapter Forty Two

Sussex Downs - 0039 BST Wednesday 22nd June

They travelled without breaking any speed limits for what, to McCabe, seemed to be an eternity but which was really only twenty minutes. The car came to a stop and the engine was switched off.

"Alright. Get him out boys," ordered the one with his foot on McCabe's head. Bishop's voice.

McCabe was roughly hauled out of the car and he glanced around. The moon was bright enough for him to see that the Mercedes had pulled off of the road and that they were in a large circle, perhaps fifty yards across, which was surrounded by a raised grass bank. In the centre of the circle was a wide grassy mound and around the perimeter of the circle was a ring of tarmac roadway the width of two cars. McCabe recognised it from the times, years before, when he and Hannah would leave their car there on sunny afternoons and walk for miles along the South Downs Way. They were at the Ditchling Beacon car park on the top of the Sussex Downs, five miles east of where he'd fired the flares, and he was sure that it was the flares that Bishop wanted. During the day the car park would have been crowded with people, and even after dark there would normally be courting couples in cars but now, in the early hours of the morning, it was deserted.

Ginger Tom forced him round to the front of the car and released him, tripping him at the same time so that McCabe fell to his hands and knees in the full beam of the car's headlights. He was dazzled by the lights and the palms of his hands burned from the abrasions caused by the tarmac surface of the car park. Raising himself to an upright kneeling position and turning he could see Bishop in front of him silhouetted by the headlights.

"You've got something of mine and I want it now."

"It's in the guitar case. It's not locked," replied McCabe.

"Well, that didn't take long. You're no hero, are you? Have a look Chancey," ordered Bishop.

They waited while Chancey went to the boot of the car, opened it and retrieved the flare pack. He returned and passed it to his boss without speaking. Bishop took it, pulled back the plastic cover strip and was silent for a moment as he studied the pack in the beam of the headlights.

"Where are they then?"

McCabe didn't reply and Bishop took a step towards him.

"I said where are they?"

"I don't know what you want," replied McCabe.

"I want my sodding drugs, that's what I want."

"Well you've got them. You can let me go now."

"I'm not letting you go, Sunshine, until I get my drugs. There's supposed to be eight in here and there's only one. Where's the rest of 'em?"

"They've been fired," answered McCabe.

"I'll fire you, you bastard," raged Bishop. "This is no sodding use to me, is it?" he screamed, hurling the flare pack at McCabe with as much force as he could muster and hitting him in the centre of his chest.

McCabe groaned at the impact and doubled up.

"What are you gonna do about it then?" yelled Bishop. "They're worth thousands they are, and you're telling me they've been fired."

McCabe made no reply but remained doubled up quietly moaning to himself.

"I said what are you gonna do about it?" shouted Bishop.

The lack of a reply added to Bishop's fury and he advanced towards McCabe.

"I'm going to kill you, you stupid bastard, and then I'm going to kill that nosey bitch girlfriend of yours."

Bishop swung his foot back like a footballer taking a penalty, intending to kick McCabe full force in the head. As he did so, McCabe raised himself to a kneeling position again, turned his body sideways, braced himself and took the full force of the kick on his left shoulder. Holding both hands high in front of him he fired the remaining flare point blank into Bishop's face, then he forced himself to his feet.

Dropping the empty flare pack, McCabe ran to the open driver's door of the Mercedes and jumped in without bothering to close it. He had been praying that the smart key, which had to be present before the engine could be started, was in the car and not in Ginger Tom's pocket. The interior lights were on, and as he settled into the driving seat McCabe was surprised to see that the starter button, which would have immobilised the car, had been removed and the smart key was in its place. He turned the key and the engine fired up immediately. McCabe put his foot on the brake, glanced down and grabbed the gear selector, pushing it into reverse which also released the parking brake. He put his foot on the accelerator and reversed away at speed, three of the car's doors still open, then braked hard slamming the doors shut which also switched off the interior lights. In the headlights he could see Bishop thirty yards in front of him, clutching his face and writhing on the ground. The two thugs had recovered from their initial surprise and were running towards him with Chancey ten yards in the lead. McCabe looked down at the gear selector again and put it into drive, pushed the accelerator pedal to the floor and, as the Mercedes leapt forward its wheels spinning on the tarmac, he aimed the car at Chancey bouncing him off of the nearside wing. As Chancey cartwheeled away into the darkness, McCabe wrenched the steering wheel towards Ginger Tom who slipped as he tried to get out of the way. McCabe felt the car lurch as both offside wheels drove over the thug's legs, and then he was away, narrowly missing Bishop and skidding and sliding through the open gate at the car park entrance and onto the road. He put his foot down as the automatic transmission rapidly changed up through the gears and the high powered Mercedes-AMG roared away into the night in the direction of Brighton.

Chapter Forty Three

Brighton - 0114 BST Wednesday 22nd June

Tricia was woken by a sustained hammering on her bedroom door.

"Who is it?" she called out in a voice sounding stronger than she felt.

The hammering stopped.

"Who is it?" she shouted.

"It's me," called McCabe. "Open the door. Quickly."

She got out of bed, noted the time on her phone and put a towelling dressing gown on, at the same time switching on the light, then she moved to the bedroom door, which wasn't locked, and opened it standing back as McCabe burst in.

"Tricia, there's no time to explain. You've got to come with me now."

"But it's one o'clock in the…"

"Tricia, listen to me. We've got to leave now. You're in danger. Trust me!"

The urgency in his voice made her comply.

"Let me get dressed," she said, and turning she hurried to find her clothes.

"Pack a bag Tricia," he called as he left the room, "but be quick."

Three minutes later she had switched off the bedroom light and was in the hallway wearing jeans and a sweater, and carrying a soft bag into which she had thrown underwear, a wash bag, and a change of clothes. McCabe switched off the hall light, opened the apartment door and looked out. The stairway was deserted.

"It's OK," he said. "Let's go."

At the bottom of the stairs, when they reached the entrance hall, McCabe opened the front door slightly and looked out into the street, which was empty except for parked cars including Bishop's Mercedes. McCabe had decided to leave it there in the hope that it would give the appearance to Bishop's people that he was still at his flat. As there was no doubt that it was McCabe who had stolen the car, there was no point in leaving it anywhere else.

McCabe waited until he was sure that nobody was waiting outside for them and then he signed to her to follow. She closed the front door behind them, and they quickly made their way across to the Mercedes and McCabe retrieved his guitar from the boot. To Tricia's surprise, instead of getting into the car McCabe ushered her across the road to a low gate set into the steel railings which surround the huge private gardens forming the centrepiece of Sussex Square and Lewes Crescent. McCabe produced a key, which opened the gate, and they passed through, closing it behind them. He took Tricia's bag from her, and they hurried on in the darkness following a steeply sloping path in the direction of the sea.

"Where are we going," demanded Tricia, "and whose car was that?"

"Its Ricky Bishop's car. I stole it and we're going to France."

"France? But I haven't brought enough things with me. I haven't brought my passport."

"We're going in Rose," he replied, as they hurried along the path. "You won't need a passport. That's the great thing about sailing between France and England, the complete lack of officialdom. You can come and go as you please, all on trust. If you have anything to declare you can call Customs and they might pay you a visit. If you don't call they leave you alone. Customs and Immigration don't have enough people to monitor it. Don't worry about your things; I'll buy you anything you need when we get there."

"But I've got stuff to do. I can't just leave everything and go to France."

"Listen Tricia, you're in danger. We're both in danger."

As they crossed the gardens, McCabe quickly told her what had happened tonight after he left Reinhardt's, and by the time they had reached the end of the path she was convinced that leaving the country for a while was a sensible option.

In front of them was what appeared to be a black wall rising above them and blocking their path. McCabe took a small torch from his pocket, switched it on and revealed a narrow, arched, brick tunnel with trees overhanging the entrance. The ground on either side of the path here was covered with ivy and formed high banks. The banks converged to funnel Tricia and McCabe along the path and into the tunnel entrance.

"Lewis Carroll's rabbit hole," said McCabe quietly.

"What did you say?"

"Sorry," replied McCabe. "Lewis Carroll often stayed here at his sister's house in Sussex Square. Apparently, he was fascinated with this tunnel and it gave him the idea for the rabbit hole in Alice in Wonderland, or so the locals would have you believe. He certainly stayed here but, according to the plaque on the wall of the house, not until nine years after the book was published."

"Where does it lead to?"

"You'll see. Come on, don't be nervous."

He walked into the tunnel entrance and Tricia followed.

Chapter Forty Four

Brighton Seafront - 0131 BST Wednesday 22nd June

McCabe and Tricia emerged from The Rabbit Hole and stopped. She realised that they had walked under the main coast road, and were now looking down at the beach. Below and to the left of them was Volk's Railway Station, and beyond that was the Blackrock car park. To their right, the tail lights of a car were receding into the distance along Madeira Drive, travelling towards the Palace Pier. Apart from that there was no sign of movement. They waited, watched, and listened. Far off to the west they could see sheet lightning flickering on the horizon, heralding a cold front which was sweeping its way towards them along the English Channel. The only sound that they could hear was the sigh of a small wave as it rolled over in the darkness and died on the shingle beach, to be followed a few seconds later by another and then others in a continuous slow hypnotic rhythm. After a few minutes, satisfied that no one was waiting for them, the two fugitives followed the footpath down to the beach and turned left along the promenade. Less than a quarter of a mile ahead of them was the seafront pedestrian entrance to Brighton Marina, and McCabe was pretty sure, even if Bishop had contacted more men to hunt them down, that nobody would follow them by the little known route that they had taken.

There was nobody about as they descended the wide flight of steps from the seafront into the marina. In front of them was the wide expanse of the Asda supermarket's car park, empty at this time of night and just a vast exposed open space. They would be easily seen crossing that if someone was waiting for them, so they avoided it by quickly turning right into the marina's multi storey car park. Climbing the car park stairs to Level 7, they hurried across the footbridge leading to the Boardwalk. They passed the closed up and silent restaurants, and then turned right heading for the security gate and the pontoons. As they walked, McCabe had been checking the wind and weather conditions and creating a passage plan in his mind. He could see that the weather was going to turn and strong winds were on the way, and normally he would have waited for it to pass before he put to sea, but they didn't have time for that. They had to get away before Bishop's people caught up with them, as they surely would.

They reached Honeysuckle Rose and, with neither of them speaking, McCabe unplugged the shore power supply while Tricia removed the mainsail cover and unzipped and unclipped the cockpit tent, laying it down flat and leaving the canvas spray hood with its clear PVC windscreen in place. McCabe fired up the engine and switched on the red, green, and white navigation lights and the white steaming light, while Tricia released the fore and aft springs. McCabe joined her on the pontoon and together they let go the warps fore and aft, then jumped aboard. McCabe pushed the Morse control lever into astern gear and they slowly backed out into the fairway. When they were clear of the pontoon he pushed the control forward and they turned and motored out into the marina while Tricia busied herself removing the fenders, stowing them in the forepeak with the warps and springs. At 0207 BST, just before high water, they passed between the concrete arms of the Brighton Marina entrance into the English

Channel and McCabe turned Honeysuckle Rose south south east onto a heading of 165° true. While Tricia took the wheel, McCabe entered their departure time and course in the log and then boiled a kettle. He returned to the cockpit with two steaming mugs of instant coffee and they sipped at them gratefully as they motored at a steady six knots across the glassy flat sea, and slowly left the lights of the sleeping city of Brighton behind them. For the first hour there was just blackness ahead of them, interspersed by the occasional red, green and white lights of fishing boats a long way off to starboard, but the sky was rapidly getting lighter and by four o'clock they could make out the water around them. For the previous half an hour McCabe had been feeling the wind on his face gradually increasing from the south west, and the sea around them was starting to move with a long slow swell. He had also been checking the boat's Oregon Weather Station, and the barometric pressure had dropped several points in the short time that they had been travelling away from Brighton.

"Have you ever sailed across the Channel before, Tricia?"

"No, only coastal."

"You'll love it. Time to get some sail up. If you stay in the cockpit I'll get up there and do it."

He went below and opened the fore hatch, and Tricia watched as he pushed the number 2 jib in its bag through the hatch and onto the deck. He closed the hatch, returned to the cockpit carrying the ropes which would be used as sheets, rigged them through the blocks on either side of the cockpit and then worked his way down the port side of the boat taking one of the sheets with him. He tied the sail bag to the guardrail, pulled the folded sail out of the bag and secured the sheet to the clew of the sail with a bowline knot, then he returned down the starboard side and repeated the process with the other sheet. Pulling the sail forward to the bow McCabe secured the tack, hanked the sail onto one of the twin forestays and attached a halyard to the head of the sail ready for hoisting. Tricia steered and kept a lookout as he returned to the mast and fed the mainsail into its track on the mast and then attached its halyard. He removed the eight sail ties which kept the mainsail lashed to the boom and hauled on the halyard until the head of the sail reached its position near the top of the mast. Honeysuckle Rose heeled to port slightly as the breeze filled the sail, and came upright again as Tricia, in the cockpit, eased the mainsail sheet to spill some air from it. On the principle that you should reef when you first think of it, and he had been thinking about it ever since he had started to watch the barometer fall, McCabe rolled the boom around using the ratcheted bronze lever at the mast end, wrapping the foot of the mainsail around it as he did so. By doing that, he estimated that he had reduced the mainsail area by about a third which would allow them to cope with the rough weather which he was sure was on its way. He wound the mainsail halyard twice around the circular bronze winch on the starboard side of the mast and then inserted a heavy steel winch handle using its leverage to haul the halyard up the last few inches and tighten the luff of the mainsail in its track. He secured the halyard to a cleat on the mast and stowed the winch handle, for ready use when needed, in a pocket fixed to the foot of the mast. Finally, he uncleated and slackened off the topping lift, the rope running from the foot to the top of the mast and through a pulley to the aft end of the boom, which allowed the weight of the boom to pull down on the foot of the sail and flatten it. As he cleated the topping lift Tricia pulled on the mainsail sheet adjusting the angle between the sail and the wind and, as Honeysuckle Rose heeled again, they both felt her surge forward at an extra knot as the wind took her. Tricia pushed the engine throttle into neutral and, as the engine noise quietened, Honeysuckle Rose slowed until she was making way through the water at two knots powered only by the reefed mainsail.

McCabe went forward again as Tricia turned the leeward jib sheet twice around the port side winch in the cockpit. He knelt by the mast and hauled on the foresail halyard, pulling the jib easily up the forestay. When the head of the jib had reached its limit he pulled the sail taut and wound the halyard twice around an empty winch on the port side of the mast. Taking the winch handle from where he had stowed it when he hoisted the main, McCabe inserted it into the circular winch and tensioned the halyard with it. He secured the halyard, still wound around the winch, to a cleat on the mast, and returned the handle to its pocket on the mast again. Then he went back to the cockpit.

Tricia switched on the autopilot and, as she pulled on the sheet McCabe took a handle from its pocket in the cockpit and wound the winch to adjust the angle of the sail in relation to the strengthening wind. When it was properly set, Tricia secured the sheet to a cleat with a figure of eight. With the sails correctly trimmed, Honeysuckle Rose surged forward again as the wind lifted her and she was quickly up to five knots, the autopilot holding her on course. McCabe pulled a toggle in the cockpit floor decompressing the engine and stopping it, and suddenly they were sailing on a starboard tack with only the trickling sound of water running past the waterline and the occasional creak of rope or timber as Honeysuckle Rose shouldered small waves aside. McCabe went below and turned the white steaming light off leaving only the red and green nav lights and white stern light on, indicating to other vessels that Rose was no longer motoring but was a sailing yacht in her natural element.

They settled down on opposite sides of the cockpit both keeping a careful lookout. By five o'clock they were in the east to west shipping lane and needed to take extra care to avoid being run down. The sun was above the horizon on their port side rising into a clear blue sky, but above them was patchy cirrus and to the west the sky was black and piled high with cumulus. McCabe switched off the navigation lights, and when he returned to the cockpit he brought with him waterproof jackets and trousers, and safety harnesses with lifelines. They put the waterproofs on then the harnesses, and clipped the lifelines to them. The other end of the lifelines they clipped to secure rings in the cockpit. Until the imminent storm had passed, neither of them would move anywhere in the cockpit or on deck without being clipped on, either to the rings or to jackstays - stainless steel wires which ran the length of the boat on both side decks and were secured to strong points. Neither of them spoke as Honeysuckle Rose continued towards France gently lifting her bow then nodding forward, comfortably pushing the sea aside with a long easy motion while the wind increased and the waves became steadily more angry.

Twenty minutes later they saw the cold front coming at them fast, a long black line of cloud and rain at sea level, and McCabe switched off the autopilot and took the wheel. To the east of them they had been observing huge container ships heading down channel towards them. Two had passed ahead and one behind them. They could still see three more ships in line astern approaching them from the east when the squall line hit them hard travelling at thirty miles an hour and trying to knock them flat, but Honeysuckle Rose wasn't having it. Her ten tons of timber, iron, steel, and rope heeled stiffly to port and then came back almost to the vertical and stayed there. McCabe pinched up as the wind hit, pointing as high as he could, and Tricia hardened up the mainsail sheet without him having to ask her. Around them the sea was being stirred into a frenzy, and spume, spray and rain lashed horizontally across the cockpit reducing visibility to almost nil. Rising up then plunging down the back of a steep wave, Rose dug her nose in and picked up a great mass of sea water with her foredeck, then she came up again and threw it behind her with contempt, shaking it off as it poured away along her deck and over the side. Where the approaching ships were they were unable to see.

For two hours they continued in that way, with McCabe letting Honeysuckle Rose have her head, tramping along sometimes at four, sometimes at five knots at forty five degrees off the wind which, even on a good day, was as high as she would point. Plunging and rising into and over the waves, Rose once more proved her worth, as McCabe had known she would when he made the decision to leave Brighton with a storm approaching. Her long keel and solid build carried them safely forward and, once Rose had settled into her groove, in a perverse way McCabe and Tricia were almost enjoying themselves. He was impressed with the way that Tricia had handled herself and the boat.

Glancing across the cockpit at her he saw that she was sitting there impassively with her arm hooked around a sheet winch, patiently keeping watch as best she could in the poor visibility. At about 0600 they passed the place where Jack's body had been discovered. They couldn't see anything through the spray and rain and McCabe wasn't sentimental enough to believe that Jack's spirit was there in any way. They discussed it and then both lapsed into silence for a while.

The ships that they could see when the squall had struck must have passed them by now and be well off to the west but they had entered the west to east shipping lane with the same hazards as the previous one but coming from the opposite direction. With hardly any visibility through the rain and spray there was no point worrying about what might be out there and Rose had a radar reflector near the top of her mast. McCabe knew that the Channel has the busiest shipping lanes in the world with over four hundred ships a day passing through, and he hoped that those on watch on any nearby ships were checking their radar screens and would take avoiding action if necessary. Some of the larger ships that travel along the English Channel are constrained by their draft so wouldn't be able to manoeuvre much anyway, and McCabe wondered whether he should have hove to between the two shipping lanes and waited for the storm to clear. Passing ships were more dangerous than the weather was. It was too late now and he realised that he was tired and making bad decisions.

Not once had Tricia complained, and she had not shown any sign of sea sickness either, which surprised him considering the conditions. He had lost count of the number of his acquaintances who had been obliged to give up sailing because of motion sickness. It was something that he could empathise with though, as everyone who has ever been on the sea for any length of time has, at some point, suffered from it. But the true overwhelming nausea brought on by sea sickness, which reduces some people to miserable retching wrecks incapable of movement and unable to help themselves in any way, is a liability on a small boat. The dehydration that it induces can even be life threatening if it continues for long enough.

The rain had stopped, visibility was improving, and the wind was calming down. McCabe switched on the autopilot and waited while it learned the sea conditions, then satisfied that it could cope, he went below and plotted their position. As he had thought, they were in the west to east shipping lane and, after he had compensated for leeway and laid off for tide, he calculated that they were two thirds of the way across it and close to the western end where ships joined it. A loud shout from Tricia sent him rushing up the steps. She was pointing off to starboard. McCabe swivelled round on the companionway steps in time to see a great grey wall of steel appearing out of the murk. A giant container ship was crossing their bow, oblivious to the little yacht's presence, and Honeysuckle Rose was tramping along towards it being steered unswervingly by the autopilot on a closing course with the ship's great frothing propellers. McCabe threw himself across the cockpit and pressed the red button to disconnect the autopilot. He spun the wheel to port and Rose instantly came about, pivoting but dead in the water as they came under the lee of the huge ship and the wind was lost from the sails. McCabe clipped his harness to a ring bolt as, on their starboard side, the ship slid past thirty yards away and the turbulence sucked the yacht towards it. They both watched helplessly as the churning propellers drove towards them and then passed them no more than twenty feet away. Rose pitched and tossed with her sails flogging, then spun around twice in the wake of the huge ship but stayed afloat and upright. As the ship steamed off eastwards following the direction of the storm, McCabe regained control of the yacht and brought her up into the wind again. They continued on their original course both too stunned to speak.

By 0900 they had cleared the shipping lane and the weather had improved considerably. By 1000 the wind had veered and lost a lot of its strength. Visibility was good and behind them, in the distance, they could see a long line of ships, brilliant in the sunshine, heading along the shipping lane where they had so nearly come to grief. McCabe broke out Honeysuckle Rose's oversized red ensign at the stern, and the sight of it cheered them up as it flew straight and flat in the stiff breeze while they sipped at cups of instant soup that Tricia had prepared.

At 1100 the wind had dropped further, the sea had calmed to a steady swell, and Honeysuckle Rose began to slow. McCabe shook out the reef in the mainsail, and hauled down the jib and lashed it to the guardrail. He replaced it with the large genoa and Rose picked up speed again. As the sun rose higher into the sky they started to feel its warmth, and with a steady breeze from the west rippling the surface of the sea they sailed on leaving a V shaped wake behind them.

At midday they were still sailing at five knots in bright sunshine having settled into a watch keeping routine of one hour on and one hour off. They had maintained the same heading since the shipping lanes and McCabe was in the cockpit while Tricia dozed on the port side saloon berth. Just like old times he thought, when with Hannah he had ranged up and down the Channel in Honeysuckle Rose. They had visited pretty well all of the French and English ports between Dover and Honfleur, with the occasional sortie as far afield as the Brittany coast and Santander in Spain when time allowed. The old team settling into an easy pattern of watch keeping and running the boat, both instinctively knowing what was required without discussion. He remembered how pleased he had been when they first sailed together, that he had found someone who shared his passion for boats.

He was woken from his reverie by Tricia who was standing at the foot of the saloon steps.

"Sandwich?" she called.

"Yes please."

She rooted about in one of the starboard lockers until she found a tin of corned beef. In the fridge she found butter and, on the shelf behind the galley sink, piccalilli and a white loaf which McCabe had bought the day before. Within ten minutes they were both sitting in the cockpit with a mug of tea each and thick corned beef and piccalilli sandwiches, which they munched happily. The autopilot was on again and Honeysuckle Rose sailed herself steadily onwards in the sunshine towards France. It was starting to feel like a holiday.

An hour later they could see the coast of France low on the horizon ahead of them and McCabe hoisted the small French courtesy flag at the starboard crosstree. He had held Honeysuckle Rose on more or less the same compass heading all the way across on the basis that they had left Brighton at around high water and, at the speed they were averaging, the crossing would take about twelve hours. It was a rough calculation, but they were cruising not racing and, if his calculations were correct, the west going and then east going tides would more or less cancel each other out. They should fetch up in France with Fécamp roughly on the nose; the same reasoning that Tiger Fish had used three weeks before, according to Allerton, but sailing in the opposite direction.

Honeysuckle Rose had a GPS satellite navigator which McCabe had left switched off, preferring to use dead reckoning whenever it was safe to do so, and however many times he did this there was always an element of doubt in his mind as to whether he had got it right. For the next hour he scanned the French coastline looking for familiar landmarks. Tricia saw it first; the signal tower on the cliff immediately to the east of Fécamp, which confirmed that they had made a good landfall. Three hours later, after a small correction to their course, they had the sails down, the autopilot off and the engine on as they motored between the breakwaters of Fécamp Harbour entrance and, at just after six in the evening local time, they rounded the wall into the harbour and picked up a visitor's berth on Pontoon C.

Twenty minutes later they had Honeysuckle Rose securely tied up and her sails stowed, and they were sitting back in the cockpit enjoying the sunshine and a bottle of Sauvignon Blanc from Rose's fridge as they shared the afterglow of a successful crossing.

Chapter Forty Five

Le Havre - 1339 CEST Friday 24th June

Two days after Honeysuckle Rose's Channel crossing, part of Gravier's team was watching the Le Havre train station and the bus terminal, both of which are approached by wide, open expanses of concrete precinct. Nobody could cross them without being observed. Other watchers were thinly spread out across Le Havre at car hire offices and the ferry terminal, and the police were watching the streets. Angelos was already nearly five kilometres away and out of the city.

The previous night, as soon as it was dark, Angelos had left the apartment, glad to be active again and free of the stink of eight days of accumulated domestic waste. Eight days of total boredom spent sleeping, eating packaged food, pacing the room, and intensifying her hatred of the world in general. With the precious abrin safely in her rucksack, and using the street map obtained from the Tourist Office, she had followed the back streets north, and climbed high above the city on the Lechiblier Stairs. From there she joined the Rue du 329ème, skirted around the Sainte-Marie Cemetery, and entered the Forêt de Montgeon which is over 240 hectares of woodland purchased by the Municipality of Le Havre in 1902 as a playground for its citizens. Having followed the network of roads and tracks through the woods, Angelos was now hidden, undetected, in undergrowth on the northern edge of the forest. She rested: sleeping, waking, eating biscuits, drinking bottled water, and sleeping again. The terrorist was waiting for the afternoon to pass until she would walk the remaining kilometre into the small town of

Fontaine La Mallet to catch the 6.19pm bus from Le Havre, which would take her the final forty kilometres to Fécamp.

This was the flaw in Gravier's plan and he had lost her.

Chapter Forty Six

Fécamp, Normandy - 1920 CEST Friday 24th June

The yacht club is called the Société des Régates de Fécamp, and it occupies the first floor of a futuristic looking concrete building which stands alone on the quay near the harbour entrance. In front of it is Fécamp Harbour, and behind it is the sea. The ground floor of the building houses the Harbour Master's office, and showers and toilets for the use of boat crews. McCabe was standing alone on the wide first floor terrace, looking out to sea with a beer in his hand, enjoying the view. In front of him was the broad pebbled beach which curved away past the town on his left towards a low line of white cliffs half a mile away. The cliffs continued the curve and stretched away into the distance in a gentle sweep forming a bay three miles wide. The sea was completely flat and the bay was dotted with an assortment of yachts, small fishing boats and speed boats, their French owners taking advantage of the still summer evening. Through the open doors behind him came a hubbub of raised voices, mostly English, shouting to make themselves heard. Fécamp Yacht Club was playing host, as it often did, to yet another fleet of visiting racing yachts from the other side of the Channel. The bar was full of excited yacht crews who, having completed their race, many for the first time, were fuelling up with beer for an evening on the town.

Two days had passed since McCabe and Tricia had arrived in Fécamp, and they had spent their time sunbathing and relaxing on board Honeysuckle Rose, with the occasional foray ashore for provisions. Chad had found a local doctor to belatedly take out his stitches and pronounce that the head wound was healing satisfactorily, and last night he had jammed at a Jazz Manouche gig in one of the local bars feeling the intense pleasure that he got from playing Gypsy Jazz in the country where it had been developed. Neither he nor Tricia had raised the subject of what they were going to do about returning to England, preferring to ignore that for the moment. One thing that McCabe was sure of though, was that when they did return he would face serious problems from Ricky Bishop and his thugs and, depending on how seriously he had injured them in the Ditchling Beacon car park, maybe from the police as well. Grievous bodily harm at least and manslaughter or murder at worst. This morning he had bought the English newspapers and searched them carefully to see if there was any reference to three injured men being found on the Sussex Downs. He had also searched the Brighton Evening Argus online, but nothing was reported. Whatever had become of Bishop and his henchmen, McCabe knew that he had made a serious enemy, but for the time being he would put that to the back of his mind. Nobody knew where he was, so it could wait until later, and he was grateful for the fact that they could sail from England to France and vice versa without meeting officialdom and being asked for passports or any other form of identification.

"Chad?"

He turned at the sound of her voice, and standing behind him was Sophie May her blonde hair pulled back into a pony tail, and wearing white shorts, a navy blue polo shirt and deck shoes.

"Sophie. What a surprise. What are you doing here?"

"I raced over from Brighton on Tiger Fish," she replied. "I was going to phone you but now you've saved me the trouble. What brings you to Fécamp you gorgeous man?"

"Holiday. A few weeks break."

"On your own?" she asked.

"No, I have a friend with me."

"Really? Female?"

"Yes."

"Lucky girl."

McCabe smiled at her, "No, nothing like that. Just a friend."

"Well I'm glad to hear that, Chad. It means I'm still in with a chance."

She gave him a seductive smile and McCabe felt an electric thrill of anticipation pass through him.

"Is she here?" asked Sophie. "I'd like to meet her."

"She's having a shower. I came up here for a beer while I'm waiting for her. Listen, why don't we meet for lunch tomorrow and…"

"Sophie!" the clipped vowels of the South African accent rang out across the terrace. "Mr Allerton is looking for you."

They both turned to see Frik Benniker filling the doorway which led to the bar.

"Bit difficult at the moment Chad," she said quietly. "Let's talk another time."

Sophie turned and Benniker stood aside as she passed without speaking to him. He kept his eyes fixed on McCabe.

"I think it would be a good idea if you kept away from her," said Benniker with menace. "She could be very bad for your health."

He stared at McCabe for a few moments waiting for a reply which didn't come, and McCabe returned his gaze without blinking.

Benniker grunted, then turned and went back into the bar. McCabe looked out to sea again determined that, as soon as he could, he would get to know Sophie better.

Chapter Forty Seven

Fécamp - 1931 CEST Friday 24th June

While McCabe was admiring the view from the Yacht Club, only a kilometre away, the bus from Le Havre pulled in to the stop on the Avenue Gambetta four minutes late. The doors opened with a hiss and Angelos stepped onto the pavement with the rucksack over her shoulder. She turned and made her way along the pavement, walking towards the town centre until, in the Rue André Paul Leroux, she found a tabac where she bought a Fécamp street map and studied it while she drank a coffee. When she left the tabac Angelos retraced her steps and then walked until she reached the Quai Bérigny.

She stopped for a few moments and looked around her, quickly taking in the harbour, the pontoons in the sunshine packed with the English racing yachts and, on the other side of the harbour, the steep green slope of the hillside with expensive houses clinging to it. The terrorist continued along the Quai Bérigny, turned left into Rue du Domaine, then turned right into Rue de Mer. The small terraced house that she was looking for was on her left. Angelos glanced around at the deserted street as she took the key from her pocket and inserted it into the lock of the front door. The door opened easily and she stepped into the hallway closing it behind her. She waited and listened but the house was silent. In front of her, on the left side of the hallway, was a narrow staircase leading to the first floor, beyond the staircase was an open door which led to the back of the house, and to her immediate right was another door which was slightly ajar. She stepped forward and gently pushed it. The door opened into a small sparsely furnished living room. Angelos eased the rucksack from her shoulder, placed it on the hall floor and then stepped into the room.

"Stop!" commanded a man's voice to her right, and she froze.

"Turn slowly towards me."

Angelos did as she was told and found herself looking at the delivery end of a Glock 23 pistol.

Chapter Forty Eight

Fécamp - 1942 CEST Friday 24th June

"I thought I'd find you here."

McCabe smiled at her as Tricia joined him on the terrace fresh from her shower. She looked relaxed and the two days enforced rest on Honeysuckle Rose had been good for her. He had already decided not to spoil it by telling her that he had just met Sophie May.

"What does a girl have to do to get a drink around here?"

"Come on," he said. "I'll buy you a drink at the bar. What would you like?"

"A dry white wine please."

Together they went into the Yacht Club and a wall of noise hit them. They worked their way through the crush of people to the bar where, after a short wait, McCabe caught the attention of one of the overworked girls who were serving drinks. In French he ordered a glass of house dry white wine and a beer pression for himself. When the drinks arrived he paid for them, passed the wine to Tricia and picked up his beer. Then they moved away from the press of people at the bar and stood by the terrace doors on the edge of the crowd.

The interior of the Yacht Club is a large, modern, open space with hard echoing floors and no ceiling, and the hollowness of the pitched roof amplifies the sound. There were at least two hundred people there in small groups all drinking, all leaning towards each other to hear what was being said, and seemingly all talking at once. The cacophony of raised voices gave McCabe the impression that he was present at some enormous Mad Hatter's tea party, and it made any conversation between himself and Tricia impossible without shouting, so they sipped their drinks and watched the proceedings for a few minutes.

McCabe scanned the room looking for Sophie and Benniker but, if they were there at all, they were lost in the crowd. A young man holding a bottle of beer and wearing the deck shoe, cargo pants, polo shirt uniform of a racing yacht crew had detached himself from one of the groups and was making his way towards them smiling. McCabe saw that it was David Anderson who he had last seen at Reinhardt's in Brighton nearly two weeks before. Then he remembered that in two days time he was supposed to play his regular Sunday gig there. He put the thought out of his mind. There was nothing he could do about it. David reached them and was saying something which they couldn't hear above the noise, so McCabe shook his head and gestured towards the doors. The three of them went out onto the terrace.

"I was saying, what a surprise to see you both here," said David, seemingly genuinely pleased to see them. "How are you Tricia?"

"Very well thank you," replied Tricia puzzled. He seemed familiar although she couldn't remember where she had met him before. Probably in a bar or club.

"Are you part of the race, David?" asked McCabe.

"I certainly am. I came over on Tiger Fish. Haven't seen the results yet but we did pretty well I think. Some of the boats are still out there and we've been in for nearly two hours."

"So, you're looking forward to a weekend in France then?" Tricia asked.

"Not really. Most of us are going back tomorrow morning. We've got taxis booked to pick us up at eleven o'clock and take us to Dieppe to catch the 1330 ferry to Newhaven. There'll be a few hangovers to be nursed I expect."

"So when is Tiger Fish going back?" asked McCabe.

"Sunday I think."

"Isn't it a bit unusual for the crew not to go back with the boat?" asked Tricia.

"It is a bit," replied David, "but we actually like it. We've done the race and we don't have to do the boring bit, cruising the boat back to Brighton. Graham pays for the taxi and the ferry tickets and we're home in half the time. More comfortable too."

"So who's sailing Tiger Fish back?" asked McCabe.

"Just the three of them. Graham, Frik, and Sophie."

Chapter Forty Nine

Fécamp - 2021 CEST Friday 24th June

Angelos raised her eyes slowly and saw that the pistol was being aimed at her by Renard who was sweating profusely. Renard visibly relaxed as he carefully returned the still cocked weapon to the shoulder holster hidden beneath his jacket.

"I am pleased to see you Angelos. Have you had a good journey?"

"It has been slow and tedious."

"Well you are here now," replied Renard, "and you are safe. Do you still have the package?"

"Of course I do, that was my mission. I was told to guard it with my life, so if I am here then so is the package."

"We are pleased with you Angelos, but France is no longer safe for you. I suspect that the dead woman in Rouen was your work and the authorities are looking for you."

Angelos did not reply.

"No matter," said Renard. "It is probably better that I do not know. Tomorrow you will rest here and you will travel to England on the following morning."

"And how will I travel to England?"

"You will be taken there aboard a yacht. The movement of private yachts between France and England is unregulated. There are no immigration controls because the Authorities depend on the honesty of boat owners to contact them if they have any foreign nationals on board. They rarely meet boats to check. This means that you can enter and leave both countries unhindered.

The people who are taking you are not supporters of our cause. They think that they are smuggling economic migrants - poor unfortunates who are in search of an opportunity. They are also very well paid for their trouble so they don't ask questions. I have been cultivating them for a long time and they have carried many people across for me in both directions. You will leave here wearing clothes suitable for a yachtswoman - I have them ready for you - and you will meet them near the harbour. I will take you there myself."

"Can these people be trusted?" asked Angelos.

"They can. They have done this for me often and would now face long prison sentences if they were caught. They will take you to the yacht and you will immediately put to sea. The crossing should take about twelve hours. When you arrive in England you will be met by one of our people who will take you by car to a safe house. There you will hand over the abrin powder which you are carrying to an expert who will distribute it to our groups throughout the United Kingdom. They will then mount coordinated attacks against the population by distributing the abrin through the air conditioning systems of offices and public buildings, particularly in the primary commercial centres, and introducing it into water supplies. If we choose the right targets the British economy will take a generation to recover because we will have killed their most talented people, but that is not the object. The object is to create terror so that the British population will never feel safe again."

Chapter Fifty

Fécamp - 2158 CEST Saturday 25th June

"What are they up to, Tricia?"

It was the following evening, and she and McCabe were relaxing in Honeysuckle Rose's cockpit, having just spent nearly two hours eating a Fruits de Mer bought earlier in the day at the poissonnerie on the quay. In front of them, on the table, were the remains of the meal, a pile of shells: crab, prawn, oyster, whelk, winkle, clam, langoustine, lobster, and cockles. The contents of the shells had been accompanied by mayonnaise, and a shallot dressing for the oysters, and eaten slowly, a little at a time. They sat back contentedly, each with a glass of chilled Muscadet, and watched the comings and goings in the harbour around them.

It was almost dark and lights had appeared in some of the boats and in the windows of buildings around the harbour, giving the whole scene an atmosphere of glamour which was not apparent during daylight. From the yacht club, and the restaurants and bars at the southern corner of the harbour, muffled outbursts of group laughter could occasionally be heard as the visiting yacht crews continued with their weekend celebrations. Above the harbour, gulls wheeled silently, gliding with their wings outstretched and looking ghostly as the light from below made their pure whiteness contrast with the darkening black of the sky above them. The fleet of racing yachts was moored, bow on, to both sides of Pontoon C, their battle flags hung limply in the still warm air, and they were packed shoulder to shoulder so closely that the forest of rigging seemed to merge into one huge web of metal and rope.

"Perhaps they're not up to anything, Chad."

"Yes they are," he replied. "There can only be one reason why Tiger Fish's crew went back by ferry today. Because Allerton doesn't want witnesses."

"Witnesses to what?"

"That's what I don't know."

"Perhaps he wants some privacy with Sophie May," said Tricia.

"If he wanted that he'd send Benniker back by ferry, as well."

They sat in silence for a few minutes and McCabe stared moodily at Tiger Fish. She was moored five boats away from Honeysuckle Rose on the other side of the pontoon. As he watched, Allerton and Benniker appeared on deck then climbed down onto the pontoon and began to walk towards the narrow ramp which led, at a sharp angle, from the pontoon up to the top of the high harbour wall. They passed Honeysuckle Rose without acknowledging McCabe and Tricia, instead carefully ignoring them. The two men reached the top of the ramp, opened the flimsy mesh gate and, as they did so, McCabe put his wineglass on the table.

"I'm going to follow them. I'll see you back here later."

As he jumped onto the pontoon, Tricia quietly called after him, "Be careful, Chad."

"I will," he called over his shoulder, and then he was hurrying along the pontoon.

She watched him until he reached the top of the ramp and disappeared from her view as he went after Allerton and Benniker.

Tricia sat quietly, taking a few minutes to finish her glass of wine. She was beginning to think about clearing the table and washing up the supper dishes and plates, when she noticed that Sophie May had appeared on Tiger Fish's deck. For a reason that she couldn't explain, Tricia felt the need to avoid her, and she stood and then stepped down into Honeysuckle Rose's saloon which was in darkness. Through one of the forward scuttles she watched as Sophie left Tiger Fish and walked quickly along the pontoon carrying a sailing bag. As Sophie passed Honeysuckle Rose, Tricia grabbed the spare boat keys, stepped up into the cockpit and locked the saloon and aft cabin doors. She waited until Sophie had reached the top of the ramp and then she followed.

By the time Tricia had climbed the ramp and reached the top, Sophie was two hundred yards away and had turned left along the harbour wall following the Quai de la Vicomte. Tricia maintained the same distance between them as she followed, and the groups of yachtsmen strolling back to their boats ensured that, if Sophie turned around suddenly, she probably wouldn't notice Tricia among the crowds of people on the quay that night. Sophie didn't turn around but walked purposefully along the quay until she suddenly crossed the road, turned right and disappeared. Tricia hurried forward, crossed the road in the same spot, and turned, where Sophie had, into a paved area taken up with tables and chairs belonging to the Big Ben Café on her right. She crossed the small square and turned left into the Rue des Prés, a narrow deserted street with a mix of terraced houses and workshops on either side, their front doors opening directly onto the pavement. There was hardly any street lighting but in the gloom a hundred yards ahead of her was Sophie, still hurrying along the street. Tricia followed.

***

McCabe stayed at a discreet distance behind Allerton and Benniker as they walked purposefully along the pavement on Boulevard Albert 1er, the seafront road which leads south west from the harbour in the direction of the casino. Benniker suddenly turned around and McCabe, feeling exposed, kept walking but Benniker appeared not to notice him and turned away again. The two men entered an upmarket café bar and McCabe stopped and wondered what to do next. He crossed the road and climbed a short flight of steps onto the promenade, following the line of the beach until he was opposite the café and could see into its wide picture windows. It was full of people standing or seated at tables, and Allerton and Benniker were nowhere to be seen. McCabe crossed the road again, entered the cafe, worked his way to the bar, and ordered a beer. He stood with his back to the room as he used the long mirror behind the bar to study it. Then he spotted Allerton and Benniker who were seated at a table at the back of the room with a red faced man in a crumpled linen suit. Allerton and the man were deep in conversation while Benniker listened, all the time studying the faces in the bar. McCabe watched in the mirror as Benniker suddenly got to his feet and began to move towards him through the crush of people. Picking up his drink, McCabe looked away and pretended that he hadn't seen him.

“You don’t listen, do you?” Benniker had spoken quietly into McCabe’s right ear, the Afrikaans accent adding menace to his words.

Looking into the mirror again McCabe watched himself as Benniker, his massive chest pressing down against McCabe’s back, a huge hand on the bar on either side of him, stooped over him like an enormous animal about to devour its prey. Behind them the other people in the bar were talking and drinking, oblivious to them. The barman was drying glasses unaware that they were anything but old friends who had just met again after a long separation.

“I saw you in the street, McCabe. Why are you following us?”

“I’m not following you.”

“Don’t you take the piss out of me, McCabe. I said, why are you following us?”

“I’m not.”

“You leave now,” ordered Benniker. “I’ll catch up with you another time.”

Benniker kept his hands on the bar, raised his head and looked into the mirror, staring directly into McCabe’s reflected eyes. McCabe stared back trying not to betray his fear. Their eyes remained locked together for a few moments but McCabe broke first and looked down at his drink. Benniker stood back and McCabe, as an act of defiance, picked up the beer taking his time to finish it. Benniker waited. McCabe turned and, ignoring Benniker, he pushed his way through the crowd and left. Benniker went back to the table where Allerton and Renard were still deep in conversation.

***

Tricia was staying close to the inside edge of the pavement hoping that, if Sophie turned around, she wouldn't see her in the shadows of the narrow street. She matched her quarry's pace, thankful that she was wearing deck shoes that made no sound. Sophie suddenly disappeared from view again. Tricia stopped. She looked around quickly but, apart from herself, the street was empty and silent. A few of the houses had chinks of light showing through their closed curtains, and from the ground floor window of the house next to her she could see blue light and hear the muted sound of a television just a few feet away. Far off in the distance a dog barked and she felt very alone. Making her way cautiously along the pavement until she reached the place where Sophie had vanished she found a narrow arched opening in the wall which formed a passageway. She waited and listened. Nothing. The passage was in complete darkness but she could see that it led to the back of the houses and, at the end of it, there was a glimmer of light. Gathering all of her courage she crept slowly and silently down the dank passage, feeling her way along the rough brickwork with her left hand. When she reached the end she stopped again. In front of her was a small, high walled, concrete yard mostly in shadow. Sophie was not there. The light was being cast from a large single ground floor window to Tricia's right. Next to the window was a glazed door and in the corner of the yard furthest away from the window she could make out a refuse bin standing in the shadows by the wall. Apart from that the yard was empty. With her heart pounding Tricia crept across the yard and stood behind the waist high bin. From here she could see into the window twenty feet away.

The room she was looking into was a kitchen. In the centre of the room was a large wooden table like a butcher's block with half a dozen wheelback chairs placed around it. On one end of the table was Sophie's sailing bag and, in three neat stacks at the other end, were twelve red mini flare packs. Sophie was standing by the bag and talking to a man in his late twenties, tall and handsome with jet black wavy hair, dressed in denim and leather, and looking like an off duty rock star. Although Tricia could not hear what was being said, she could see that they were comfortable with each other; he stood close to Sophie as if they were old friends. As they talked Sophie unzipped the sailing bag and from it she took twelve flare packs identical to the ones already on the table. She stacked them in front of her, reached into the bag again and took out five bundles of banknotes which she placed next to the flares, then she passed the bag to the man. He walked to the other end of the table, picked up the duplicate flare packs, placed them in the bag, zipped it up and then walked back and put the bag on the table in front of Sophie. Tricia watched them, framed in the window like a tableau being acted out without sound as the man crossed the room and disappeared from sight for a few moments. He reappeared with a bottle of red wine and two glasses but Sophie was smiling, shaking her head and refusing the offer as she looked at her watch. He looked disappointed as Sophie picked up the bag and moved out of sight, and then the door was suddenly opened and the yard was flooded with light. Tricia dropped onto her haunches behind the refuse bin, pressing herself into the shadows against the wall, the blood pounding in her head.

She heard the man say, “Bonne nuit, Sophie. Toujours un plaisir.”

“Merci, Jean-Charles,” was the reply, and Tricia watched Sophie’s silhouette as, carrying the bag, she walked across the yard and turned into the passageway to the street.

The door closed and the yard was in semi darkness again. Tricia waited for a minute while her heart rate slowed and then she carefully stood up. Through the window she could see Jean-Charles, now seated at the table and sipping a glass of wine as he stared into the distance, lost in his thoughts. Tricia moved silently across the yard and into the darkness of the passageway terrified that somebody would discover her there, and she breathed a sigh of relief as she reached the still deserted street. She leaned against the front of the house until she had recovered her composure, then she turned right and hurried back towards the harbour. As Tricia reached the Quai de la Vicomte she saw Sophie in the distance walking along the harbour wall, still holding the sailing bag. Tricia watched her walk down the ramp and along Pontoon C, then Sophie boarded Tiger Fish and was lost from view.

As she made her way down the ramp Tricia could see that Honeysuckle Rose’s cabin lights were on. She hoped that it meant that Chad was back. She walked along the pontoon and, when she reached Honeysuckle Rose, she was relieved to see him sitting in shadow in the cockpit.

“There you are. I was wondering where you’d gone,” he said.

She climbed aboard clearly excited.

“You’ll never believe what I’ve just seen!” she exclaimed. “I can’t tell you out here, let’s go below.”

Tricia went down the steps into the saloon and turned, "Well? Come on then."

McCabe got to his feet and followed her and they sat at opposite sides of the saloon table.

"How long have you been back?" she asked.

"About ten minutes."

"Did you see Sophie May walk past?"

"I did. Just after I got back."

"I followed her, Chad. After you left she came along the pontoon from Tiger Fish carrying a bag, and I followed her. She went to a house in one of the streets that run parallel to the harbour, and I watched her give a man some flare packs and he gave her some flare packs and…"

"Slow down, slow down," said McCabe, "and start again slowly."

Tricia looked exasperated.

"About five minutes after you left to follow Allerton and Benniker… Where did they go by the way?"

"I followed them to a bar along the sea front. They met a man there and then Benniker spotted me and told me to clear off."

"Did he realise you were following him?"

"He did. He was quite threatening."

"You'd better keep away from him then. Anyway, it's not him that was up to no good tonight. It was Sophie May."

"Go on," said McCabe.

"After you left I followed her to a house and watched her through a window. There was a man waiting for her there. He was French. She took a load of cash and some flare packs from the bag she was carrying and gave them to him. He replaced them with new flare packs, and then she left. I followed her back here."

“Were all the flare packs similar?” asked McCabe.

“As far as I could see they were identical. Do you see what it means?”

“Does it mean that the flare packs were out of date and she’s bought some new ones?”

“Very funny Chad.” she said with a look of contempt. “I don’t think she’d get them from a private house in the middle of the night. Do you?”

“Sorry,” he replied, “I’ll be serious. What do you think it means?”

“Drugs.”

“Go on,” said McCabe.

“The flare pack that Jack had was full of drugs, wasn’t it?”

“Right.”

“And where did he get the flare pack from?”

“Assuming it wasn’t his own then he would have got it from Tiger Fish’s inventory,” replied McCabe.

“Correct, but why would the flare pack that Jack had in his pocket contain drugs?”

“You tell me,” answered McCabe.

“Because all the flare packs on Tiger Fish have drugs in them. I’ve just seen her take twelve normal packs into Fécamp and bring back the phoney ones. Sophie might just be running an errand for Allerton and she’s too dumb to realise what’s going on, but they’re smuggling heroin across the Channel in mini flare packs, Chad.”

McCabe thought for a moment, “You could be right.”

“Of course I’m right. All we’ve got to do is prove it. Then we’ve got them.”

“Do you think they killed Jack because he found out what they were doing?” asked McCabe.

"I don't know," she replied, "but we have to get on board Tiger Fish and check those flare packs. If they've got drugs in them we'll call the police and then we can get them arrested and questioned."

"Only this time," said McCabe, his expression grim, "we'll find out the truth. Tomorrow we'll keep watch on Tiger Fish, and if they leave her I'll see if I can get on board and have a look round."

Chapter Fifty One

Fécamp - 2349 CEST Saturday 25th June

It was nearly midnight when Angelos heard a key being turned in the front door lock of the safe house. She moved quickly and silently across the living room and waited behind the door with the knife in her hand. The front door closed and she heard Renard's voice.

"It is me."

Angelos relaxed and moved back across the room as Renard bustled in, out of breath and sweating.

"It is all arranged my friend. You will leave tomorrow."

Angelos looked at him impassively.

"Sit," said Renard, collapsing into an armchair. "I will give you your final instructions."

He waited until Angelos had seated herself in the other chair.

"In the morning we will leave here and you will follow me at 100 metres distance to the end of this street, where it meets the harbour. We will walk towards the sea and when we reach the Boulevard Albert 1er we will turn left. I will show you on your street map. A short way along that road we will come to a cafe, I have just been there myself. Outside, at a table by the pavement, will be two men drinking coffee. So that you will recognise them I can tell you that one of the men is very large with blonde coloured hair, South African. The other man is English, white haired, and short. So that you can be sure that they are the correct people I will join them as you walk past. After a minute or so, you will return and they will stand up and leave the cafe while I will stay there. You will follow them to a yacht called Tiger Fish which is moored in the harbour. When you reach the yacht you will go below and it will immediately leave the harbour. You will be in England by tomorrow evening and will be landed at a city called Brighton. There is a large marina there and, as soon as you arrive, you will leave the yacht and walk unchallenged along the jetty and through the security gates until you reach the road. I have done this myself several times, and it will be clear to you when you get there. When you reach the road you will be met by a car and taken to a safe house in Brighton. At the house you will meet your new Controller and you will give him the abrin powder which you are protecting. Is all of that clear?"

Angelos nodded.

"Then there is nothing more to be done." Renard got to his feet, "Sleep well my friend. Tomorrow you have important work to do."

Chapter Fifty Two

Fécamp - 0845 CEST Sunday 26th June

The following morning, McCabe and Tricia saw Allerton and Benniker leave Tiger Fish, climb the ramp to the harbour wall and disappear from their view. For nearly two hours they had been taking turns to watch through Honeysuckle Rose's port saloon windows, waiting for an opportunity to get on board Allerton's yacht and examine the flare packs. Only Sophie May was still on Tiger Fish and they could see her reading in the cockpit. There was no activity on the other boats around them, mostly English yachts, their crews sleeping it off after the festivities of the night before.

Tricia continued to watch, while McCabe made coffee for them both and then sat quietly playing through chord sequences on his guitar. Ten minutes later Sophie suddenly stood up and went below returning immediately with keys in her hand and her shoulder bag. She locked Tiger Fish's cockpit door, climbed down onto the pontoon and walked towards the ramp with her bag over her shoulder.

"She's leaving," exclaimed Tricia.

McCabe put down the guitar and they both moved to watch Sophie from Honeysuckle Rose's starboard windows until she had reached the top of the ramp and was out of sight. Excited, Tricia spun around and stepped up into Honeysuckle Rose's cockpit.

"I'm going to have a look," she called over her shoulder.

"Wait," called out McCabe, but she had gone, rushing down the pontoon towards Tiger Fish, ignoring his protests.

Cursing quietly to himself McCabe jumped onto the pontoon and hurried up the ramp after Sophie. When he reached the top he could see her walking along the Quai de la Vicomte towards the town. Looking down at the pontoons he could see Tricia lifting Tiger Fish's fore hatch which had been left open a couple of inches for ventilation. If Sophie looked to her left she would see Tricia on Tiger Fish's deck. He watched as Tricia lowered herself into the forward cabin, pulling the hatch down behind her. He looked up again but Sophie had not seen her and he descended the ramp and returned to Honeysuckle Rose to keep watch.

In Tiger Fish's forepeak Tricia had stopped to get her bearings. She was conscious of the silence inside the boat. The cabin she was in was lined with rich mahogany panelling, and had white vinyl ceiling panels and a teak floor. She was standing in the vee formed by the berths on either side of the cabin. The berths met at the bow end and had thick bunk cushions on them covered with expensive blue fabric. At ceiling level, on either side of and across the forward end of the cabin, were lockers with mahogany louvred doors, six in total. The port berth was completely covered by five large sail bags which contained Tiger Fish's selection of foresails. The starboard berth had a red Helly Hansen holdall on it, a man sized T shirt, a grubby pair of shorts, two pillows and a folded sleeping bag. So this was where Benniker slept.

Tricia opened each locker in turn. They were all empty. She looked aft along a mahogany lined passageway through the centre of the boat, which led to the saloon, and she followed it. To her left, on the starboard side of the passageway, was a sofa berth with blue cushions, and on the right was a door. Behind and above the sofa were three large locker doors. Tricia opened each one in turn. They were empty. The full height door on the opposite side of the passageway revealed a spacious shower and heads completely lined with white laminate. She moved on into the saloon.

The mahogany and blue colour scheme was continued in the saloon. To Tricia's right, on the port side, was a long L shaped sofa berth and, in line with it at the other end of the saloon, was a mahogany navigation station. To her left was a straight sofa berth beyond which was a well fitted out galley, again all in mahogany. In front of her between the port and starboard sofas was a large mahogany dining table slightly offset to port. Above the sofas were six more lockers. Tricia stepped into the saloon and began to search through them, one by one.

***

McCabe anxiously watched Tiger Fish from Honeysuckle Rose's saloon. Ten minutes had passed since Tricia had dropped through Tiger Fish's fore hatch. How much longer was she going to be? He silently cursed again, angry that he hadn't stopped her.

"Come on Tricia." he muttered. "Get out of there."

Suddenly, four people walked past Honeysuckle Rose's bow and into his line of sight. Allerton, Benniker, and Sophie May carrying four sticks of French bread. They were followed by a woman that McCabe had not seen before, who was wearing sailing clothes and carrying a rucksack over her shoulder.

McCabe's blood turned cold, and a chill of horror gripped his stomach as he watched them hurrying towards Tiger Fish.

***

Tricia's careful search of the saloon lockers had proved fruitless. They contained books, safety harnesses, plates, cups, saucers, glasses and all of the usual paraphernalia needed to keep a crew comfortable in harbour and at sea, but none of the lockers contained flare packs. She turned and surveyed the saloon her gaze resting on the navigation station. She crossed the saloon and examined it.

The nav station was on the port side of the boat facing forward and was a built in unit about three feet square which was attached to the hull lining. It comprised a mahogany top fitted with a lifting panel rather like an old fashioned school desk and, in front of it, was an upholstered bench seat for the navigator with a full width backrest. Below the desk, and an integral part of the unit, was another locker door. In front of the navigator's seat, behind the desk, were a radar screen and GPS display. To the left of the navigator's seat, built into the hardwood hull lining, was a large black control panel with switches and circuit breakers from where all of the boat's electrics could be monitored.

Tricia lifted the top of the navigation table and, inside, she could see a stack of charts a couple of inches high on top of which were a protractor and a parallel rule. She closed it again. Crouching, she opened the locker door in the front of the nav station and inside she found a large yellow plastic container with a wide red screw top lid. She pulled the container out, unscrewed the top, and inside she discovered a set of full sized parachute flares. Not what she was looking for but flares nevertheless. She replaced the container and closed the locker door. In the side of the nav station was a set of drawers. She pulled one open and, as she did so, she heard voices and the sound of feet on the deck above her. In front of her the open drawer revealed a dozen neatly stacked mini flare packs. As she reached into the drawer and was about to pick up one of the flare packs she heard the sound of a key in the lock of the cockpit doors six feet away from her. She grabbed a flare pack, closed the drawer, stood up, and noiselessly crossed the saloon towards the front of the boat, pushing the flare pack into the pocket of her fleece jacket as she went. She reached the start of the passageway as the cockpit doors were pulled open and by the time Benniker had reached the bottom of the steps, Tricia was in the forward cabin. He would see her through the open door when he looked forward and, as he did, she threw herself into the pile of sail bags on the port berth, burrowing and covering herself with them. Benniker hadn't seen her. As the rest of Tiger Fish's crew came down the steps into the saloon she lay in the forepeak, hidden by the sails, her heart pounding as she realised that she was trapped and began to imagine what they would do to her when she was discovered.

In the darkness, under the sail bags, Tricia listened to the muffled voices of the crew, unable to make out what they were saying. She felt a slight vibration through the boat as the engine was started and, suddenly, she heard Benniker's unmistakable Afrikaans accent right next to her as he shouted to someone.

"I'm going to rig the genoa."

He would find her when he sorted through the sail bags.

She heard Sophie's voice above, calling through the hatch to Benniker.

“Graham says he wants you on deck, Frik, to help cast off.”

“Well I wish he’d make his bloody mind up.”

Had he gone? He wasn’t moving the sail bags. She lay there, waiting, for what seemed to be an interminable length of time, and then she felt Tiger Fish moving with the slight up and down motion which meant that they had left the mooring and were motoring out of the harbour.

In the saloon, twenty feet away from Tricia, Angelos sat on the starboard sofa berth clutching the rucksack containing the abrin powder, and she was already beginning to feel sick. At the back of the spacious cockpit, Graham Allerton stood behind the wheel as he steered Tiger Fish between the pontoons towards the harbour entrance. On Tiger Fish’s deck, Benniker and Sophie were removing the fenders and warps ready for sea. From different vantage points around the harbour, three of Gravier’s watchers, who had followed Renard from Paris, looked on. One of them was talking into his mobile phone.

Chapter Fifty Three

Fécamp - 0921 CEST Sunday 26th June

McCabe was beside himself with fury and frustration as he climbed the ramp up to the harbour wall and ran past the yacht club, along the Quai Vauban, towards the huge breakwater that formed the harbour entrance. What the hell had he been thinking of to let her get on board Tiger Fish? Why hadn't he rushed forward and stopped them from sailing? The only consolation he could see was that they didn't appear to have discovered her. Tricia must have hidden when they returned, but there aren't many places to hide on a yacht the size of Tiger Fish, and it could only be a matter of time before she was found. And then what? If they really were smuggling heroin into the UK, then they weren't going to take kindly to an uninvited visitor who had been searching the boat while they were away. From his previous contact with Ricky Bishop, McCabe new that these people were capable of anything and presumably Graham Allerton would be as ruthless as Bishop had been if he thought that his plans were being thwarted.

He reached the end of the breakwater and looked down at the sea. It was flat calm here protected from the easterly wind by the high cliffs to the north of the town. Two hundred yards away Tiger Fish, also in the lee of the cliffs, was motor sailing on a north north westerly heading with just her mainsail up. A mile beyond her the sea, no longer in the lee of the headland, was chopped up and the occasional white horse suggested that the wind strength out there was at least force five. He could make out Sophie and Allerton in the cockpit and Benniker standing by the mast making adjustments to the mainsail halyard tension with a winch handle. McCabe had to act. He could call the police but by the time he had explained, and even if they believed him, when they took action Tiger Fish would be half way across the Channel. If the Tiger Fish crew discovered Tricia in the meantime, they were just as likely to drop her overboard. Is that what had happened to Jack? He had to go after them in Honeysuckle Rose.

McCabe turned and ran back towards the pontoons. Could he catch them in Rose? It was doubtful. They would have a theoretical top speed of nearly ten knots, and he would only overhaul them if they were in no hurry and sailed at a leisurely pace while he motor sailed at Honeysuckle Rose's full hull speed of eight knots. Even then, if the wind kept its present strength they would probably outrun him, but he had to do something, and at least once he was underway he could use Honeysuckle Rose's VHF radio – no, not the radio, Tiger Fish would hear it. Use his mobile phone to telephone for help before he was out of range. If he could keep them in sight he could guide the police to them. He reached the top of the ramp and ran down it holding onto the handrails and almost falling headlong as he reached the bottom. McCabe sprinted along the pontoon and, as he reached Honeysuckle Rose, he saw that the berth recently vacated by Tiger Fish was now occupied by a small, dark blue sports boat. The two Frenchmen who had just arrived in it were standing on the pontoon talking, warps in hand but not tied to the cleats. The engine was still running.

McCabe made the decision without any conscious thought. He continued at speed along the pontoon and leapt between the startled Frenchmen, landing awkwardly in the boat. Turning, he grabbed the wheel and pulled back the throttle, switching the drive from neutral to astern. The boat reversed away from the pontoon and the two men held fast onto the warps, leaning back and sliding forward like the losing team in a tug of war. McCabe increased the revs and they quickly began to slide towards the water until they both finally gave up at the same time, releasing the warps as the boat surged astern. He reversed the boat away from the pontoon and, ignoring the shouts and curses of the angry Frenchmen, he engaged forward gear and moved slowly away. He pushed the throttle into neutral briefly while he recovered the warps and pulled them inboard to avoid fouling the propeller. Leaving the two fenders to hang over the side, he settled into the driving seat, opened up the throttle again, and pushing a white bow wave in front of him he headed out fast towards the harbour entrance ignoring the angry shouts of moored boat owners caught in his wash as he passed. When he reached the entrance McCabe could see Tiger Fish nearly a mile away, low on his apparent horizon and still heading north north west. He opened up the throttle fully, brought the powerful boat up onto the plane and, with fenders flying, skimming across the flat sea at thirty knots he went after her.

***

"She's going green," laughed Benniker.

"Well, if she's going to throw up, she'd better not do it in the saloon," replied Allerton turning to look astern. "We're clear of the land now. Tell her to come up into the cockpit."

Benniker went below and immediately reappeared at the bottom of the saloon steps, ushering their passenger up the steps and into the cockpit. Angelos, still clutching the rucksack, sat down heavily on the port side of the cockpit by the wheel, and turned sideways to face forward. She looked disoriented, occasionally puffing out her cheeks and blowing out air as she fought the urge to be sick. Sophie, seated on the port side of the cockpit by the saloon steps, regarded her with distaste. Angelos looked at the beautiful arrogant woman in front of her and thought how much she would like to cut her throat. Then, no longer caring about the abrin, she dropped the rucksack, turned, knelt on the cockpit cushion, and began to heave the contents of her stomach over the side deck.

Allerton switched on the automatic helm leaving it to steer the boat, and letting go of the wheel he sat down on the starboard side of the cockpit.

"While you're down there, Frik," he called, "you can get the genoa up. We'll be out of the lee of the headland soon and we'll get some wind, so we need a foresail hanked on."

Benniker, resisting the temptation to say that he didn't need to be told, made his way forward, stooping slightly to avoid the saloon ceiling an inch lower than his height. He reached the forward cabin and stood by the port bunk as he checked the pile of sail bags. Identifying the genoa bag, he pulled it away from the others and uncovered Tricia lying on her back, her eyes wide with terror. Benniker's huge left hand reached out and grabbed her throat, pinning her to the bunk.

Chapter Fifty Four

Fécamp - 0930 CEST Sunday 26th June

Four hundred yards separated McCabe from Tiger Fish and they had still not noticed him approaching. As the gap between the two boats rapidly closed he saw Benniker emerge into the cockpit dragging a struggling Tricia by the collar of her fleece jacket. Tiger Fish was still motoring with just her mainsail up and was now heeling slightly to port as she left the lee of the cliffs and felt the wind. With two hundred yards to go McCabe also felt the wind as the sea changed instantly from a flat calm to a force five chop. The sports boat began to bounce as it leapt over the wave tops but McCabe kept the throttle fully open as he watched, furious and powerless to intervene, while Benniker manhandled Tricia on board Tiger Fish. With fifty yards left between the two boats, the crew of Tiger Fish were suddenly aware of him as he aimed at their port side. With thirty yards to go McCabe pulled back the throttle and stood up. At an angle the sports boat cannoned into Tiger Fish's side with a bang and, as it ricocheted away, he was thrown onto her, falling awkwardly with his midriff on top of the guardrail, rolling over it and landing face up on the side deck.

Ignoring the pain from his stomach muscles McCabe struggled to his feet, hanging onto the steel standing rigging for support. He looked back under the boom towards Tiger Fish's cockpit, taking in the scene like a snapshot. Tricia was on the cockpit sole where Benniker had thrown her and was struggling to get to her feet. Next to her was a rucksack. Allerton had jumped up and was standing behind the wheel. Sophie May was seated on the port side of the cockpit and had turned to look at him open mouthed. The woman he had seen boarding in Fécamp was kneeling on the port side deck and vomiting over the side. Benniker, with a look of hatred on his face, was climbing out of the cockpit onto the starboard side deck.

As Benniker worked his way forward, McCabe crabbed up and across the coach roof of the heeling boat on his hands and knees, stopping by the windward side of the mast and leaning against it as he knelt there. Benniker stepped onto the coach roof and towered over McCabe as, using his left hand against the mast to steady himself, he leaned down with his right fist raised and clenched ready to beat McCabe into submission. From its pocket on the starboard side of the mast, where Benniker had stowed it, McCabe pulled out the heavy winch handle and with both hands he hammered it into Benniker's left kneecap, both dislocating and breaking it at the same time. Benniker gave out a huge roar of pain and, as his knee gave way under him, he pitched forward head first over McCabe, crashing onto his face on the foredeck. McCabe jumped to his feet then knelt beside him and, with as much force as he could, he clubbed Benniker across the side of his head with the winch handle, twice. Benniker lay still and at that moment, in his rage, McCabe didn't care whether he was unconscious or dead. He turned and advanced slowly down the starboard side deck towards the cockpit still holding the winch handle in his right hand, and glared at Allerton with a look of malevolent fury on his face.

"Are you alright Tricia?" called McCabe.

"I'm OK. They haven't hurt me," she replied as she pulled herself up to a sitting position, still on the cockpit sole.

"Right," said McCabe. "Turn this boat round Allerton. We're going back to Fécamp."

"Can't do that, I'm afraid," replied Allerton. "I've got an appointment in Brighton."

Without really taking it in, McCabe noted, along the coast, the grey shape of a naval patrol boat two miles away to the east and making towards them at speed.

"Allerton," snarled McCabe, "I've just got rid of your bully boy. If you don't want me to start on you, you'd better do as I say."

They stared at each other while Sophie and Tricia remained still and Angelos retched onto the deck. McCabe moved towards Allerton with the winch handle raised.

Allerton caved in, "Alright, alright, no need for violence."

He pressed the button to switch off the automatic helm and turned the wheel hard to port, steering Tiger Fish rapidly through 180 degrees until she was heading back to Fécamp. The boom thrashed across the boat as she gybed, but not quickly enough to hit McCabe, who ducked under it, and Allerton was out of options.

"No," shouted Sophie. "We're not going back."

She had moved out of the cockpit and was standing on the port side deck, her left hand holding on to the windscreen as Tiger Fish heeled to starboard. McCabe stepped down into the cockpit keeping his eyes fixed on Allerton who stared back at him.

"Shut up Sophie," said Allerton.

"No," her voice was raised in temper. "I said we're not going back. Turn this boat round now."

McCabe and Tricia turned to look at her while Allerton continued to stare at McCabe. Angelos, in her own wretched world, stayed still with her head hanging over the rail and groaned quietly.

Sophie was holding a small semi-automatic pistol in her right hand as she glared at Allerton.

"I said turn the boat round."

"Be quiet Sophie and sit down," ordered Allerton.

There was a sharp crack and a short spit of flame from the gun, and Allerton fell back onto the cockpit bench clutching at the small calibre bullet hole in his chest, a surprised look on his face.

"Turn the boat around, Chad," ordered Sophie quietly and pointed the gun at him.

McCabe stepped up to the binnacle and pressed a button on the autopilot panel twice. Tiger Fish's bow began to swing out to sea again and she kept turning until she resumed her original course away from Fécamp. McCabe noted that the patrol vessel was still closing with them, now a mile away, but the others were too preoccupied with what was happening on board Tiger Fish to have noticed it.

"You stupid bitch," shouted Allerton. "You've shot me."

"Be quiet Graham, or I'll shoot you again."

Allerton didn't reply.

"Now what?" asked McCabe.

"You're going to sail us to Brighton. Graham obviously can't and you've made sure that Frik is out of it."

"And what if I refuse?"

"Then I'll shoot your girlfriend. What was she doing on board Tiger Fish anyway?"

"I was looking for the flare packs with the drugs in them?" replied Tricia.

"What drugs?" sneered Allerton.

"The drugs you're smuggling across the Channel," answered McCabe.

Allerton winced at the pain in his chest.

"Don't be ridiculous. I wouldn't have anything to do with drugs. Too many people get hurt by them."

"He means it," said Sophie. "His speciality is people smuggling. Like this thing here."

Angelos was kneeling on the deck facing her, watching Sophie with hatred while she fought back the nausea. This woman was shooting people and trying to prevent her from fulfilling her mission.

Sophie pointed the gun at Tricia, "And what were you going to do when you found them?"

"We were going to go to the police with them," replied Tricia, "and ask them to question you all about Jack's death."

"Ah yes, Jack," said Sophie. "I was sorry about that. He realised that we had two illegal immigrants on board and talked to me about it while we were on watch together. It was obvious that he was going to inform the authorities when we got to Brighton. Well I couldn't have the police swarming all over the boat could I? He was hanging on to the backstay having a pee over the back. Why do they do that macho crap? It was pretty much as I told you Chad, except that I gave him a shove and helped him overboard. The main difference was that it happened two hours after the beginning of our watch and I didn't raise the alarm until two hours later at the end."

"So by the time you raised the alarm you were two hours away from where Jack went overboard. That's why the positions were all wrong and Allerton didn't find him when he turned back and searched," said McCabe.

"Afraid so," replied Sophie, "and then there was the problem of recovering the flare pack that he'd had in his pocket. Have you any idea how much that was worth?"

"So you searched Jack's house," replied McCabe.

"I didn't, but I got a professional to do it. We didn't really expect to find the flare pack there but we had to try. It was after that when I realised that you must have been given it with Jack's things, so it might be on your boat."

"So it was you who searched Honeysuckle Rose," said Tricia.

"And shot me in the head when I turned up and interrupted you," added McCabe.

"But it's such a thick head that you survived," Sophie laughed. "Such a thick head that you even asked for my help, wondering where Jack got his drugs from. He got them from Ricky Bishop's pushers - I gather you've met Ricky. He's not very happy with you."

Allerton was staring at her in amazement, "Why?" he asked.

"For money Graham, why else? Every time we crossed the Channel with your illegal immigrants I've been making ten times the amount you have by smuggling heroin."

McCabe had already realised that Sophie had decided that none of them were going to survive, otherwise she wouldn't be telling them all this. Still holding the winch handle he made a move towards her and she swung angrily pointing the gun at him.

"Don't," she said, and then she saw the Royal Navy patrol vessel four hundred yards away, its white ensign streaming as it launched a fast RIB with five black clad figures in it, and she knew that she was cornered.

Sophie held the gun extended in front of her as she looked from one to the other in her confusion. Angelos had also seen the patrol boat and she staggered unsteadily to her feet, vomit smearing the front of her jacket. She raised her right arm and the knife was in her hand as, with a huge effort, she launched herself at Sophie. At the same time Sophie fired the gun sending a bullet spinning towards the terrorist from close range. A hole appeared in Angelos' face and her knife plunged into Sophie's beautiful throat as her momentum carried them both over the rail and into the sea. McCabe put the throttle into neutral, then killed the engine. He hauled on the mainsheet to ensure that it was as tight as it could be and let Tiger Fish heave to as she turned up into the wind.

The RIB closed with them rapidly and four armed marines from the French Commando Jaubert swarmed aboard wearing black combat kit, training their weapons on everyone and shouting at them in English, ordering them to lie face down. McCabe and Tricia complied, but Allerton was unable to obey and Benniker was dead or unconscious. All of them, including Benniker, had their hands secured roughly behind their backs with cable ties, and while two of the marines kept them covered the other two quickly searched the yacht, immediately finding Angelos' rucksack and appearing satisfied with the contents. McCabe and Tricia were efficiently body searched and the flare pack was removed from her pocket. The P2000 Class, 20 metre Fast Patrol Boat came alongside and they were rapidly passed from hand to hand across to it by the French marines, and were again forced to lie face down on the green painted deck.

A Royal Navy medic boarded Tiger Fish to check on Benniker and Allerton, and a helicopter was called which would airlift them to hospital.

The patrol vessel wallowed in the choppy sea as McCabe lay there listening to the mixture of English and French voices and wondered what was about to happen to them. Then he felt the cable tie holding his wrists being cut and one of the marines was helping him to his feet. Tricia was also being released. McCabe massaged her wrists to help the circulation and did the same to his own. He heard a voice that he recognised.

"I told you to try and stay out of trouble, Mr McCabe."

He turned, and standing there, one hand holding a handkerchief and the other gripping a grab rail on the patrol boat's superstructure, was Detective Sergeant Barnard of the Sussex Police.

Chapter Fifty Five

Fécamp - 0936 CEST Monday 27th June

Detective Sergeant Barnard took a sip of coffee, then replaced the cup and looked at them both. They could already feel the heat in the early morning sun as they sat at a table outside the Big Ben Café where McCabe and Tricia had arranged to meet him. They were both still tired, having spent a large part of yesterday being interviewed and making statements to the French police. The occasional car passed but Fécamp was still waking up, and in front of them the harbour looked peaceful and half empty as most of the racing yachts had returned to England.

"So, what can I tell you?" asked Barnard.

"You could tell us why you happened to be passing in a Royal Navy patrol boat yesterday," replied McCabe. "I'm glad that you were."

Barnard smiled, "Ok, but everything I tell you, and I can't tell you everything, must remain confidential. Agreed?"

"Agreed," answered Tricia and McCabe together.

"For over a year we've been watching Allerton and Benniker, and monitoring their activities as they ferried illegal immigrants across the Channel to England. Of course they weren't aware that we were keeping tabs on them. Allerton's an idiot. Even with all his wealth he couldn't turn down a bit of easy money. He assumed that they were all economic migrants and was quite happy to pick up a few thousand pounds for each trip; the going rate at the moment for an illegal cross Channel trip is €8,000. All of them were terrorists. Some were UK citizens who didn't want us to know that they'd been abroad, and others were of foreign make. It suited us, once they reached the UK, to let these people run while we keep them under observation. They can lead us to bigger fish."

"Who do you work for?" asked McCabe.

"Sussex Police, you know that. I can't tell you which branch but anti terrorism is my main interest."

McCabe decided to let Barnard talk rather than pursue the question.

"Anyway," said Barnard, "the operation was going fine until your son's death drew attention to them. We thought that they might curtail their activities for a while, but they didn't. Then we got intelligence that there was a particularly dangerous terrorist loose in France. The French were after him, or her as it turned out. She was completely unknown to them or us, but she appeared to be making for this area. We surmised that she might be crossing the Channel to England and, if that was the case, that Allerton and Benniker might be taking her, which is why we had a patrol vessel standing by. The French Authorities tracked her to Fécamp and watched her board Tiger Fish, and they told us when she left harbour. They also supplied the marines that you met. She was too dangerous for us to let her loose in England which is why we intercepted you yesterday. We did the right thing."

"Why was she so dangerous?" asked Tricia.

"I can't tell you that I'm afraid. Like so much of what we do, the public will never hear about it. If they knew everything that goes on there would be a mass panic. I can tell you that her body was recovered from the sea yesterday because she was wearing a flotation jacket, but we haven't found Miss May yet."

"What's happened to Benniker and Allerton?" asked Tricia.

"Benniker and Allerton are under arrest in hospital. When they recover they'll be extradited to the UK and tried for aiding and abetting terrorism. They can expect to spend a long time in prison."

"We thought it was all about drugs," said Tricia.

Barnard looked grim.

"Sometimes we have to make tough decisions. We knew about the drugs. It was important but it wasn't our priority. We had to let that continue so that we could monitor the terrorist threat. If we'd closed down the Tiger Fish route - the Normandy Run as we know it - that particular group would have found another way to enter the UK and we would have lost contact with them. What amazes me is that Sophie May was doing all of that under Allerton's nose and he wasn't aware of it."

"So she was a courier?" asked McCabe.

"No, she was more than that," replied Barnard. "She was the wholesaler, buying heroin in France, transporting it to Brighton and then selling it. Do that run once a month and you're into big money. Ricky Bishop, who I know you've met, bought it from her and then distributed it to pushers."

"So she didn't work for Bishop?" said McCabe.

"No. At times Bishop worked for her. When she wanted some muscle, for example," he looked intently at McCabe. "It's starting to make sense to you isn't it?"

McCabe slowly nodded.

Barnard continued, "We estimate that the heroin we recovered yesterday from the flare packs on Tiger Fish is worth at least six figures in Brighton."

McCabe thought of his meetings with Sophie and had the sudden realisation that she had set him up each time. “I think that we must be on Bishop’s hit list now,” he said.

“You are,” replied Barnard, “but he has other things to think about at the moment. Brighton police arrested him last night, and his two heavies. They have no chance of bail and are facing a long sentence. One of his lads is singing his heart out. Apparently you nearly blinded Bishop, you crushed one of his heavy’s legs, and broke the other one’s ribs. You’re a dangerous man when angered, Mr McCabe, but they’re not pressing charges and we have no interest in prosecuting you. Not surprisingly, none of that was reported to the police at the time and they were all treated in a private clinic in Hove, which we knew about, although we didn’t know how they’d got their injuries. We’ll be putting them away for quite a while but Bishop’s memory and reach will be long. Watch your backs.”

“We will” replied McCabe.

“You’ll be pleased to know,” said Barnard, “that the French Authorities will cover the damage to the sports boat and square it with the owner. We don’t want him suing you and drawing attention to our operation.”

“Thank you.”

“I’m sorry that I was obstructive when you came to us asking for your son’s death to be investigated, but we couldn’t do anything to panic them. In fact, I took everything that you said very seriously, but I had to ask the Coroner to delay the inquest. As it is, when I get back to England I’ll speak to the Coroner and tell him what we know. I’m sure that you’ll get the result you want.”

“I find it hard to believe how any woman could be so cold blooded,” said Tricia.

“Sophie May?” asked Barnard.

Tricia nodded.

"She was a sociopath," said Barnard. "We did some checks on her. Full name Sophie Elanore May, thirty two years old, only child, born in Arundel, West Sussex. Her father was an army officer who died when she was five. She was beautiful, persuasive with men, and used charm on everybody. Popular, fun, attractive, well spoken, cultured. Product of a first class boarding school which she left as the girl most likely to marry well, although she never did. She had an aristocratic mother who died four years ago leaving her a substantial sum of money and a house in Arundel, which Sophie sold. With the proceeds she bought a large period farmhouse in Ditchling. At the time that she bought the farm house she was working as a PR Consultant for a drug company which specialised in women's health products, planting stories in the press, entertaining, that sort of thing. A good salary, but not enough to support her lifestyle. Through the drug company she worked for she made contact with pharmaceutical people all over the world, and particularly some dodgy characters in France who were prepared to supply her with heroin in bulk.

"Allerton was easy. We don't know where they met but, once she'd found him, she had her route to get the drugs from France to England. He just thought she was an air headed bimbo. She found Ricky Bishop who strong armed the competition in Brighton out of the way and she was in business.

"We estimate that each flare pack contained about 40 grams of heroin. So at €120 a gram in France - it varies all the time, but that's a reasonable guess - each flare pack would cost Sophie May about £4,000, or whatever that is in Euros. At that price you can see why she was so keen to get the missing flare pack back, as well as the fact that her method of transporting the drugs would be blown if anyone discovered what was in it, which you did, of course.

"All twelve flare packs added together on each of her trips amounted to nearly half a kilo of high quality heroin, white not the usual brown stuff; top quality product which would cost her maybe £50,000. The heroin that goes onto the street isn't pure, so when she got it back to England it would be cut by adding powdered milk, or talcum powder, or anything that looks similar and bulks it out. Say it's cut to 50% pure, she now has twice as much product and it's sold as smack to Bishop for twice what she paid for it, say £100,000. More if the purity is less than 50%. Each drug delivery across the Channel by Tiger Fish was worth at least £100,000, so Tiger Fish's trips to France and back each month were not only taking terrorists into the UK but also over £1,000,000 worth of smack heroin in a year.

"When we compare the rifling on the bullet that's been dug out of Allerton I'm sure we'll find that it matches the one that bounced off of your skull. We already know that the gun that shot you is the same one that killed Harry the Swish."

McCabe carefully avoided Barnard's gaze.

"Oh yes, Mr McCabe, we knew that you'd found Harry's body, and we're pretty sure that the match with the Allerton bullet will confirm that he was shot by Sophie May to stop him talking to you. Why do you think I bumped into you in The Cricketers half an hour after you found him? Coincidence? After you got out of hospital I had people watching you to see what you were up to and whether you were likely to blow our operation. I called them off that night when you told me that you'd decided to give up your search. I believed you, and you were on your own after that."

"I was trying to find out about Jack's involvement with drugs."

"Jack wasn't involved with drugs. He was a police officer working for me," replied Barnard. "If he had any meetings with drug dealers it would have been to help our investigation."

McCabe was stunned, "… but Jack left the police six years ago. He only did it for a couple of years."

"No," said Barnard. "He went undercover six years ago. Jack was a very experienced officer with eight years of service."

"What about his job with the yacht broker, though? Did they know that he was a police officer?"

"No, Mr McCabe, even they didn't know. As you are aware, anyone taking goods or people that require clearance into the UK are expected to phone the National Yachtline and report their arrival. A lot of people don't do that, so the majority of our work depends on intelligence. We get it from various sources: members of the public, other police forces in the UK and abroad, but a large amount of what we learn is from our own officers working undercover, particularly regarding immigration. We know how porous our borders are so all of the UK ports, airports, and marinas have police, customs, and Border Force officers working at them just observing and gathering information. You know who they are but you don't know what they are. That's part of the cover. In marinas they mix freely with the boating community, they join yacht clubs, they talk, they listen and they watch. The yachtsman who's been your friend for years may well be one of our officers. In Jack's case he worked for a yacht brokerage, which allowed him to visit marinas all along the South Coast of England and blend in with the background. He did some very useful work, not least identifying and tracking the Normandy Run. You should be very proud of him."

"I am," replied McCabe, still trying to take in the fact that for six years he'd had no idea of what his son had had been doing. "I always have been."

A large black Peugeot pulled up to the kerb in front of them and the driver got out and stood by the rear nearside door. Barnard stood up.

"I have to go to Paris now. I may need to talk to you both again, but I'll find you if I do." Tricia and McCabe stood and shook hands with him, "Remember what I said, Mr McCabe. Try to stay out of trouble."

Barnard smiled then turned and crossed the pavement, pulling his handkerchief from his pocket as the driver opened the back door. He got into the car, the driver closed the door and then got into the driving seat. As the car pulled away Barnard raised his hand to them sneezing at the same time, and then he was gone.

"Well," said Tricia as they sat down again, "so now we know."

"We do," replied McCabe.

They finished their coffees gazing out over the harbour, both absorbed with their own thoughts, until McCabe turned to her, "Ready?"

They stood as McCabe pulled out his wallet and put some Euros on the table.

"What are you going to do now, Tricia?"

"I don't know really. My life's going nowhere. I've got elderly parents who don't care about me, a sister who makes porn movies and doesn't like me, no job, no ties. I can do anything I like."

"We get on well together, don't we?"

"We do, Chad."

They crossed the road and, as they strolled slowly arm in arm in the sunshine along the deserted Quai de la Vicomte towards Honeysuckle Rose, McCabe made up his mind about something that he had been considering ever since they arrived in France.

"Ok, Tricia. We've got time and we've got a boat. Where would you like to go?"

The End

Also available in this series

The Fleischer Menace

Printed in Great Britain
by Amazon

41426162R00162